The Tender Heart

Carter Saga: Book 1

Noelle Jane Myers

Cover designed by Lisa Bennett

This book is a work of fiction. Names, characters, places, and incidents either are products of the author's imagination or are used fictitiously. Any resemblance to actual persons, living or dead, events, or locales is entirely coincidental.

Noelle Jane Myers
Visit me on Facebook: https://www.facebook.com/noellemyersauthor/

Printed in the United States of America

First Printing: April 2018
Three Pens Publishing

ISBN-9781980828525

To my parents, and my crazy, wacky, wonderful tribe – too many to mention – who have believed in me far more than I deserve.

Preface

J amison Carter stared at the kind doctor in disbelief. The infant's wails echoed off the stone walls of their home.

"No. She cannot be gone." His gaze flickered to his wife's still form. Her pale face was beautiful, even in death. The thought that he would never see the lively sparkle in her emerald eyes took his breath away.

"Pa, look. She has red hair like Ma." His youngest son's words penetrated the numb fog that surrounded him and he turned to look at his boys. They all stood somberly at the foot of the bed. They knew. They accepted, so calmly.

The baby squalled again. A single red curl peeked out of the blanket the infant was wrapped in. Rage replaced the blankness.

"Get her out of here. I don't want to see her." The big cattle rancher kicked a chair in the direction of his children. He was vaguely aware of someone ushering them out of the room. "Oh Eileen, what will I do without you? My love." He took her limp hand in his. It was as though he could feel the warmth draining from her. She was gone, and that child had taken her from him.

"What will you do, Jamison?" Despite the kindness in Doc Warren's voice, there was a hint of steel underlying his words.

Jamison knew he was out of line. It wasn't the child's fault. This was life here on the range. If his wife's death was anyone's fault, it was his. Eileen had had a rough go with Sawyer's birth five years ago, and Doc had warned him about what could happen if they had another child.

"I can't take care of a baby, Doc. I can't. I have five sons and a ranch to run. I cannot add a baby girl to the mix." Jamison glanced at the door to the bedroom. "I will send her to my mother, back East. She is a wealthy woman, and she and my sister can raise the baby. They have plenty of money, and the child will get the best care and schooling." He ran a hand through his hair.

"Her name is Megan. Eileen named her before she died. She is your daughter, Jamison. The people here will help you. I will help you."

"Megan." The name sent rage coursing through him. No, he could not face the thing that killed his beloved. He would not.

"I will make arrangements to send her out on the first stage East," he growled.

"Jamison, you must wait a few weeks. The babe isn't strong enough to travel." Doc's horrified expression nearly changed his mind, but a glance at the pale woman on the bed strengthened his resolve.

"My mind is made up. She goes the minute I can arrange it." Jamison flung the bedroom door open and froze. Sawyer stood by the fireplace holding the infant, whose copper hair could be seen from across the room. Caleb was feeding her a bottle of milk, and her brothers were all cooing over her.

For a brief moment he hesitated. Compassion warred with rage in his soul. He tamped down his feelings mercilessly. "We are not keeping her." Jamison flung the words over his shoulder as he stalked outside to get some air.

∞ ∞ ∞

Adelaide Carter looked at the scruffy messenger in disbelief. "You cannot be serious." Her daughter, Amelia, peered over her shoulder.

"I am, ma'am. Carter give me a letter to show ya. He paid me one hundred in gold coins to make sure the kid got here all right." The man held out the basket and the sealed envelope. Adelaide tore the envelope open and read the short missive.

"Jamison wants me to care for her. Her mother died in childbirth," she summarized for her daughter, who had taken the baby from the basket.

"Mother, she has red hair, just like Eileen." Amelia's delighted squeal sent chills down Adelaide's spine.

"No. I won't take any child of that... that wench." Adelaide moved to shut the door.

"What'll I do with her?" the messenger asked.

"Take her to the orphanage. Or to a church. I don't know. I don't care," Adelaide sneered.

"Mother, I am ashamed of you. If you turn this child away I shan't ever see you again." Amelia stood in front of her, hands on her hips, eyes blazing with fury. "I know you hated Eileen, but she was kind and wonderful. She made Jamison a better man. It is our Christian duty to care for this child as we are able."

The messenger shifted his feet and cleared his throat. Adelaide's face flushed with mortification that this lowly scrap of a creature was witnessing her argument with her daughter. "You just had a baby. How will you take care of Helena and a rambunctious two-year-old in addition to this child?" Adelaide protested.

"We can do it together, Mother. I live just down the lane. The babies can play together. Please, she is just a child. She deserves as much love as we can give her."

Adelaide never could refuse her daughter. She acquiesced with a grunt. She would do her duty by the child, but no more. Any love would have to be given by Amelia.

Chapter 1

Megan raced through the wet, slippery streets, skillfully dodging the polished hansom cab and the huge horses that pulled them. She had spent far too long with Tony the grocer, his wife, Maria, and their brand-new baby, Geno. He was so adorable, with his thick dark hair and chubby cheeks. She had completely lost track of time. If she didn't get home soon, her grandmother was going to beat her something awful.

She dodged around another cab, crossing the busy street. It was freezing out and she could feel the water seeping in the cracks in her shoes. As Megan pulled her threadbare shawl a little tighter around her neck, she slipped on the slick cobblestones and fell hard. Her basket of groceries scattered across the sidewalk.

"Oooh. Miss Megan, is you all right?" Grubby little hands reached out to help her to her feet. Several small children scrambled to pick up the food and return it to her basket. Their dirty faces stared with longing at the fruits and vegetables as they gave them to her.

"Thank you, Johns, I am fine. I really appreciate your help. I wish I had more to share with you today, but I just don't. But here is an orange Tony gave me, and a bright new penny I have left from the grocery money our cook sent with me." Megan pulled the littlest girl into her arms for a quick hug. She always felt terrible for the children on the streets, especially on days like this, huddled under newspapers in stairwells, with their bare toes and dirty faces.

Johns, the leader of the urchins, gave her a big grin of thanks and the four children crouched back under the wet paper, carefully segmenting the orange. Megan checked her basket to make sure she had everything, then hurried on her way.

She burst through the back door of the huge old house and nearly collided with Moriah, her grandmother's pleasantly plump cook. The women laughed as they tried to keep their footing.

"Child, you are all a mess. What happened?" Moriah's eyes twinkled with merriment.

Megan knew her friend was aware she had stayed to see the baby. That was why she had sent Megan to the grocer this early in the day.

"I fell." Megan said lightly, brushing at her dress. "The baby was so cute, so pink and round and healthy. Maria looked good too. Tony was so proud. I think he nearly popped his buttons when he showed me his son for the first time," she said, twirling around the kitchen.

Moriah laughed and handed Megan a biscuit hot out of the oven.

"Eat it quick, child. Before your grandmother sees you. She is in quite a mood this morning," Moriah ended in a whisper.

"Has she been asking for me?" Megan paused mid-bite as Moriah nodded. That couldn't be good. She wolfed down her biscuit and a slice of warm, salty ham before she hurried to the parlor where she knew her grandmother would be waiting.

∞ ∞ ∞

Adelaide Carter stood in front of the crackling fire in the austere room.

"Come here, girl," she said harshly

Megan hurried to stand before her, and Adelaide looked down at her granddaughter, a frown on her thin face.

"Well, I should expect nothing less. You are a mess as usual. Can't you do anything with that hair of yours? And at least have the decency to put on a clean dress." Adelaide looked her up and down with a look of disgust.

Megan was used to these morning beratings and said nothing. If she uttered a word her grandmother would take it as disrespect. Listening to how worthless her grandmother thought her to be was far better than getting beaten again.

She often wondered what it would be like to have Moriah as her guardian instead of Adelaide. Or what it would be like to have a mother, like those children who she saw walking in the park in their starched pinafores with their beautiful curls. Not that she wasn't grateful for what she did have. It was better than being on the street, like the precious children she loved so much.

After a few more minutes of lecturing, Adelaide gave Megan a list of instructions for her day, and Megan's heart sank. It was several pages long. She was glad she had gotten to see the baby this morning.

Adelaide had listed fixing up the guest room as her first chore. That meant Helena was coming for the weekend. She inwardly groaned. Helena was the same age as she was, and they were cousins. That was the end of their similarity. Adelaide adored Helena and doted on her every whim. Megan was another story. Megan knew there was no love in Adelaide's heart for her. Every day she was a reminder of the fact that her father had left his mother for "that woman," as Adelaide called her. Megan was the picture of her mother, according to Moriah, and that renewed Adelaide's hatred every time she saw Megan.

Adelaide had never forgiven "that woman" for luring Jamison out West. An Irish woman and a serving girl, Eileen McDougal was not classy enough for Adelaide's son. Not in Adelaide's eyes. When Megan had arrived on her doorstep nearly eighteen years ago, Adelaide would have put her out on the street. But Helena's mother, Amelia, had convinced her to keep the child out of "Christian Duty." Amelia had doted on the two girls, and they had been friends when they were small. Then Amelia had died, and Adelaide in her grief chose to focus on her hate. So Megan had been allowed to stay, but only as a poorly treated servant.

Megan's gaze traveled farther down the list and a smile crept onto her face. She was supposed to fix up all three guest rooms. That meant Uncle Henri and her rakish cousin Titus St. James would be joining Helena. Uncle Henri was a kind soul, though he was a bit absentminded. And Titus just made Megan smile. He was a gambler, and a rogue, but he had always shown her kindness. In fact the two had been great chums all their lives. Memories of some of their escapades drifted through her mind. Megan caught herself before she began to giggle. Adelaide was in a foul mood, and she did not want to exacerbate it.

"Well, go!" Adelaide dismissed Megan with a wave of her hand, and Megan hurried to get started. The chores would take her all day and possibly late into the night if she were going to finish them all.

It was very late when Megan finally crawled between her thin covers. She wasn't going to get much sleep, but the prospect of seeing Henri and Titus made some of her exhaustion melt away. Helena was becoming more and more like Adelaide, and she tended to make Megan's life miserable when she was around. The two women would gang up on her and delighted in bullying her.

Megan shivered and burrowed farther into her bed. The attic was always either cold or sweltering, but these damp nights were miserable.

As she lay in bed shivering, she let her mind drift. On nights like this it was easy to think about what could have been. What her family was like. Her mother, her father, her brothers.

She knew what her father looked like, at least as a boy and a young man, because Adelaide kept his portrait in the upper hall. He had blue eyes, like Adelaide's in color, but different in the kindness they held. The entire family in the portrait had the same blond hair and blue eyes. A stark contrast to Megan's coloring.

Megan barely remembered Amelia, and she had no recollection of her father. Adelaide had reminded her often that her father had sent her away when her mother had died in childbirth. She wondered what her brothers looked like and if she resembled any of them. Drifting into sleep she prayed someday she would meet her family.

Megan twisted her face into a grimace as she tried to tame her coppery curls into a neat braid. It didn't work. It never did. Her curls always pulled loose, and her grandmother had threatened to have her head shaved more than once. She finally managed to subdue her locks into some semblance of order, then hurried downstairs to help Moriah with breakfast.

She had overheard Adelaide telling Rollins, the butler, that the St Jameses would arrive on the morning train. She hoped Adelaide would give her some time with Uncle Henri and Titus. Helena, however, would want little to do with her.

Moriah met her at the bottom of the stairs with a glass of cold milk, and a piece of warm cornbread drizzled with maple syrup.

"Megan!" Adelaide's shrill voice echoed throughout the house just as Megan finished eating. Megan sighed and swiped the crumbs from her face with the back of her hand, then hurried to find her enraged grandmother. She found her in Helena's room.

"You call this clean?" Adelaide was as angry as Megan had ever seen her, only she didn't know why. She had cleaned the room from top to bottom.

"Yes, ma'am, I cleaned in here," Megan protested.

Adelaide turned around, holding out a white-gloved hand before her. She raised a finger, on the tip of which was a black spot of dust.

Megan closed her eyes. She knew she had missed something. It had been so late when she finished cleaning last night that she had forgotten the baseboards and windowsills.

"If you can't do your job, I don't know why I should keep you on. You are worthless," Adelaide began.

"Grandmother, I am sorry. It was just so late and I was so very tired. I still am, in fact." Megan forgot herself for a moment and spoke up. She clamped her hand over her mouth as she realized what she said. But it was too late. Adelaide stormed toward her, her face purple with anger.

"Don't you talk back to me. Don't you ever talk back to me." Grabbing Megan by the arm, Adelaide's face twisted with hate, then relaxed into a catlike smile. Megan shivered in fear. When her grandmother smiled at her it was never a good thing.

Adelaide's grip tightened painfully, causing Megan to wince and try to pull away

"If you are in need of a little rest, I am sure a week at Blackwell's would help you get your strength back. Don't you?" Adelaide sneered.

Megan's blood ran cold. She had gone to the home for the insane once with her grandmother to plant a tree for the Ladies' Aid Society, as a token of their support for what they called the "poor unfortunate inmates." It had been a sham. A nice luncheon for the ladies, and a nice lesson for Megan.

Ever since that day, Adelaide had threatened to take her there every time she was angry, and Megan knew it was no empty threat. The screams that had echoed through those cold, drafty halls still haunted her.

"No, ma'am. I am feeling fine. Please, Please. I will clean the baseboards and windowsills now," Megan pleaded.

"Then get to it." Adelaide released her with a shove.

Megan hurried to gather her cleaning supplies, then scrubbed the room until every surface shone. She even got Rollins, who was also Moriah's husband, to help move the heavy four-post bed to get the baseboards behind it.

Megan finished cleaning just as Adelaide returned. Rollins ducked behind the door as she entered the room. Her wide brimmed hat was so large the older woman had to tip her head to get through the door, and prevented her from seeing the lanky butler.

"I suppose it will do. Now go. Cook has an errand for you." Adelaide swept out of the room with barely a cold glance at her, and Megan relaxed. Rollins winked at her has he hurried down the back stairs. Everyone in the household would gladly face Adelaide's wrath to help Megan, but no one could afford to lose their job.

Megan hurried downstairs behind Rollins, to the kitchen. Moriah took the cleaning supplies out of Megan's hands and shooed her and Rollins into the pantry, where she gave each of them a warm cookie straight out of the oven. They enjoyed their cookies for just a few minutes while Moriah bustled about.

"Megan, your grandmother wants me to make a special meal for your uncle Henri and your cousins. I need a few more things from the market, and your grandmother has been complaining of a toothache and wants you to pick up some laudanum at Dr. Franks's." Moriah pushed a basket into Megan's hands. It felt a little heavy, and Megan lifted the towel covering it. Inside, she found a dozen warm cookies and some assorted breads.

"I know you feed some of the street children," Moriah murmured, touching Megan's shoulder. Megan smiled at her in thanks, then hastened off toward the market. If she hurried she might get to spend a little time with Titus and Uncle Henri before dinner.

She dashed straight to the austere offices of Dr. Wilhelm Augustus Franks, doctor to those who lived on the Upper East Side. She always felt snubbed when she walked into the office, even when she came in the side door the servants used.

True to form, Doctor Franks glared at her and held out the medicine with two fingers as though he would contract some deadly disease if their fingers should accidentally brush each other's.

She shoved the tiny bottle of laudanum deep into her basket and hurried on her way. It was another chilly day, and she wanted to get to Johns and the children before the cookies got cold and hard. The street kids would love them either way, but Megan wanted to give them the pleasure of having a fresh warm cookie — one she was certain several of them had never had. She hurried through the stalls at the marketplace, picking up the necessities Moriah had instructed her to get: onions, greenhouse tomatoes, a few herbs, and a nice block of sugar.

It took her a few minutes to find Johns and his ragtag crew. They were selling newspapers on a different corner than usual. Her heart constricted at the sight of their little toes and fingers nearly blue from the cold. She sat on some nearby stairs and handed the goodies over. Moriah had packed the cookies well. They were still slightly warm and chock-full of nuts and plump raisins.

Johns divvied up six of the cookies and wrapped the remaining ones in a newspaper and put the bundle under his hat to save for later. The children scarfed the cornbread and buns Moriah had sent as well. Underneath it all they discovered a jar of milk. Megan nearly cried at Moriah's thoughtfulness.

She handed the jar to Johns, who held it as if it were made of gold. He carefully helped the children drink from the jar, starting with Anna, the youngest, then Joey, Charlie, Bethy, and Davis. He took his share last, as he always did, but not before offering Megan some.

"You sure you don't want none, Miss Megan? I knows you don't get much foods, either," he said solemnly. Megan pulled Anna into her lap, giving her a fierce hug, and Joey and Bethy snuggled in close. She looked at Johns tenderly.

"You go ahead, I have had plenty this morning. Moriah made sure of that." Megan smiled. Johns gulped down a few swallows, then gave the remainder to Anna and Joey to share. Megan used her fingers to gently detangle Anna's hair, then carefully put it into a braid. Anna smiled up at her, a look of adoration in her eyes. Megan gave her one last hug as she tucked the jar that had held the milk back into the basket.

"I have to go. I will try and find you again soon. Be careful and try to stay warm."

Megan waved as she hurried back home. The wind was bitterly cold, and Megan pulled her shawl up to try to keep her neck and back warm. Her feet and legs were nearly numb when she got back to the house. Her shoes and stockings were soaking wet, and so was the bottom of her dress. She shut the kitchen door and went right for the stove.

"Hi, Squirt." A silky-smooth, buttery voice warmed Megan almost as much as the fire from the stove. She turned with a grin to find her favorite cousin sitting at the kitchen table, his shiny shoes jauntily propped on its surface.

"Titus," she breathed, her smile nearly splitting her face. He stood and took one step to stand before her.

Megan laughed. She still came to about the middle of his chest. He wrapped his strong arms around her and gave her a crushing hug. She squeezed him back, sinking into his warmth. His smart taffeta vest was scratchy against her face, and he smelled of sweet tobacco and strong coffee. She rested her face on his chest and could hear the steady rhythm of his heart.

"It is so good to see you. You are looking quite... dapper." Megan smiled.

"I wanted to say hello, but I can't stay. I've got a busy night ahead of me. Got an invite to play with some of the boys at an exclusive game at the St. Nicholas. Only the best players will be there." Titus's face was flushed with excitement.

Megan was slightly disappointed he was leaving so soon, but she didn't let it show on her face. Titus brushed a kiss on her forehead and was out the door before she could blink.

Moriah gave her a look of sympathy as she took the basket from Megan and silently continued her dinner preparations

One of the bells above the stove broke the peaceful business of the two women, and Moriah sighed as she wiped her floured hands on her apron and left the room. A tap on the back door drew Megan's attention.

She wiped her hands on the flour-sack towel hung by the door and opened it. She was surprised to find Davis standing in the doorway and pulled the shivering boy into the warmth of the kitchen and over to the stove.

"Davis, what are you doing here? Is everything all right?" Megan grasped the thin boy by the shoulders.

"Yes, miss, you just dropped this and Johns thought you might need it." Davies dug in his threadbare pants and pulled out the small bottle of laudanum from Dr. Franks's office.

"Oh Davis! Thank you." Megan slumped in relief as she took it from the boy. She would have been in all kinds of trouble if she had lost the laudanum. She'd reached above the stove to grab a fresh roll to give to Davis when the rustle of taffeta distracted her. She turned to see Helena smirking in the doorway.

"Well, who is this filthy little ragamuffin? Does Grandmother know you feed the little rats?" Her face was twisted into a mask of disgust and revulsion.

"I don't need it, miss. I has had enough." Little Davis's chin jutted out defiantly, even as his stomach loudly protested.

"Take it, Davis," Megan said kindly as she turned to her haughty cousin. "Leave him alone, Helena. He isn't taking anything from anyone. Would you begrudge the boy some food? You have more than you could ever need." Megan stepped in front of Davies. She would not allow Helena to bully the child. She had little choice but to respect Adelaide. Helena was a different story.

"You dare speak to me that way?" Helena's voice rose.

"I am your cousin," Megan protested

"You are nothing but a servant," Helena spat back.

"You can't talk to Miss Megan that way. She is nice, and kind and loverly, and you, you is mean and nasty and... and... and ugly." Davis came out from behind Megan's skirts and stood arms akimbo facing Helena.

Helena was shaking with rage, and before Megan could stop her she hauled back and slapped Davis. The child fell hard against the stone wall.

Megan watched in horror as Helena walked toward him. She reacted without a second thought and pulled her cousin back. Helena broke free, but Megan got between her and the boy and slapped the older girl across the face. When that didn't stop Helena, Megan tackled her.

"Get off me you dirty thing," Helena shrieked.

"Will you leave him alone?" Megan kept her arms wrapped tightly around her nemesis. If someone called a policeman, Davis would be in a lot of trouble. The street children were often accused of crimes and punished severely. Only last week a ten year old boy was hung for stealing a pair of shoes.

"I am going to teach him a lesson on how to treat his betters," Helena ground out.

The two girls struggled for a moment before Megan was hauled unceremoniously off her cousin.

"What exactly do you think you are doing?"

She turned to face Adelaide, who was purple with rage. Megan had never been so frightened in all her life, but she was more afraid for Davis.

She looked over Adelaide's shoulder and was relieved to see Moriah helping him out the door. Her arm was beginning to throb where Adelaide's nails were digging through her thin blue dress. She didn't dare move; she barely dared to breathe.

Helena got up and brushed herself off. She opened her mouth to say something, but the look her grandmother gave her sent her flouncing out of the room.

Adelaide let go of Megan. "Get upstairs to your room." Her voice was a low hiss.

Megan picked up her skirts and ran for the stairs. She caught a glimpse of Moriah's pale face as she left the kitchen. She was in trouble, and Moriah knew it too.

Chapter 2

Megan stared at her grandmother and the rotund officer in horror. "What?" she breathed, her heart pounding.

"Get. In. The. Wagon." Adelaide's face was devoid of emotion.

Megan saw neither compassion nor kindness on the police officer's flabby face. She caught the conspiratorial glance between him and her grandmother and her stomach lurched. Adelaide had hauled her downstairs before dawn lightened the sky. Megan's head was still fuzzy from sleep, and she couldn't believe her grandmother had called the police over last night's argument with Helena.

The officer twisted her arm painfully and hauled her to the police wagon, where he shoved her inside. Megan scrambled into the cold and damp box as the door clanged shut. She sat down just as the wagon lurched forward. Megan slid off the narrow bench onto the wooden floor. The other two women in the wagon helped her up. They appeared as frightened as she felt.

Megan clung to the iron rings screwed into the wall as they bumped along the streets. Time and time again they lurched forward only to stop a short distance down the road. Megan covered her nose more than once as they traded passengers. Several of them were quite ripe. Women were dropped off at various jails, hospitals, and "homes for troubled women." From her perch inside the wagon, Megan thought the homes looked more like gloomy prisons.

As they rattled along, Megan listened to the conversations around her. She learned that the constable who had grabbed her was named Officer Pietro. He treated all the women with the same roughness as he had her that morning. The driver seemed to be a little kinder. Whenever they stopped, he would turn around and look through the barred window at the women inside and inquire how they were doing. He even smiled at Megan once.

Officer Pietro finally hauled Megan from the wagon late in the afternoon. The fading sun was bright after the dark of the paddy wagon. When she could focus, she realized they were at the docks. The smell of the river made her gag. She was exhausted and faint from hunger. Not so much as one drop of water had been offered to her, let alone food.

Officer Pietro kept an iron grip on her arm as he steered her through the crowd milling about and toward a small boat. The sign over it read: Blackwell's Island. Panic threatened to choke off her air. She pried at the fingers locked around her arm, pulling her entire body back.

"Please, no, you can't. I don't belong there. I am not crazy." She kept her voice low, so as not to draw attention to herself. If she created a scene things would only get worse. She struggled silently as the policeman dragged her closer to the docks.

Officer Pietro cuffed her behind her ear, stunning her.

"There is no call to treat her that way!" a deep voice interrupted their struggle.

Megan looked up to see a handsome stranger striding toward them. He had an air of confidence that commanded the attention of everyone in the vicinity. Even the doxies stopped their calling to watch him. His western-cut suit hugged his broad shoulders, and the dark navy fabric accentuated his kind gray eyes.

Megan recognized something else in their depths: profound sadness, a feeling she knew well. He turned those sad eyes to her, and a new emotion flickered across his face. Anger. This was also something Megan was familiar with. She took a step back as he reached for her. In his hand was a white linen square.

"I will not harm you." He held the handkerchief out.

Megan was confused. Did he want her to blow her nose?

"Who are you to tell me how to treat this crazy chit?" Officer Pietro had recovered his wits and thrust himself between Megan and her would-be rescuer.

"I am a lawman like yourself."

Officer Pietro dropped her arm, but the stranger's words sent new fear slithering down her spine. Surely this man was not similar to the evil policeman hauling her toward the boat to the insane asylum.

Megan did not hear the words the two men spoke, or rather, she did not understand them. She felt as if the words buzzed in her mind like bees around honey, never lighting long enough to make sense. Hunger gnawed at her stomach, making her nauseous.

A warm tickle crept down her neck, distracting her from wanting to chew her arm off from hunger. She reached up to scratch the irritation but found her hand blocked as the stranger pressed the damp handkerchief behind her ear. The throbbing pain changed to a sharp sting as cold water seeped into the cut Officer Pietro's ring had left on her neck. She stared at the kind stranger dumbly as her brain tried to wrap around what he was saying to her captor.

"I may not have authority in this precinct, but I assure you, I have friends on the judicial circuit who will hear about your brutality."

The man turned to her and patted her shoulder. "Miss, I am sorry you have been treated so poorly."

"Thank you, sir, for your kindness." Megan tried to push the handkerchief back into his hands, but he would not take it.

"Keep it. Please. I wish I could do more." His large, rough hands curled her small one around the damp cloth.

Megan barely had a chance to smile her thanks before Officer Pietro snatched her arm roughly and pulled her away. The dock swayed under her as she tripped on the rough boards. He hauled her on board the boat and shoved her into the single cabin.

"Keep your mouth shut or you will never get out." The menace in his voice frightened her.

He slammed the door, shutting her in.

One beefy attendant, a single bunk that reeked of sickness, and four women filled the cramped space. One of the women lay unconscious on the bunk.

As the boat left the dock, a breeze came through the single window where the attendant leaned against the sill. The smell of whiskey from the intoxicated man hit Megan full in the face, and her eyes watered from its potency.

Between her empty stomach, the smells in the room, and the rocking of the boat, Megan had all she could do to keep from vomiting. One of the women sitting on the floor smiled at her shyly and handed her a wax-paper-wrapped peppermint candy. Megan took the sweet and popped it in her mouth before the attendant could protest. She needn't have worried; he was too drunk to care.

The peppermint helped a little with her nausea, and she tolerated the boat ride without an incident. The other women were quiet; no one seemed to be in the mood to talk. The one who had given Megan the peppermint sat rocking herself, and Megan tried not to stare at the others.

The moment the boat slowed next to the dock on Blackwell's Island, Officer Pietro was back. He once again seized her arm in a grip so strong Megan expected to see bruises when she dressed for bed later. She remembered this horrible place from once when Adelaide had brought her to that luncheon and started shaking, more from fear than cold.

As they left off the boat, her captor pulled Megan one way, while the other passengers were herded down another path by the drunken attendant. Craning her neck, she tried to see where they were being taken, but she soon lost track of them.

A round woman in nurse's dress and a linen cap met them at the end of the dock. Judging by her smile and familiar greeting, she was friendly with the policeman. The imposing building loomed in front of them like some horrific yawning monster. Megan barely had time to register the words emblazoned on the metal plaque above the arched doorway. Lunatic Asylum. The nurse led them down a dark hallway that smelled of sweat and urine. Two huge iron, padlocked doors were at the far end, and down a little side hallway sat an ornately carved door.

The nurse led them to the oak door and knocked, and a muffled voice told them to enter. On the other side of the door was a lavish office. The sign on the desk said Superintendent Richards.

"Sit down and keep quiet." Officer Pietro shoved Megan onto a chair by the door before sauntering to the desk to talk to the pale, thin man behind it. He took a wad of bills from his pocket and peeled several off, then handed them to the superintendent, who pocketed the money.

"I don't belong here." Megan's protest sounded hollow even to her own ears.

Richards was being paid for his silence. He smirked and yanked a bell cord behind his desk.

A burly attendant and the nurse who had greeted them came through the wooden door.

"Take this one to see Dr. Giles in Admitting. She will be with us for a while." The man gave her a condescending smile.

Megan fought the urge to protest; it would only fall on deaf ears. The desire to kick, scream, and run was overwhelming, but any such reaction would only solidify their claims, and she wouldn't be able to get off the island even if she could escape from the asylum

"I don't belong here. This is not right." Megan kept her voice calm as she made direct eye contact with the superintendent and the police officer. Officer Pietro glared back at her, but Superintendent Richards at least had the good grace to look ashamed. The brawny attendant snatched her arm like she was a rag doll.

Megan glared at him. "I am not resisting. You don't need to be rough," she said with as much dignity as she could muster.

The brute laughed and gripped her arm tighter, nearly lifting her off the ground as he walked down the gray hallway. She struggled along on her tiptoes while the nurse puffed as she ran to keep abreast of his lengthy strides. The hallway seemed to stretch on for eternity.

Finally the attendant lugged her through the double doors and shoved her onto a narrow wooden bench. "Sit here until the doctor is ready to see you," he growled.

The nurse wheezed from exertion as she waddled to the desk at the front of the room. Megan peered around the room, but it was bare and empty, save for a run-down harpsichord in the center. Curious they would have an instrument here. It was a long, bare room, with yellowed benches encircling it. These old and straight benches were far too over crowded.

The stark white walls were somewhat relieved by three small paintings. Megan squinted to see them. All three were landscapes. Even the paintings were dull and barren. She sighed.

There were a few other patients in the intake room, but most were doing their best to be inconspicuous. One young woman was weeping quietly into her hands. Several nurses played cards at a table at the front of the room, seeming to ignore their charges.

A piercing scream from the yard drew Megan's attention. A woman with matted hair and rotten teeth clutched the bars from the outside. Her glassine eyes flickered to and fro wildly, never focusing. The woman was hopelessly insane. Two sturdy nurses peeled her away from the bars and hauled her off kicking and cursing. Fear once again clutched at Megan's stomach.

A shapely blond nurse came out of the door to what Megan assumed was the doctor's office.

"That one is next." The heavyset nurse at the desk pointed to her.

The blonde beckoned for Megan to follow.

She considered refusing, but the rough attendant was still standing next to the door, so she chose to keep her dignity and entered the doctor's sparse office.

Dr. Giles was a slightly balding, middle-aged man who paid the voluptuous nurse far more attention than he did his patient. His heavy, cloying cologne hung in the stale air, turning Megan's stomach.

The nurse and doctor flirted with each other while performing a cursory examination. Megan's height, weight, and general coloring were noted. The doctor glanced inside her mouth at her teeth, and made a few more notes in his book.

She finally mustered the courage to speak. "I am not sick, and I do not want to stay here. No one has a right to shut me up in this manner."

He took no notice of her, and the nurse roughly shoved her back into the waiting room.

The nurses sitting at the head of the room ignored her, so she walked to the harpsichord and ran her fingers over the keys. A small metal plate was screwed into the casing. Donated by the Ladies' Aid Society. Ah, that explained the out of place instrument.

"Do you play?" a dark-haired young woman asked.

Megan smiled at her. Her plain clothes identified her as an inmate, but she was better dressed than most of the women in the waiting room. Her eyes were bright and inquisitive, and she was the first friendly face Megan had seen here.

"Oh, yes, ever since I was a child." Megan's mind drifted back to the times she had spent enjoying the piano when her grandmother was off on one of her trips to Europe, or at a society party.

"Please play," several women insisted. A few leaned forward, hope spreading across their faces.

Megan sat gingerly on the rickety wooden chair before the old harpsichord. She struck a few notes, and the ill tuned response sent a grinding chill through her. She played for a few moments while she took in the waiting room.

The woman who had spoken to Megan carted a chair over to the piano.

"Everyone here calls me Miss Nell," she whispered.

Megan scrutinized her for a few seconds as she continued to play. Miss Nell didn't look her in the eye. Instead, she fixed her gaze to the side or looked at Megan's hands. She seemed to fear that meeting Megan's gaze would come across as a challenge. One glance at the nurses confirmed her hunch.

The nurses at the front of the room reminded Megan of a picture she had seen of a pride of lionesses in one of Helena's books. They sat glaring at the women in the waiting room, and if one dared meet their gaze, they would cuff them behind the ear or push them to the floor. Megan paused for a moment, and Miss Nell finally peeked at her and smiled.

She is pretty when she smiles. I wonder why she is in this dreadful place. She seems as sane as I am.

"I am Megan, Megan Carter." Megan smiled back as she started another melody.

"Everyone into the hall." The order came abrupt and harsh

The women shuffled reluctantly into the dingy hallway. The barred windows were not covered, and the crisp evening air whistled through them. Most of the women were clad in only thin gowns, with no shawls. The nurses, however, had floor-length woolen dresses and overcoats. Megan rubbed her arms to try to stay warm, staring at the nurses with longing.

The nurses kept the women waiting in the hall for half an hour before the padlocked doors at the far end were finally open. A viselike grasp seized her hand and tugged her forward.

"Stick with me," Miss Nell said.

Rushing forward as smoothly as she could with Miss Nell towing her, Megan found herself being steered toward an uncovered metal table in the corner of the room beyond the doors, which was lined with several plates. Megan studied the meal sitting before her: a piece of gray boiled meat, stale bread with what she judged to be rancid butter, a single boiled potato, and a dish of what appeared to be stewed prunes. All of it stone-cold.

Megan was starving and tried valiantly to eat, but she couldn't do it. She offered her bread to a young blue-eyed girl at the next table whose bread another woman had taken. The girl couldn't have been much older than fourteen or fifteen. A few inmates, in contrast, appeared to be in their seventies.

"You must eat to keep up your strength. I know it is awful, but try," Miss Nell urged.

Megan choked down a few bites of the wretched food but was afraid what little she got down would come right back up. The women at her table grabbed for it gratefully when she pushed it away, not at all taken aback by its horribleness. Miss Nell sighed but didn't press the issue.

One of the women at her table appeared particularly frail. Tillie, she said her name was, and she had given Megan the peppermint on the trip to this dreadful place. Her husband had said she was sick and needed rest and to be taken care of. Tillie had had a fit of hysteria when her three-year-old son had been taken from her arms as she was placed in the ambulance, and they had brought her here instead of to the hospital in the city.

"I panicked. It has only been a few weeks since we buried our little Sarah, and having him snatched from my arms brought back many memories of losing her. I miss them so much. I have never been apart from my son overnight, and I am afraid my husband won't know where I am." Tillie's lower lip trembled, and she began crying silently. Megan was horrified. She was truly frightened for Tillie in this horrible place.

Miss Nell gallantly offered the young girl her cup of hot water masquerading as tea. At least it was hot.

There was little talking during dinner. The nurses marched around the room, giving orders and boxing women about the head if they had the least little complaint.

A woman at one of the tables near the front of the room began screaming and fighting the nurses as they forced the women sitting there to stand and leave. Megan and Tillie clung to each other in fright as a few of the other patients muttered to themselves. Megan caught the word bath.

Whatever could be so terrible about a bath? What scared her most, however, was Miss Nell's reaction. Her face had gone pale, and her lips were pinched in a thin line.

"I have to go now. Whatever you do, don't fight them. Do what they say. It will only make things worse if you don't," Miss Nell said.

Megan didn't understand where she was going, but one of the other patients told her Miss Nell was a paying patient, which meant she was kept in a different ward. All the patients spent their days together, but Megan ascertained after talking to a few of the other women, that wasn't the same at night.

A nurse motioned for everyone at their table to go through the door next. Everyone was fairly docile and left the room with no resistance.

Her group had a dozen women, she figured as the nurses herded them back down the cold dark hallway to a door she hadn't seen before, then drove them into the room beyond. After the dimness of the hallway, Megan shielded her eyes against the bright lights. When they had adjusted, she saw why the other woman had panicked. The nurses hauled the woman ahead of her stark naked out of the bathtub. Her lips were blue, and she did not appear to be conscious. The horror of the scene took Megan's breath away.

"Take your clothes off." The rough, red-faced nurse pulled Megan into the center of the room.

"I beg your pardon?" Megan did not understand. She searched around for a screen of some sort to duck behind, but there was no such luxury. The only tub was in the center of the bare, wet room. A woman with a tangled nest of hair rocked next to the tub, muttering to herself as she toyed with the stained washcloth in her hands.

The nurses descended upon her, pushing and pulling her this way and that. One yanked her feet out from under her and jerked her shoes off, while another pulled her dress over her head in one swift tug. Megan clung to her shift, but that was soon removed with a slap on her hands and a knock upside her head for good measure.

The crazy woman with the discolored washcloth chuckled fiendishly as Megan gawked around in horror. The other women were staring at her, most in abject terror; Megan was afraid Tillie was going to faint dead away. She was soon standing in front of more than a dozen women with not a stitch of clothing on.

"Please, please make the others go away. Can they not wait outside the door?" Megan pleaded.

"Shut up," one of the nurses said, shoving her toward two women standing beside the tub.

She didn't wait for them to put her in the tub, but jumped right in, more out of wanting to escape everyone's gaping stares than wanting to cooperate.

Gray, soapy film covered the top of the frigid water, and the bottom of the tub was gritty with the filth from the previous bathers. Megan gasped as a bucket of even colder water was dumped over her head. The insane woman scooped soft soap, or at least Megan prayed it was soap, from a tin bucket and proceeded to scrub Megan from head to toe as two nurses held her still.

Three more buckets of ice water were poured over her head in quick succession, and the water invaded her every pore. A moment of relief came as she was dragged, gasping from the tub. She had no doubt she must look absolutely insane at the moment, gulping for air and flopping like a fish. Her arms and legs were numb, blue with cold, and covered with goose bumps as big as mountains. Another few minutes in the frigid water and she suspected she would have been rendered unconscious.

Her clothes were put in a box, and labeled clearly with her name, but were not given back to her. She stared longingly at the white linen handkerchief that lay folded on top of her skirt. It was more than a piece of fabric now; it was another piece of humanity being stripped away from her.

Megan was handed a short cotton slip and instructed to put it on and follow the nurse. One of the white-capped women led her through a door marked Lunatic Asylum, BV Hall Six. With a shove, the nurse sent her sprawling into what Megan could only assume was a bed.

A burlap sack stuffed with straw for a pillow and a slick oilcloth covered a thin, musty mattress on the thick wooden board. A single woolen blanket was the only other covering. The minute she lay down, her wet hair flooded the straw pillow with water, and her woolen blanket was soon damp. Tillie was soon shoved into the bed next to her, and Megan could hear her teeth chattering.

No one got much sleep. The nurses talked loudly all night, and their heavy shoes clunked on the wooden floors as they walked the uncarpeted room regularly checking on their charges.

Megan's head was throbbing and her throat burned by morning Tillie was alarmingly pale in the morning light. Megan took her hand when to the time came to get out of bed. It was icy-cold. Megan's were not much warmer.

They were shown to a table at the end of the room.

"Wash yourselves and get dressed," one of the night nurses instructed with a bored expression. "Your clothes will be brought when you are done washing."

Megan was aghast when she realized the bowls of water had a thin layer of ice on them.

"Why do you not warm the rooms?" she asked the nurse.

"You are in a charity ward of the hospital. You should not expect royal treatment," the nurse scoffed. "Besides, the board of trustees says we cannot turn the steam heat on between March and October, and the pipes need repairing." But her face softened as she followed Megan's gaze to the delicate Tillie.

Megan did her best to wash up a little, but there was no helping her hair, which hung in wild ringlets around her face. No matter how she begged, the nurses would not give her a ribbon or even a piece of string to tie it back.

Megan returned to the bed she had occupied the previous night, which was closest to the double doors. She turned in surprise at the sound of a key in a padlock. The day nurses were unlocking the doors so they could bring them their clothes. Megan shuddered. They had been locked in the room all night.

A wad of clothes was tossed unceremoniously on her bed, and Megan scrambled to put them on. The underskirt was only a thin dark cotton, but it was a little warmer than the light shift she had worn to bed. The outer dress was made of white shapeless cotton and had a large black stain on it. Megan adjusted it the best she could, tying a knot at the waist to give herself a bit of shape. As she was fiddling with it, she found the underskirt was several inches longer than the outer dress.

There was no use in crying about it, so Megan continued dressing. She was getting ready to put on her stockings when she glanced at Tillie. The poor girl was shaking violently and couldn't get her dress buttoned.

Megan clutched the stockings in her hand with longing, but instead of putting them on, she helped Tillie button her dress, then handed them to her.

"Here, put these on over yours. They will help a little," Megan said with a smile.

"Aren't you cold?" Tillie could barely get the words through her chattering teeth.

"I don't typically get cold. Besides, you need them much more than I do," Megan assured her.

The night nurse stopped beside Tillie's bed. "I don't usually allow this, but here, take this. You won't last the week without it." She handed Tillie a gray, moth-eaten shawl. "Don't expect any more kindnesses from anyone here," she warned harshly as she clumped out the door.

Megan counted forty-five beds in Hall Six as the nurses marched them outside for their morning exercise. She noted, by both her nose and her eyes, that not all of the inmates had been bathed the night before. Miss Nell was in a group of women coming out of a slightly better kept building on the east side of the island.

A nurse instructed Megan and her group to stay on the walkway and follow a certain path. Miss Nell joined Megan and Tillie and they sandwiched Tillie between them, to try to warm her and to shield her from the nurses, who appeared to delight in randomly striking their patients.

As they rounded a corner, Megan caught sight of a strange procession heading toward them on another path. Several women were attached to a thick rope by leather belts, and two nurses oversaw the patients from a wooden cart at the end of the rope. Some of the patients were yelling and screaming, some were cursing, and some were singing, praying, or preaching. They had a horrific, vacant wildness in their eyes.

"Who are they?" Megan whispered to Miss Nell.

"Those are the most violent and dangerous patients, the ones deemed criminally insane," she whispered back, averting her gaze.

"Be careful, missy. You wouldn't want to find yourself in that ward," one of the nurses crept close and whispered loudly in Megan and Tillie's ears. Megan understood the woman's threat: behave, or you might find yourself in with those women. Tillie's pale face telegraphed her terror. Miss Nell looked at them with compassion but pretended not to hear. Megan understood: she had to protect herself.

Long before Megan was ready, they were told to return to the cold, damp halls of the asylum. They were forced to wash once more, forty women with only two towels afforded them. Megan shuddered as she observed women with open sores and women with clear, clean skin using the same towel. She carefully washed her face and used her underskirt to dry it as much as she could. She urged Tillie to do the same.

Breakfast was cold gruel, and lunch was not any better than dinner had been the night before. Boiled cabbage proved to be a staple at the institution. After eating, the women were forced to sit on the straight, wooden benches for hours with no activities provided them.

The nurses then allowed them another outing to walk for a few precious moments before it was back to the benches, which were positioned in front of the windows. The windows were always left wide open.

Day after day, this was the routine. Eat, walk, sit, eat, walk, and sit. Megan lost track of how long she had been in the asylum after the second or third day. She did what she could to keep Tillie's spirits up, but the poor girl was freezing and could barely sit up.

During one of their afternoon sessions sitting on the benches, the doors at the end of the hall opened, and the pompous doctor who had admitted her into the asylum strode through. With him was a much younger doctor with a kind face. Megan took a chance and called out to them. Nurse McCarten immediately struck her a vicious blow on the back of her head, but Megan was not deterred.

"Please, Doctor, my friend is ill," she said, trying to prop up Tillie as the delicate girl listed against her.

"Let her fall. It will teach her a lesson." The older doctor rolled his eyes. "Charity patients," he ground out to the young doctor.

The other man, however, did not appear to share his opinion, as he came straight to Megan and Tillie. He took Tillie's pulse, checked her eyes, and examined her tongue. Dr. Giles loomed over them, a disapproving frown plastered on his face.

"Have you no warmer clothing for them?" he asked the nurse as he also examined Megan.

"Sir, this is a charity ward. We do the best we can for the poor dears," Nurse McCarten simpered.

Megan covered her snort with a cough, trying not to get herself into trouble. The doctor caught it, though, and his eyes twinkled.

"My name is Dr. Kent. What is your name?" he asked the two women.

Megan knew Tillie was painfully shy and could not bring herself to answer. "My name is Megan, and this is my friend, Tillie," Megan said for them both.

"Nurse, you should close those windows. You will have several cases of pneumonia if you are not careful." He smiled at Megan and patted her shoulder.

"Dr. Giles, this girl seems to be quite well. Indeed, she shows no signs of insanity. Her eyes are clear, her answers precise. For what has she been brought here?"

Dr. Kent began talking to the other doctor before they were out of earshot. Megan leaned forward, keen on hearing Dr. Giles's answer.

"You mustn't put much stock in that. We get women here all the time who for a short period will appear as sane as you or I...." The rest of Dr. Giles's response was lost as they walked through the doorway.

Nurse McCarten turned to Megan. "It will be bad for you if you keep making trouble. Don't make me do something you will regret," she hissed.

And so the days passed. Megan couldn't remember how long it had been since she talked with Moriah. A week? Two? If she stayed much longer, she would go insane. The only things that kept her from drifting into the abyss of despair were her two friends and the memories of the kind gray-eyed stranger. She dreamed of him often.

Kindness was in short supply during her waking moments. She was horrified when one day, several nurses goaded a woman into hysterics and hauled her into a closet. Her cries grew softer and softer until Megan could no longer hear them. Several hours later the woman rejoined the others in the main room, and Megan could see finger-shaped bruises on her throat.

There was one nurse who cared for the patients with kindness and compassion. The young woman who had given Tillie the shawl the first day was on duty most nights. She would pull an extra blanket out for a frail inmate, or tenderly comfort a crying woman when she walked the wards. All of her actions were covered with brusqueness, but Megan could see the kindness beneath them.

How hard it must be for her. A place like this could kill any bit of kindness in the soul.

Dr. Kent was another exception to the heartless staff. He checked in on Tillie and Megan almost every day, but although he was caring, he did not offer to help either woman out of her predicament.

Few women ever had visitors, but Miss Nell was an exception. Megan, Tillie, and Miss Nell had been taking their afternoon stroll when Nurse McCarten came over and told her she had company. Megan and Tillie had not seen her until dinnertime. She joined them at the table, her eyes red-rimmed from crying. When pressed, she told Megan her husband had come to see her.

"He refuses to have me released. He is too busy courting society women. He doesn't want me anymore," she sobbed.

Megan was heartbroken for her. If she ever got away from this horrible place, she was determined to help both her new friends.

The nurses delighted in tormenting their patients. Every day someone would disappear from their group. Megan was terrified Tillie would be next.

Today was bright and sunny, and the three friends were happy to be walking instead of sitting inside the dark, dank building. Just ahead of them, a tall, thin woman, who had been admitted the night before, broke down in a fit of crying.

Megan froze in horror as the nurses descended upon her, hitting and kicking. One nurse hit her repeatedly with a thick wooden broomstick.

Ignoring her friends' warnings, Megan dashed forward to help. She ducked under a pair of restraining hands and tackled the woman wielding the broomstick.

"Stop, stop, you are killing her!" Megan screamed as she scrambled to her feet, her arms outstretched as she blocked the nurses from injuring the poor woman on the ground any further.

"You will pay for your interference, my pet," the nurse snarled.

Megan didn't even have time to shield her face before the broomstick cracked across her skull. The world went black.

Andrew Summers groaned as he stepped out of the hansom cab. He would rather be in the saddle on his horse than bound up in these fancy duds and stuffed into these cracker-box carriages. Several days on a train lay before him, but he couldn't wait to get out of the city and back home. The wide-open range was far more welcoming than the oppressive concrete and noise here.

"Wait for me, driver. I will only be a moment."

"Sure thing, mister." The grizzled old man grinned down at him.

Andrew walked through the cemetery gates, across the open grass and up the hill to the large oak tree standing like a silent sentinel over the gravestones. He stared down at the dark mound of earth with its plain wooden cross. It was the only grave in this corner.

"I think you would like the view here, Mother. I wish I could take you back with me; you would love the mountains in the spring. I am sorry we did not have more time." He spent a few more minutes saying goodbye before he folded himself back up into the cab and instructed the driver to take him to the train station.

The smell of sewage flowing through the streets turned his stomach. Or was that grief? He stared out the window, unashamed of the tears that streamed down his face. The sonorous bellow of the ferry horn shook him out of his sorrow for a moment, and he reached into his pocket for his handkerchief, but his fingers found only emptiness. His mind drifted back to the day his mother died. Had it only been a week? Ten days? He couldn't remember.

Julia Summers had died in his arms as the sun crept over the horizon, at peace and happy. His father had been gone for many years, and he was now alone. Andrew had walked for blocks, thinking and remembering his childhood. He clenched his fist at the memory of the policeman and the girl.

The girl's silent struggle hit him harder than any scream would have, and her pleading emerald eyes had drawn him to her.

He wished he could have helped her more. Something had definitely been amiss there, but the uniformed officer had been right: Andrew had no jurisdiction. He wanted to think about it further, but the cab rolled to a stop.

"We'se here," his driver announced. "I'll take yer bag into the station."

Andrew climbed from the cab. He turned to thank the man and slammed into a well-dressed dandy in a taffeta vest. He had seen enough men in his travels to know this was a gambler, and a wealthy one.

"Excuse me, sir." The young man surprised him with politeness.

"My fault, I wasn't watching where I was going." Andrew laughed off the apology, but the young man truly looked distressed. Much more distressed than running into a stranger should cause. The young man was pale and his face held a haunted look. Closer inspection revealed the gambler had several days' worth of blonde stubble, and dark circles under his eyes. "Is there anything I can help you with?" His job was helping people, whether here or at home.

"I am looking for my cousin. Maybe you've seen her? A petite redhead?" Hope crossed the young man's features.

"When did you lose her?" Andrew turned to scan the crowd.

"She's been missing for over a week now."

"A week? Have you called the authorities?"

"Yes, but they won't do anything without my grandmother stepping in, and she is certain Megan ran off."

"Did she take any trunks or things with her? Surely the stationmaster would remember a redheaded girl traveling in the last few days."

A strange expression settled on the gambler's face. Not until the gentleman spoke again was he able to define the look: shame.

"Megan is a servant girl in my grandmother's household. She wouldn't have any luggage, not even a spare dress. She was wearing a blue dress the last time I saw her."

"A week ago, you say?" Surely it couldn't be the woman he had helped on the docks.

"About that, I am not really sure how long she has been missing."

Andrew's eyebrows arched toward his hairline. He tried to school his features, but the other man blushed anyway.

"I do know that an Officer Pietro is the one looking for her. He was at my grandmother's house yesterday with a report. He has had no luck."

"I happen to know who Officer Pietro is." Andrew clenched and unclenched his fists. It was the same woman. He had gotten the abusive policeman's name during their encounter.

"That does not sound good." The way the young man blanched gave Andrew some hope that he truly did care for his cousin.

Andrew paid off his driver and took the young man aside to tell him what he knew. Twenty minutes later, Andrew boarded his train to finally head for home. He spent some time praying for the young man he had sent racing toward Blackwell's Island and the beautiful, copper-headed woman.

"Megan, Megan, are you all right?"

Megan touched her face. It burned as if it were on fire. She expected to see blood on her fingers, but there was none. Miss Nell and Tillie were bending over her, their gazes filled with concern.

"I am all right." Megan's head throbbed. Her friends helped her to her feet. Megan could see Tillie was terrified, and she did her best to act like she was okay.

"Keep walking." One of the nurses who had participated in the beating shoved Megan hard and her ribs screamed in protest. The nurses had clearly turned their anger on her, even though she had been unconscious. At least they had stopped beating the other woman.

Megan couldn't take this place much longer. She would go truly insane.

"Megan Carter," a strident voice called.

She turned toward it, and stomach clenched in fear. It was the nurse who had wielded the broomstick.

"Yes." Megan strode forward bravely, shaking off her friends' protestations.

"Come with me. You are wanted in the superintendent's office," the nurse ground out.

"Megan, please don't go. I am afraid for you." Tillie plucked at Megan's sleeve.

"If I don't go willingly, they will only force me to go." Megan sighed. She smiled at her friend—a smile she didn't feel—and hugged her tight.

The nurse sighed and tapped her foot impatiently. "Don't let me hurry you," she sneered.

Megan followed her back into the dark building.

The minute they were out of sight of the others, the nurse turned on her, and her hammy hands wrapped around Megan's throat. Her vision blurred and her knees buckled, and Megan cried out as the woman struck her in the stomach with a vicious blow. When the nurse let go of her, she sank to the floor retching.

"Keep your mouth shut if you know what is good for you, dearie. I don't want to get nasty, but I will."

She was hauled to her feet by her hair, one arm twisted painfully behind her back, and marched through the frigid hallway to the superintendent's office. The nurse slapped her soundly a few times before opening the door and shoving Megan inside.

Megan stumbled a few steps and fell against a broad, solid chest. The familiar scent of tobacco and strong coffee struck her nose as she flailed to gain her footing. Strong hands grasped her upper arms and righted her.

She tipped her head back and found herself staring into the steely gray eyes of her cousin Titus. He lifted her easily in his arms and placed her on the settee in the corner. His gentleness belied the anger blazing in his eyes.

Megan's head was spinning and she struggled to catch her breath. Closing her eyes, she took a deep breath, trying to stop the spinning. A cool cloth was placed on her head, and a glass pressed to her lips. She took a sip, but the strong liquid burned her throat and she shook her head to get away from the offensive beverage.

"No, chérie, you must drink this." A familiar voice echoed through the room.

"Uncle Henri?" Her eyes flew open, sending waves of pain through her head.

"Yes, ma petite. I am here."

When Megan could focus, she searched around the room. Titus stood over her, shoulders rigid, his very stance telling of his fury. Uncle Henri was kneeling beside her, and behind him in the shadows stood a sober Helena.

"Oh, Helena, I am sorry I struck you. It was wrong of me," Megan said when she came into view. Helena hung her head in shame.

"Sir. This is indeed my niece. And as you have no paperwork stating she is here, I presume it is all right for us to take her home?" Henri rose and turned to face the fat man behind the desk.

"I don't understand how something like this could have happened," the man blustered. It was a lie. Megan had seen him accepting money from the officer who had brought her, but she held her tongue. It would be better not to speak of it at the moment. She wanted out desperately.

"I don't either, and believe me, we will be making inquiries." Titus's voice was cold. Henri St. James stood tall and distinguished next to his son, nodding in agreement.

"You may, of course, take her home, and please accept our humblest apologies," the superintendent mumbled. "Ah, here are her things."

A nurse Megan had never seen before came into the room carrying a box with no name on it. Megan opened it and found her belongings inside. She distinctly remembered when her clothes were put in the box. It had been clearly labeled with her name. The superintendent was covering his tracks. If they hadn't known her name, they couldn't be held responsible for holding her against her will or without cause.

Her fingers brushed the precious embroidered handkerchief sitting on top. She had dreamed of that little square of fabric every night.

Titus directed everyone out the door as he spoke. "Helena, you help Megan dress. The rest of us will wait outside."

The nurse and superintendent hurried ahead of Henri and Titus, leaving the cousins alone. Neither girl spoke as Megan slipped into her old blue dress. Her stockings were missing and she would have to go barelegged under her clothes, but the thought didn't bother her. She was going home.

Helena plucked a small mirror and a comb from her reticule, and Megan winced as she inspected her face in the mirror. A black-and-green bruise was forming on one cheekbone. Her cheeks were red, but her face pale, and her hair was a disheveled mess. Megan tried to work the comb through, but she couldn't make her hair do anything, so she handed the comb and mirror back to her cousin with a little shrug.

"May I?" Helena surprised Megan by asking. At her nod, Helena swiftly and expertly combed through the unruly mass of curls and twisted them into an elegant chignon. A few pins and they were ready to rejoin the men. As they were leaving the room, Helena stopped Megan with her hand on her arm.

"Megan, I am sorry. My behavior has been inexcusable lately. Mama would be ashamed of me. I should never have been so unkind to you or the little boy. I am truly sorry. I didn't know what happened that night after I left the kitchen. You must believe me. I can't believe Grandmamma would send you here, either. Not if she understood what it was like. She must not have known." Helena's expression begged Megan to tell her she was right.

Megan's heart wrung with compassion for her cousin. She was fairly certain her grandmother had known exactly what was in store for Megan when she had sent her with Officer Pietro that day. Seeing how Adelaide reacted to having her home would be interesting.

Chapter 3

As they walked down the hallway, Megan grew dizzy with hunger and the pain in her head. She glanced out the window as they walked, trying to focus on something else. At the sight of the nurses herding the women back indoors, she remembered Tillie and Miss Nell. She turned to go to them, but Titus gripped her hand.

"Megan, we need to get you out of here. No detours," he whispered.

"I can't leave Tillie and Miss Nell. I can't," she whispered back, trying to pull away. The effort of simply walking was wearing on her. Her head was pounding, and she didn't have the strength to fight her cousin.

The door was a few steps ahead, freedom was in sight, but she felt as though she was betraying Tillie and Miss Nell. They didn't deserve to be there any more than she had.

Titus waved Henri and Helena ahead as he turned to Megan. He put his hands on her upper arms and bent down until his face was even with hers.

"Talk to me, cousin. What is wrong?" His voice was gentle, and his eyes, like molten lead, bored into her soul.

Tears streamed down her face as she fought to get the words out.

"Hey, hey, Squirt, stop... stop." Titus took her face in his hands and brushed her tears away with his thumbs. He drew her into a gentle hug. Megan glanced around, but no one was in sight. When she had stopped crying, Titus offered her a handkerchief. Megan blew her nose loudly, and they both laughed at the sound echoing through the hall. She winced, grabbing her side. Her ribs would be sore for a few days.

"Now, try again. What is wrong?"

Megan could hardly think. Between crying and the last few hours, her head felt like it was going to fall off. She felt the darkness crowding in as her knees buckled.

Titus gathered her in his arms and held her close. "Hang on, cousin. We are almost out." He headed for the dock as swiftly as his legs could carry him.

Megan fought to stay conscious, her head swimming as Titus carried her. She could see the concern in his expression as he smiled down at her. Henri came forward with a restorative as Titus boarded the boat with his precious bundle. Helena hovered nearby.

Megan soon recovered enough to sit on her own and was happy to see the boat they were taking off the island was much nicer than the one that had brought her. Henri told her he had chartered it specially to get her; they were the only passengers.

Despite the cool air, Megan begged to sit on the deck. Titus stayed with her while the others went into the wheelhouse to get warm. Megan was still in a lot of pain, but she had to talk to Titus. She started and stopped several times, choking tears back, but by the time the boat docked back in the city, she had gotten the entire story out.

"Please, Titus, I can't leave them there. I am sure Tillie's husband doesn't know what kind of an awful place she is in. Tillie won't last long; she isn't strong enough. I have to do something. Please."

"I will help them, Squirt."

Megan loved it when he used his childhood nickname for her.

"I promise, I promise I will get Tillie out, even If I have to stage an invasion at midnight. I will find a way to help her and Miss Nell. I swear."

His voice was sincere as his gaze held hers. Searching his face for a moment, Megan nodded.

The captain told them the boat was secured and they could disembark. Megan was dreading going home. She moved to stand, but her head swam and her legs wouldn't hold her. Titus scooped her up and carried her to the waiting hansom cab, and Henri wrapped his wool outer coat around her shoulders to make her more comfortable. Helena had not said a word since the island. Megan assumed it was only because she was upset about what she had seen.

Megan was lost in her misery, but soon, they were pulling to a stop in front of her grandmother's house. Titus wouldn't let Megan attempt to get out of the carriage on her own. Henri paid the driver, and the four of them entered the house. Walking through the front door was strange because Adelaide had always insisted she use the kitchen entrance with the rest of the servants.

Helena went straight to her room. She did not even greet her grandmother as she came down the stairs.

Adelaide froze at the sight of Megan. Her face turned first white, then green, then a strange shade of gray as she struggled to contain her emotions.

Megan shrank into Titus in fear. He kept his hold gentle, even as his jaw clenched in anger. The glance he shot to his father told her Titus had his suspicions about how she ended up on Blackwell Island, and Adelaide's reaction had confirmed it.

∞ ∞ ∞

Adelaide considered the stony faces of her son-in-law and grandson. She had to find a way to cover her guilt, and quickly, lest they take Helena and leave. She could abide anything, but the threat of not seeing her favorite grandchild was unbearable.

"Megan, there you are. We have been worried sick. Wherever did you find her?" she said with feigned concern, even mustering a few tears. Megan's appearance was shocking; she had a nasty bruise on her face, and one eye was swollen shut.

I hope she has learned her lesson. Now she knows I mean business. Adelaide hid the ghost of a smug smile behind her delicately scented handkerchief.

"Megan was badly mistreated and she needs her rest." Henri's chin jutted out, and his voice made it clear that he was unmoved by her attempt at sorrow.

"Of course. Take her right upstairs to... oh... well, perhaps Megan would feel more comfortable if Moriah were to help her." Adelaide rang for the cook. She didn't want the men to know that Megan slept in the drafty room upstairs, or that she had precious few belongings.

∞ ∞ ∞

Moriah's face lit up with relief and joy when she saw Megan. Despite Adelaide's protests, Titus insisted on carrying Megan to the top of the stairs. Helena met them there and handed Moriah a velvety flannel nightgown from her own closet.

"Megan, I am so sorry. Will you forgive me?" Helena whispered.

"Of course I do."

Moriah hated knowing that the young woman was hurting, but it might be a good thing if Helena learned what her grandmother was really like.

Soon Megan was ensconced in the warm nightgown, and Moriah tucked her under her threadbare covers.

Megan sighed. "It feels so good to get back in my own bed." Her eyelids slid shut, then popped open again. "Moriah, did Davis get away okay?"

"Yes, the children are fine. Rollins made sure he got back to the others safe and sound. I have much to tell you, such wonderful things. But you need your rest. I am glad you are home and safe. We were worried."

Moriah hugged her friend fiercely. She determined no matter the consequences, Adelaide would not hurt Megan again, not if Moriah had the power to stop it.

Megan laid her head on her pillow and was asleep before she could take another breath.

∞ ∞ ∞

Megan woke with a start the next morning, then she remembered where she was. She burrowed further under the thin blankets, reveling in their warmth. She had always been happy to have them but was even more so this morning. After over a week in the asylum, she would never complain about her quarters again. She kept her eyes closed and listened as the city awakened with the sunrise.

The clip-clop of horses' hooves, combined with the creak of the milk carts jingling, was soon drowned by the knife grinder's cry.

"Knives? Any knives to grind? Sharpen your knives for a penny." His rich, deep voice carried from the square nearby. The distant sound of a train whistle drifted through the crisp morning breeze floating through her window.

Megan took a moment to enjoy the pleasant sounds. Was it only yesterday when the noises that had woken her were moans and screams echoing through the asylum? She opened her eyes in a panic, fearing her pleasant morning was nothing but a dream, then relaxed as soon as she spotted Titus sitting near her door.

"Good morning, Squirt," his deep voice rumbled through the attic room.

Megan sighed and stretched her arms above her head. "Good morning, cousin."

"How are you? How is your headache?" Titus came and sat on her bed.

"Better. Is Grandmother terribly angry?" Megan was more concerned about Adelaide than the faint lingering headache.

"I think she is, for now. She will get over it." Titus shrugged. "She certainly put on a good act last night, didn't she?"

Megan nodded. Yes, Adelaide had put on a good act last night, but she was still concerned because she knew her grandmother would not "get over it." The minute the others left, Megan would be in at her mercy again. Helena's attitude was changing, but Megan wasn't convinced it was enough to prevent retribution from her grandmother.

"I need to get ready and see what Grandmother wants me to do today." Megan slid her feet from under the covers and pressed herself to a standing position. Her head swam and she tipped over. Titus was right there by her side, steadying her. It took a moment for her head to clear. She waved Titus out the door assuring him she was fine.

Megan washed up and put on her old blue dress. It hung loosely on her too-thin frame. It had always been a little big, but she must have lost weight at the asylum. She then opened the drawer of her bedside stand and grabbed her last pair of stockings. Staring at them for a moment, she shivered, remembering her friend back at the asylum. They had been so cold. She pulled her woolen stockings on, sending a prayer heavenward for Tillie. *She must be terrified. Please keep her safe until Titus can find her husband.*

She plaited her wild hair back into a braid and tied it with her one remaining precious blue ribbon. Titus had given it to her many years ago for Christmas and it was one of the few presents she had ever received.

Her gaze dropped to the square of linen neatly folded on her nightstand. That bit of fabric meant much more to her than she wanted to admit. The stranger's kindness had planted a seed of hope in her heart, one she never wanted to forget. She would repay his kindness, if not to him, then to others in turn.

She picked up the handkerchief and looked at it carefully for the first time. It was slightly stained with her blood. Moriah would be able to fix that. A monogram, AJS, was expertly embroidered in one corner. She wondered if the man had a wife who had lovingly stitched those initials into the fabric. Was it terribly selfish of her to hope not?

She set the square back down next to two of her most precious possessions on the nightstand: her brush and her Bible.

Megan headed downstairs to the kitchen, where she hesitated in the doorway. Adelaide stood across the room, near the door between the kitchen and the dining room. Titus and Moriah were chatting next to the stove, and Titus waved her in.

"Megan." Adelaide's voice was stiff but held little of her usual harshness.

"Yes, ma'am." Megan didn't quite know how to respond to the change in tone.

"I need you to fetch me more laudanum from Dr. Franks's office. Please." Her grandmother's voice cracked on the word please. It wasn't one she used often. Megan glanced at the cook, whose eyebrows were raised in surprise. What had Titus said to Adelaide to get her to act this way?

Megan didn't trust her voice, so she nodded. Adelaide nodded curtly in return as she left the room. As soon as she was out of sight, Megan relaxed.

"Here, Megan, have breakfast." Moriah was ready with a glass of milk and a hot biscuit.

Megan took both gratefully. When she bit into the flaky, buttery goodness of the biscuit, tears she didn't understand choked her. She took a moment to gain control over her raging emotions.

"I missed your cooking," she said around another mouthful of biscuit.

The cook smiled and hugged her.

Megan leisurely ate her breakfast, enjoying every bite, before sailing out the door with a smile and a wave to Moriah. After the last few weeks, not even the thought of walking into Dr. Franks's office could dull her joy.

Adelaide sat in her study and seethed. Every time laughter echoed from the kitchen, the barbed wire of hate twisted around her heart. She had never hated anyone as much as she hated Megan at this moment. She wouldn't be able to go shopping with Helena if she didn't calm down.

She plucked her last bottle of laudanum from the desk and poured a generous draught into the glass of sherry sitting near her blotter. She drank it in one swift gulp. The sweet burn of the alcohol masked the bitterness a little. Adelaide grimaced and poured herself another glass of sherry. She sipped at this one, trying to get the harsh taste of opiate out of her mouth. She peered at the bottle of laudanum. She had enough for one more dose.

Good thing the little brat was back. Dr. Franks had delivered a new bottle twice while Megan was away, and Adelaide's busybody neighbors were whispering. Well, now the nosy old bats wouldn't know she was still taking it.

Adelaide pressed her cold hands to her flushed cheeks. She remembered back to a week ago when Titus had roared into the room demanding to know where Megan was. She had never seen him this angry. Henri too, showed rare anger and had threatened to take Helena back to France. The risk of losing Helena had stirred her into suggesting that Titus check with Officer Pietro.

Adelaide told her son-in-law the policeman was the one who often patrolled the nearby neighborhoods. She knew that the corrupt policeman would send them looking in the wrong direction. An honest officer might find the little chit.

Helena had given her such a baleful look, Adelaide knew her granddaughter had figured out she was lying. But she said nothing, and things between them had stayed the same, so Adelaide bore little guilt for her actions.

Adelaide opened her paper fan and waved it in front of her face briskly, trying to cool down. The laudanum raised her temperature for a few minutes, but the relief from her toothache and her nerves made the warmth worth the trouble.

"Grandmamma, are you ready?" Helena's cultured voice broke through her thoughts.

"Yes, darling, of course. Rollins has the coach waiting for us." Adelaide smiled genuinely at her favorite grandchild. Helena was the picture of her mother, which endeared her to Adelaide that much more.

Adelaide would shower the girl with anything she desired. Helena had always idolized her grandmother, but she knew her perfect image had cracked a little after the incident with Megan. Adelaide knew Helena had her eye on a new silk dress down at Madam Amile's, but it cost more than her father was willing to pay. She was certain she could get back into her granddaughter's good graces with the purchase of the dress.

Chapter 4

Titus tiptoed through the house and eased open the door to his grandmother's study. He was in the middle of a losing streak, and his father had already refused his pleas for money. He would only borrow a little from Adelaide. She would never miss it, and even if she did, he could explain and would pay her back when he won.

His luck was going to change, he was sure of it. A couple hundred dollars should set him back on his feet. He shut the door, careful not to let the latch click. He navigated to her desk by moonlight. He cast another glance at the door to make sure it was secure before he lit a match.

He rummaged through the desk drawers as quietly as he could. Adelaide kept a money box in the desk, but he didn't know where. Titus nearly dropped the match when it burned his finger. He shook it out and lit another. He didn't dare light a lamp. Adelaide was a light sleeper, and the bedroom door was cracked open a few inches. If his grandmother caught him, she would be furious.

Titus finally found what he was looking for in the back of the last drawer and carefully placed the box on the top of the desk. He sighed with relief when it wasn't locked. When he opened it and reached for the money, an envelope addressed to his cousin caught his attention. Why would Adelaide hide a letter to Megan? He decided to take a chance and light the lamp. Turning it down as low as he could, he sat on the edge of the chair and read the letter.

Dear Megan,

I am sure you have wondered about us, as we have about you. I regret to inform you our father has died. We thought you should know. Father kept in touch with Grandmother and frequently told us how you were doing. We were hoping you would be willing to visit us here at the ranch. We would so love to meet you. Unfortunately it is not feasible for us to come to the city at this time, but we would love to have you and Grandmother visit us here. We are busy with the spring roundup but should be able to take a break soon.

Please come visit us, Megan. Father would never let us send for you, saying you were better off in school back East. Life is hard here. But it is good too. We would love to meet you and show you where you were born. We have enclosed enough money for two train tickets from New York to the end of the line. You will need to take a stage through the mountains, and then it is another day's journey to Coldville. I know it is a long journey, but we are longing to meet our little sister. Please consider our proposal. We await your letter and hope to see you soon, dear sister.

With love,

Your brothers

Five signatures followed.

Titus sat back, stunned. Despite never having met them, he recognized the names of his cousins: Riley, Morgan, Logan, Caleb, and Sawyer. No money was in the envelope. He peered into the money box again and saw another paper.

He took it out and gasped. It was another letter. This one was from Adelaide. To a police officer. An icy chill crept into Titus's bones.

He had always known his grandmother was capable of cruelty; he had seen her use her words to cut people to the quick many times. He even suspected she had known Megan was in the asylum. But this was madness. Adelaide was planning to permanently commit Megan. She referenced his interference and laid out plans to make sure that their tracks were well covered.

The letter was unfinished, but Titus got the feeling Megan would "disappear" inside those walls. This letter was proof of how far Adelaide would go. She had not always been this way. When his mother was alive, Adelaide had treated Megan more like an equal to Titus and Helena. The older his cousin had gotten, though, the harsher his grandmother had behaved toward her.

Titus took a deep breath. He blew out the lantern and sat in the darkness trying to gather his thoughts. He had to do something; he owed Megan that much. Aside from his mother, she was the only other person who had ever believed in him. Henri and Helena did in their own way, but Megan made him feel like he could do anything. He was ashamed he had not spent more time with her.

He would get Megan on the train West, and he needed to do it now. Adelaide's letter was not dated, but he knew she would finish it in the next day or two. Titus carefully counted several hundred dollars from the cash box and put everything back into the drawer. He then unlocked the door that led from the salon to the balcony and slipped outside.

As a child, he had climbed the trellis many times, but he was far too large to try it now.

It would be dawn soon. He had to hurry. He went back into the study and carefully left the same way he had entered. Adelaide never stirred, but Titus's heart quickened with every creak of the house and squeak of the floorboards.

As soon as he was away from Adelaide's door, he took off his shoes to reduce the sound of his footsteps and sprinted for the kitchen and the servants' stairway. In seconds he was at Megan's door, where he paused, second-guessing himself. How was he going to get her out of the city? Her shabby clothes would attract too much attention at the train station, especially since he wasn't ready to send her emigrant class. He retraced his steps and went back down the stairs.

He needed to talk to his sister. After seeing the conditions at the asylum, she would help him. Titus hurried up the main staircase and knocked lightly on her door, then cracked it open.

"Helena?" he whispered, thinking she might be sleeping.

"Titus? What are you doing? It isn't even dawn," Helena hissed back. She lit the lamp beside her bed, then propping herself up, she motioned for him to come in. "If this is regarding money for one of your games, I don't have any." She flopped back on her pillows with a sigh.

"This isn't concerning money. It's about Megan." He explained to his sister what he had discovered in their grandmother's desk.

Helena's eyes widened with each word. "She wouldn't do such a thing. Would she?" Helena's voice trembled and tears pooled in her eyes.

Despite her protests, Titus knew that in her heart, Helena knew the truth.

"What are we going to do?" she asked.

"We?" Titus had to double check.

"Yes, of course, we. She is my cousin too. Even if I haven't acted like it lately." Helena took his arm.

He smiled down at her, and a spark of comradery flickered between them. He had missed his sweet sister the last few years.

"A single woman traveling alone is going to draw attention. If she travels emigrant class the trip will take a lot longer. I read the other day it can take twice as long since they unhook the lower-class cars if they need to add cargo cars," Titus said.

"She will have to go second- or first-class," Helena agreed. "Oh, I understand. Her clothes. She will stand out in the wrong way if she travels in her blue dress. It is hideous. Does she even have any others? I have only ever seen her in...." She stared at Titus, guilt written all over her face.

"Oh Titus, we have been awful. She is our own cousin. Why did we not ever do anything before? I am ashamed of myself." She turned her face into her brother's chest, crying.

"Me too, sis. Me too. We have both been selfish." Titus wrapped his arm around her, hugging her tightly. "We need to get Megan away now before the house is awake."

"Yes. Grandmother wakes early, so we will need to hurry." Helena threw off her covers and slid her arms into her robe, then wrapped it around her. "Bring Megan here, to my room. I have a dress she can have for traveling and a few other things she will need." She was already digging through her trunks.

Titus left his shoes in Helena's room and retraced his steps to Megan's door. He knocked lightly and simultaneously entered the room. She was asleep with her head on the pillow, but her legs dangled over the edge the bed, as though she had sat down and fallen asleep.

Titus lit the lamp on her rickety table. His guilt grew as he beheld the bare room and shivered. It was freezing in here. He perched on the edge of the bed, which was more of a cot. It creaked and groaned so loudly, Titus was afraid it would collapse. He knelt in front of his cousin and smiled. With a streak of stove black on her nose, and her face relaxed in sleep, she seemed much younger than she was. He gently shook her.

"Megan. Megan, you need to wake up."

She sat bolt upright. "Titus? You scared me. What are you doing here? What time is it? Oh no, am I late? Grandmother is going to kill me." Megan stumbled to her washbasin and began to scrub her face. Titus put his hands atop of hers.

"Megan, stop. It is still early. No one is awake but us. I need you to listen to me. Stop. Stop and listen. Please."

Megan did as Titus asked and sat on her bed while Titus explained.

"Wait, what? My brothers wrote and asked me to come visit?" Hope and fear mingled in her voice.

"Yes. Come with me now. Helena is going to help you get ready. We need to leave this house. It is no longer safe for you here." Titus took her small, icy hand in his.

Megan opened her mouth, as if she were going to ask another question. She must have seen the answer in his expression. She pressed her lips together and nodded. She snatched up her few precious belongings and wrapped them in her shawl. Titus grabbed her shoes and motioned for her to follow him.

They crept through the dark halls to Helena's room. Helena peeked out, watching for them and opened the door quickly, then closed it softly behind them and turned up the light.

"Megan, I am so sorry. I have acted horrendously. Can you ever forgive me?" Her eyes were still red from crying.

"Of course, Helena. I am glad to be friends with you again."

"Titus, you can't be in here. Megan is going to have to change." Helena shooed him back out into the hall.

Megan ducked behind the screen while Helena shooed Titus out the door. She yanked off her threadbare dress but left her underthings and stockings on. She felt awkward standing there in nothing but her underclothes, but fortunately, Helena tossed a navy taffeta day dress over the screen.

"Do you have a crinoline?" Helena asked, leaning close to the screen.

"No. I don't need one normally. Do I need one with this dress?"

"Let me see." Helena peeked around the dark wood panels.

Megan turned around carefully to face her cousin. She caught a glimpse of herself in the mirror and stopped. The dress fit her well. Snug at the waist but not too tight and with enough room in the rest of the dress that she could move fairly easily. Helena eyed her critically and motioned for her to turn. Megan obliged, the fabric swishing loudly.

"I think for on the train this will be fine. The dress is long enough that we won't need to worry about your shoes. I don't think mine will fit you, but let me grab gloves and a hat. You will draw too much attention if you don't have those." Helena drew her into the middle of the room and dug around in the wardrobe for a moment before pulling out a pair of dark gloves and a hat that matched Megan's gown.

Megan sighed with relief when her cousin handed her the little hat, which was adorned with a small peacock feather, a wisp of veiling, and black trim. Helena had been known to wear outlandish and elaborate hats, but this one was modest.

"Here, let me help you." Helena laughed as Megan struggled to put up her hair and fasten the hat. With a few expert twists and a few pins, Helena soon had Megan's hair tamed and the hat safely secured.

"Take a look." She turned Megan toward the mirror once more.

Megan hardly recognized herself. The colors in the dress and hat made her skin pale like porcelain and accentuated her green eyes. Helena's reflection beamed at her, and Megan smiled back.

Helena called for her brother.

Titus opened the door and silently slipped back inside. He scrutinized her from head to toe. "You are pretty, Megan," he said with no trace of his usual teasing.

Helena hugged her, then Megan and Titus sneaked down the hall to the back stairs. Megan was barely in the kitchen when Moriah hauled her into a fierce embrace with tears streaming down her cheeks. Rollins wrapped his arms around them, and Megan allowed the tears to come. She was going to miss her friends.

"I am sorry to cut this short, but we need to leave," Titus said, holding out her shoes.

Megan sat to put on her shoes. While she laced her boots, Moriah set a reticule down on the floor beside her.

"It isn't much since we didn't have much notice, but I pulled together a few things. Should be enough for breakfast today and maybe tomorrow."

Megan peeked inside the bag. Moriah had wrapped several items in brown paper. There was plenty of room for her other belongings as well. She tucked them in carefully and stood.

"Do you have enough money?" Rollins asked.

Megan looked to Titus for the answer.

"I have enough for her ticket, the cab, and a little besides. The poker game pretty much tapped me out, and I don't dare take more money from Adelaide. I am afraid she will accuse

Megan of stealing it and send someone after her." Titus hung his head.

"I don't have much. We don't get paid until tomorrow, but please take this. It is a lengthy journey, and you will need money." Rollins handed her a few coins and a few bills.

Megan accepted them graciously. To refuse them would be rude. I must remember to pay them back someday.

She hugged Moriah one last time.

Titus took her little bundle and pulled her out the door. The sky was beginning to lighten and the spring air was brisk. He kept tight hold of her hand and hurried down the street.

Megan ran to keep pace with her long-legged cousin. By the time they got to the bottom of the hill, she was out of breath and her ribs were screaming at her. They were still not healed from the beating. She wrenched her hand out of Titus's and stopped at the corner.

"Titus, I can't. Please. I need a moment." She leaned against one of the gaslights along the street.

Titus glanced around. "Come on, it is only a little farther. I have a hack waiting around the corner," he encouraged.

Megan took his hand once more and gamely trudged along. Sure enough, they rounded the corner, and a carriage was parked and waiting. Titus helped her into it, gave instructions to the driver and joined her on the upholstered seat.

"We are headed for the train station. The first train headed west leaves at six fifteen. We should have plenty of time to get there," he said.

Megan was still too short of breath to answer and could only nod. She let her head fall back onto the cushion.

Far before she was ready, the hack stopped at their destination. Megan had finally caught her breath and was both dreading and looking forward to this new adventure.

∞ ∞ ∞

The driver opened the door and lowered the step for his passengers to disembark. Titus climbed down and offered Megan his hand.

"Come, Helena. We have to hurry if we want enough time to reach the train, my dear," he said with a wink. By addressing her as his sister, he hoped to throw off track any search Adelaide might instigate.

Megan stared at him wide-eyed, and he took her arm and tucked it through his. Titus paid the cabbie, and the cousins walked into the station. Megan was shaking so violently that Titus worried she would faint, so he guided her to a bench near the door.

Despite the early hour, the line for the ticket window was long. If she fainted, they would draw too much attention. The bench provided a good place for her to rest, and he would be able to see her while standing in line.

The longer he waited, the more nervous Titus became. Any minute now his grandmother could awaken and find Megan gone, then she would call her crooked policeman. One of the first places they would check would be the train station. It was the first place he had checked when Megan had disappeared.

He kept glancing back at Megan to make sure she was safe. A clock in the center of the square clicked away the minutes that seemed like hours before he stood before the ticket agent.

"Where to?" the man behind the glass asked.

"My sister is off to visit our elder brother in Coldville. We need train tickets to Denver, then tickets for the stage from there."

"Train now goes through to Georgetown. She'll take the stage through the mountains. Coldville is on the other side of the mountains. Trip takes three days by stage. There will be two overnights. One night in the Haven way station, the other on the trail. The Haven costs an extra ten dollars if paying with coin; twenty if you only got paper money," the agent droned. He sounded bored out of his mind. Titus attempted to follow the man's finger tracing the map, but it was too confusing.

Titus dug in his pockets and pulled out his money. He had enough for the tickets, and now the way station. He hadn't been prepared for that. The extra stop would take almost the rest of the money, not leaving much for food. He counted the bills for the ticket.

The man stamped a few papers and handed them over.

"These here are the tickets for the train. Them's the tickets for the stage. She will have to pay for the lodgings when she gets there, or stay on the stage overnight. Train leaves platform three in ten minutes. These tickets is for second-class, but second class-car won't be added until

Omaha. Lucky you, your sister can ride in first-class until then. She will be in car A. I have already stamped her tickets with the upgrade." The ticket agent motioned for the next traveler to step forward.

∞ ∞ ∞

Megan waited nervously for Titus to return. When he did, he took her arm and steered her toward the platform farthest away from the station, where the train waited.

He handed her the tickets, which she put into her reticule.

"You will be staying overnight at a way station. That should cost ten dollars in gold coin. Keep this much separate so you will have it when you need it." Titus waited while Megan tucked the coins away.

Titus explained what the ticket agent had said and handed her a few more coins. "I am sorry, this is all I have to give. It should be enough to get you food on the trip, though. You are fortunate; the second-class car won't be added for a few days. You will be able to eat in the dining car with the first-class passengers until then."

Megan was wide-eyed, trying to take in the information as they walked down the platform.

"Here it is... Car A." Titus stopped at the rear of the train car.

Fear hit Megan hard, taking her breath away. She turned to Titus, her eyes filling with tears.

"I don't think I can do this," she whispered and buried her face in Titus's chest. She only came to the top button on his shirt. He wrapped his strong arms around her and crushed her to him.

Megan squeezed him back, sinking into his warmth. His smart taffeta vest was scratchy against her face, and he smelled of sweet tobacco and strong coffee. She rested her face on him and listened to the steady rhythm of his heart. Breathing deeply, she cemented this moment in her memory.

"Megan. If you don't go, if Grandmother gets her way, you will disappear forever. The only way to protect you is to get you away from here. I am sorry, but you have to do this." Titus held her at arm's length. "You are strong. Stronger than any of us. You can do this. I read the letter. Your brothers want you to come. They are excited to see you. No matter what life is like there, it will be better than what you will most certainly face if you stay here."

"All aboard!" The conductor's call interrupted them.

"Titus?" Megan stepped onto the stairs leading into the train, her voice wavering with uncertainty.

"I promise I will write you and let you know what happens with Tillie and Miss Nell. I have not forgotten them. I will help them. I know where you'll be. You know our address in Boston. Mail your letters there."

"I will. Thank you, Titus. I love you," Megan said as the train slowly pulled away from the station. She stayed on the stairs, clutching the rail until the conductor called her away.

∞ ∞ ∞

Titus stayed rooted to the platform until the train disappeared in the distance. When it was gone, he turned on his heel and strode to the telegraph operator next to the ticket window.

"I want to send a telegram."

"Write it out and fill out the form, please. It will be one dollar." The agent didn't even glance up. Titus took the form and wrote.

RECEIVED MESSAGE STOP ARRIVE STAGECOACH COLDSVILLE SIXTH MAY STOP MEGAN.

The telegraph operator raised an eyebrow as he signed the telegraph with Megan's name, but didn't comment.

Titus checked his pockets as he left the station. After he paid for the ride home, he would have fifty cents to his name. Dawn was breaking and the streets were coming alive. The train station was in the middle of the city, and people were setting up shop everywhere.

Titus recognized one of his gambling buddies teetering drunkenly down the street. Titus grinned. Perfect timing. He could convince Tommy to let him share a cab, and they could find another game of poker to get his pocket money back.

Chapter 5

Adelaide groaned as she dragged herself out of bed. Between her ear and her toothache, she could hardly handle the pain. She stumbled to her desk and pulled out the vial of laudanum. She didn't bother to dilute it but took the rest of the bottle in one swift gulp. The liquid burned all the way down her throat, but she was beginning to enjoy the bitter taste.

She followed the medicine with a quick drink from the sherry bottle. Minutes later her pain began to subside. She dressed slowly, her mind returning to the letter she had received last night. By the time she was fully ready for the day, the pain was gone.

She would not send Megan to her brothers. Officer Pietro would have no problem with taking the little piece of baggage back to Blackwell's. She could finish the letter tonight and send it tomorrow. After her soft-hearted son-in-law and grandson left, Officer Pietro would have the arrangements already settled for Megan to disappear. By the time they knew to look for her, the little chit would long gone.

Adelaide had received the telegram telling her of Jamison's death the night before she had sent Megan to the asylum the first time. She couldn't stand the sight of the girl anymore. It was that girl's fault Jamison hadn't come back to visit for over twenty years. Now her son was dead, and there was no reason to keep Megan any longer. She wished the girl had never been born, and she was going to make Megan wish the same thing.

She marched down to the kitchen where Moriah was busy making breakfast. Adelaide ignored her cook as she made her way to the bottom of the stairs.

"Megan," she shouted. There was no answer. No movement from the room at the top of the staircase. "Megan," she tried again. Nothing. Lifting her skirts, she stalked up the stairs.

"Megan." She pounded on the door, then flung it open and barged in. At the sight of the empty bed, she stopped. Megan was not in her room. Adelaide stormed back down to the kitchen.

"Moriah, did you send Megan on an errand this morning?" Adelaide stood in front of her, arms crossed.

"No, ma'am. I did not," Moriah said, her voice calm and level.

Adelaide narrowed her eyes.

Rollins entered the kitchen and walked over to stand beside Moriah.

"Do you know where Megan is?" Adelaide turned her focus on the butler.

"I do not. All I know is she left this morning." Rollins put his arm around his wife's shoulders.

"I don't believe you. I think you helped her leave. She is my servant, and you let her walk away?" Adelaide shouted.

"No, Mrs. Carter. She is not your servant. She is your granddaughter. We did not help her, as we should have, I am ashamed to say. We did not stop her, either," Rollins said.

"You dare speak to me in such a manner? You are lying. I will have the law on you. You are fired!" Adelaide's voice ended on a screech.

"Grandmother, they didn't help Megan leave." Helena's voice came from the dining room doorway.

Adelaide whirled toward her granddaughter. It took her a full minute to speak. When she did, her voice was harsh. "Do not get involved in this, Helena. If you want your pretty silk dress on order from Madam Amile, don't you say another word." Adelaide experienced a tiny bit of remorse over the shock on Helena's pretty face, but a satisfied smile snaked across her thin lips as Helena clamped her mouth shut.

"As for you two. Get out. Get out before I call the police." Adelaide turned back to her former cook and butler.

"Grandmother, they didn't do anything. I did." Titus's voice matched Adelaide's in rage.

"All three of you get out. I don't want to see any of your faces again," Adelaide spat.

Helena's face blanched and she opened her mouth to say something, but before she could speak, Titus caught her attention and shook his head.

She pressed her lips together and kept silent. Adelaide smiled smugly. Helena would not buck her.

"We will be gone within the hour," Rollins said with dignity.

"Fine." Adelaide flounced toward the main stairs. "Helena, come." Her strident voice echoed through the house. She turned when she realized her granddaughter was not behind her.

"I'm sorry," Helena mouthed to the other occupants of the kitchen before following her. Adelaide silently stalked away from the kitchen.

"I'm sorry too. Do you have someplace to go?" Titus's voice carried up the stairs to Adelaide's room.

"Yes. My sister lives outside the city. They have an apple orchard and have often asked us to come stay with them. We have been wanting to get away from the hustle and bustle of city life, and it will be a nice change."

Adelaide had heard Rollins's answer before she slammed the door. Helena had retired to her own room in tears. This entire kerfuffle was all Megan's fault. She paced around her room, fuming as the shadows lengthened.

The sound of a carriage pulling away from the house enticed her toward the window. Moriah and Rollins were leaving. *Good. Now I can hire decent servants for a change. As for that brat, she won't get away that easily.* With a self-satisfied smile, Adelaide put on her hat and set off to find Officer Pietro.

Chapter 6

After a slow day of travel, Megan sat cross-legged on her little bunk, struggling to remove the jacket of her blue taffeta dress. The curtains kept the air in here still and thick, and while the little kerosene lamp set in the glass niche inset lit the space, it rendered it hot and smelly. A small ventilator near the ceiling would allow for fresh air, but Megan couldn't get the cover to budge.

The wood walls were smooth and hard with no place to hang anything, and Megan was oddly thankful she owned few possessions. One woman had already caused a hullabaloo when she had crawled out, half-undressed, and bumped into a portly Southern gentleman going to heat water at the front of the car. Their shouting had drawn everyone's attention. All over a sleeping cap left in a suitcase.

Megan contemplated her little sleeping area. The flickering light from the lamp reflected off the polished wood and the brass accents sparkled in the golden glow. If only the curtains covered the entire area. The heavy fabric had been stored improperly and was wrinkled and did not hang straight. The large gaps caused by the wrinkles in them exposed her to anyone walking by.

Megan knelt on the edge of the bed and tucked the jacket over one of the curtain rods, then shimmied out of the skirt. Clad in her underpinnings, she tucked the wide skirt around another curtain rod and sat back feeling pleased with herself. That took care of two problems. Now her sleeping area was more private, and her traveling dress would not be a wrinkled mess in the morning.

It had been amazing watching the porters change the car from a day car—with plush velvet seats, gold railings, and polished wood paneling—to a sleeping car, with beds stacked two high the entire length of the train car.

Most of the passengers had been shooed to the dining car while the porters completed the transformation but Megan hung back and watched, fascinated by the process. The polished wood panels hung from chains attached to the wall, providing the base for the upper bunk.

Porters placed another piece of paneling across the seats to make the bottom berth. They brought in thin mattresses from the cargo car to cushion the bunks, and heavy curtains were hung for privacy.

The bottom bunks afforded more privacy than the upper berths. The seatbacks created walls at the head and foot of the bunk. Those bunks cost more. Upon returning to the car after dinner, the porter showed each guest to their place and helped them in the upper bunks if necessary. Small ladders were moved around to allow people to climb in and out of the top berths.

Megan was glad she was short, she was a little cramped, but had she been much taller, she would have been extremely uncomfortable. As it was, she fit neatly on the upper birth.

As Megan leaned forward to adjust the curtains, the car lurched and she tumbled from the upper bunk right into the arms of a handsome young gentleman.

"I beg your pardon." The man craned his neck and averted his eyes, but he did not drop her.

"I am so sorry!" Megan stammered, mortified.

"Pardon my familiarity, miss." The poor man turned three shades of pink as he made a valiant effort hold her while Megan flailed in an attempt to get back behind the safety of the curtains.

The porter chose that moment to come down the aisle. He paused, watching them, with an amused smile.

After finally wriggling back into her bunk, Megan lay still for several minutes, not trusting herself to move. The stranger's face would be indelibly stamped in her mind for the rest of her days. If only it had been the handsome stranger from the docks whose arms she had fallen into.

Where had that thought come from?

Her face heated again as she dug for the linen kerchief in her reticule. She kept it with her at all times now, as a small reminder of the kindness that still existed in the world. She rubbed her thumb over the smooth stitches in the corner and willed herself to calm down.

Megan finally allowed herself to take a deep breath. Her gaze fell onto the light seeping into her bunk and she gasped. Her fall had ripped the curtain open. It had been too short to cover the entire width of her bunk, and now the tear exposed her to anyone walking by as if there had been no curtain at all. Her skirt was still draped along the one side. Thankfully that hadn't fallen to the floor.

Searching for anything to close the gap, she remembered her hairpins. Megan jerked the fabric together and pinned the tear together. For added security she also attached one end to the curtain on the other side, and the other to her pillow. She wasn't certain this was the best idea. As a restless sleeper, she would toss and turn all night, but this was the best solution she could come up with. Between the brass plating and polished wood, the bunk had no other place to attach anything.

A glance down at the foot of her bed revealed a similar yawning aperture. She plucked a few more pins from her hair and secured the gaping curtain to her blanket and her mattress. Megan sat back to rest for a moment, winded after wriggling around in the cramped space. She leaned back against the wall, then jerked forward, giving an involuntary scream. The kerosene lamp had turned the glass scorching hot, and she had burned her elbow.

"Is everything all right, miss?" a friendly voice asked from the bunk below her.

Megan flinched, and due to her cramped position, fell over, splitting the side curtain right in the middle. Again. Her hairpins flew everywhere.

An arm reached up through the middle of the curtains from the bottom berth. "Did you drop these?" A well-groomed, masculine hand held three of Megan's hairpins. She recognized the voice as belonging to the man who had caught her only a few minutes before.

"I am well, thank you. Yes, those are mine." Her voice was barely audible as she plucked the hairpins from his fingers.

The hand disappeared back through the curtains.

With a disgusted sigh, Megan blew a strand of hair out of her face. The evening couldn't possibly get any more embarrassing. A glance at the curtains told Megan they were still too short to close completely. She worked to unpin the far corner at the foot of her bed and re-pin the middle securely shut. With a huff, she fell back onto her pillow, exhausted.

Her mind buzzed with everything that had happened over the last few weeks, and her fingers found the handkerchief again. Stroking the embroidery calmed her down. What did the monogram stand for? Aaron Smith? Alexander Silvan, Aiden Shaunessy, Alfred Storm? Names floated through her mind. It was almost like counting sheep. She tossed and turned for a while before finally falling asleep.

In the middle of the night, Megan woke to find the air in her little space stagnant and uncomfortably warm. She unpinned the middle curtain and poked her head out. A hideous chorus of snores vibrated throughout the car. Boots, both men's and women's, sat beside each berth. The air was not much better in the narrow aisle. Megan assumed the other passengers had their ventilators shut.

She securely re-pinned the curtain and wriggled her way cross-legged to the window at the foot of her little space. She pushed and pulled, but the window wouldn't move. She adjusted her grip and shoved as hard as she could. Her hand slipped, and she skinned her knuckles.

Biting her lip to keep from crying out, she jerked at it this time. Her fingers slipped off the tiny metal lip and smacked her hand against the unyielding wooden wall. A glance at her hand told Megan she had broken two of her already-ragged fingernails.

She grasped the little metal edge as tight as she could and rocked her body back and forth, trying to coax the stubborn cover to move. It finally budged, and one last herculean heave made it fly open. A fierce, icy blast blew cinders into her mouth.

"This will never do," she muttered. She broke another nail in the process, but eventually inched the window partially closed.

Megan snuggled into the blankets, breathing deeply. As she drifted back to sleep, something tumbled off her bunk. She prayed it was her boots and that somehow they'd missed her neighbor's head. Visions of the handsome stranger in the blue suit and cowboy boots filled her dreams.

Megan sat straight up, forgetting for a moment where she was. Morning light seeped through her curtains, and the cacophony of snores had lessened. She peeked around her little cubby and discovered that her traveling bag had fallen out of the bunk, and she could only find one shoe. Her imagination ran amok as she stared at the open window. Some poor farmer would likely find her boot in the middle of his field. As calmly as she was able, she put her dress on and shimmied out of the bunk.

She glanced toward the dressing room at the end of the car. A woman pushed the door open and Megan could see a couple of women were already inside. She searched around fruitlessly for her missing shoe. It was nowhere to be found. *I will have to worry about this later.* Megan brushed herself off and headed to the dressing room.

One shoe or two, she needed to at least be presentable when the rest of the car woke up. She slipped into the washroom. One woman was at the washbowl, and two others were waiting, all chatting with the comradery of fellow travelers. Megan sat on one of the valises and patiently waited her turn.

"Well, I got along perty well," said one, "'til somebody opened a window, and after that, I thought I should freeze to death. My husband, he called the conductor up, and they shut the ventilators but I shivered all night. Real good soap this is, ain't it, now?"

Megan flushed with guilt but kept her thoughts to herself, not wanting to accept the blame.

"I wa'n't too cold," said the woman at the washbasin, as she held her false teeth under the faucet and swished them from side to side. "But I'll tell you what, in the middle of the night, I felt something against the top of my head. And what do you think it was? 'Twas the feet of the man in the next section. Well, this is more'n I can stand, and I give 'em a push. I reckon he woke up, for I never felt 'em no more."

Megan could not stand to listen any longer. Standing near the door and using the reflection off the polished silver plate near the washbasin, she put her hair into some semblance of order and flew out the door. The three women cackled still as she walked back to her seat.

The porter had already changed the bunk back into seats, and sitting on one velvet covered cushion was her other shoe. Embarrassed by the state of it, Megan quickly put the cracked and dirty shoe on and hid it under her skirts. Worse than the condition of the shoe, there was a neat little pile of hairpins on the seat. Megan glanced around in horror. The nice gentleman who had helped her the night before was nowhere to be seen, much to her relief.

The dark-skinned porter making the bunks back into seats was the same man who had witnessed her humiliation last night. Megan mustered her courage and walked toward him. "Excuse me."

"Yes, ma'am, how can I help you? Is you needin' somethin'?" he asked.

"I merely wanted to say thank you for your help. It must be a lot of work to set up and put away those bunks each night. Also, to thank you for finding my shoe, and my hairpins."

"It was my pleasure, ma'am. I don't know too many jobs what offer a man as much travel and scenery like this one. First time I e'er been thanked for doin' my work. I appreciates it, miss. But I don' want to take credit from sumpin' I did'na do. Them hairpins were already in a neat little pile on the bottom bunk, but I did finds the shoe." His face split wide with his grin.

Megan smiled back at him, fully able to appreciate the humor now it was daytime. People were stirring, so she returned to her seat and stared out the window for a few minutes. The train appeared to be slowing.

"Time to wake up. The train is pulling into Omaha. Everyone must disembark. Breakfast can be purchased at the restaurant at the station. Passengers must disembark here. Everybody up." The conductor walked through the car repeating his announcement several times.

Megan dug through her traveling bag. She had already eaten the biscuits Moriah had sent. She still had an apple, a small packet of dried fruit, and a roll, left over from dinner in the dining car last night.

She dug a little deeper and finally found the schedule for her trip. She had the ticket for Omaha to Denver, and then on to Goodrich. Titus had told her she would need to change cars here in Omaha. She surveyed the car as she tucked the schedule back into her bag. It was difficult to believe they had traveled so far in such little time.

On the first night there had been no sleeping car, so everyone had slept the best they could sitting up. She wasn't sure on which night she had slept better: the first night sitting up or last night with its misadventures.

Megan rested her head back against the plush velvet of the seat. The grittiness in her eyes was painful, and her head and neck ached. She was tempted to skip breakfast and walk around on the platform to get some fresh air.

By the time the train stopped at the station in Omaha, the rest of the passengers were out of their bunks and the car had returned to a sitting car. Megan was one of the first onto the platform. She turned her face toward the sun, enjoying its warmth. The day was stifling already, and the sky was clear and blue with not a cloud in sight. She was definitely going to skip breakfast. Instead, she selected the apple from her bag.

Megan was fascinated as the train inched forward, then went backward several times coupling on two passenger cars and several cargo cars. Megan was so intrigued she lost track of time as she watched the men work until the conductor called all aboard. She hadn't even taken a bite of her apple. Her stomach growled as she hurried to reboard the train. The conductor inspected her ticket and pointed her to one of the newly added cars.

"You need to hurry, miss. This is the last call." He continued his walk down the train, shouting, "Last call, all aboard."

Megan boarded the car the conductor indicated. Almost all of the seats were full, but she spotted three open spaces near the end of the aisle. Two were next to a beautiful blonde in a bright green-and-black dress and a magnificent hat. The other was right across the aisle, next to an older woman in a plain traveling dress. Both women glanced up and smiled at her. Megan smiled back and turned toward the two empty seats next to the younger woman.

"May I sit here?" Megan asked.

"You don't want to sit next to her," the older woman said, loudly enough that several people turned in their direction.

"I beg your pardon?" Megan was stunned.

"I can see you have been raised to be a proper young lady. No young lady of breeding would sit next to the likes of that." The woman's face twisted into a cold and haughty sneer.

Megan peered back and forth between the two women. The younger woman turned away and stared out the window, ignoring the speaker's tirade. Megan was aghast at the public spectacle the older woman was making.

"Why ever would you say such a thing?" Megan kept her voice low.

"She is a harlot. Look at the brazen low cut of her dress," the woman spat. "Well-bred young ladies do not consort with her kind."

Megan had had enough. Disregarding the faces turned their direction, she said, "What right have you to judge yourself to be better than her?"

"Well," the woman sputtered. "I am a Christian. I thought you were too."

"Does being a Christian somehow give us the right to judge others?" Megan held on to the seat as the train lurched forward.

"Christ said in the Good Book that... that kind of behavior is an abomination. A stench in God's nostrils," the woman railed.

"He also said, 'Let he who is without sin cast the first stone' and 'Judge not lest ye be judged,'" Megan countered.

The woman opened and closed her mouth a few times like a fish out of water. Several of the other passengers chuckled, and most turned back to their own business. The older woman flushed a bright red. With a huff, she turned her back to Megan and glared out the window.

Megan turned back to the gaily dressed young woman studying her with curiosity and something akin to admiration.

"May I sit here?" Megan repeated her earlier question.

"Please do. I am waiting for my fiancé, but there is more than enough room for the three of us here." She smiled and gestured for Megan to take a seat near the window opposite her.

"My name is Megan. Megan Carter." She offered the other woman her hand.

"Clara Smythe." The woman smiled, clasping Megan's hand firmly.

"And I am her fiancé," a deep voice interjected.

Clara's face lit up as a tall, dark, handsome cowboy slid into the seat next to her. She intertwined her fingers in his as he leaned in for a kiss.

Megan was more than a little intimidated by the man. There was a tough look in his blue eyes, but his face softened every time he glanced at Clara. He wore a gun slung low across his hips and embodied what Megan had imagined a gunslinger to be. Even through the shirt and leather vest, she could tell he was lean and chiseled.

"Megan, this is Gage Reagan, my fiancé." Beaming with pride, Clara reached for Megan's hand. "Gage, this is my new friend, Megan."

More than a few heads whipped around to stare at them when Clara introduced Gage. Perhaps she was correct about him being a gunslinger. Megan ignored their stares as she shook the hand he offered. Her small hand was swallowed in his large one.

"I heard what you said earlier." Gage leaned over to Megan. "Thank you for standing up to that woman."

The conductor stopped at their seats and asked for their tickets, and further conversation was impossible for a time. Clara and Gage were soon engrossed in each other, and Megan was left to her own thoughts.

Three more days of train travel, and at least two more by stage. Megan mentally calculated what little money she had left. Judging by the prices on the dining car menu posted on the station wall in Omaha, she would have to be frugal to have enough for her trip.

She still had the apple she hadn't eaten for breakfast, and she could save it for lunch.

Maybe if I sleep more, I won't be as hungry. She wasn't feeling well. Her eyes were still gritty, and her head was beginning to pound in earnest. Rest would do her good. She took off her gloves and pressed icy fingers to her eyes. Megan longed to let her hair out of the pins and get the soot out of her eyes and nose. She leaned her head again the smooth glass of the window and closed her eyes to sleep.

∞ ∞ ∞

Clara glanced at Megan, then sighed and put her head on Gage's shoulder.

"What is wrong?" He glanced down at her.

"She seems awfully young to be traveling West alone."

"She is older than you were the first time I met you."
Gage remembered that first meeting well. The gunslinger
and the saloon girl; it was a story worthy of a dime-store
novel.

"This is different. Something isn't right here. Tell me you
don't see something that doesn't add up," Clara insisted.

"What do you see?" Clara had good instincts about
people, and Gage respected her intuition.

"Look at her dress. It is good quality, but out of style. It
doesn't fit her, either. No seamstress of quality would make
a dress that ill-fitting. Plus, look at her shoes. You can see
her stockings peeking out of the toes. They must be several
years old to be that well-worn," Clara whispered.

"Yes. I saw her standing on the platform. She doesn't
appear to have any luggage beyond the small bag on her
lap." Gage agreed with Clara. There was much more to this
girl than met the eye.

"I am worried about her, Gage." Clara peered up into his
face, her furrowed brow mirroring the concern in her voice.

"You met her not even three hours ago." Gage smiled at
his tenderhearted bride-to-be. Clara put on a brash and
brazen front, but underneath the makeup and bright clothes,
she was sweet and kind.

"She hadn't met me yet when she defended me. You are
the only other person who has ever taken my side."

"She could be a mail-order bride," Gage suggested.

"I hope not." Clara wrinkled her face. Being a mail-order
bride was not as romantic as some made it sound. Men out
West could be rough, and Clara had more than her share of

experience with the rough side of life. Gage clenched his jaw as he thought about it.

The first time they met, Clara had been running from an abusive customer. She had knocked him off his feet and taken his breath away in more ways than one. He put his arm around her and drew her close.

"Can we help her?" Clara's words were filled with pain.

"We will try." Gage hugged her tight.

Soon their conversation turned elsewhere, and before they knew it, it was time for lunch. Megan still appeared to be asleep, so they headed for the dining car to let her rest.

∞ ∞ ∞

When Megan finally opened her eyes, Clara and Gage were gone. Their belongings were still there, and Gage had left his Stetson on the seat. She rubbed her eyes. They still felt a little gritty, but her headache had dulled to a mild throbbing. There were several empty seats, and many of the people still sitting there were eating. Her stomach rumbled as if to confirm it was lunchtime.

Megan took her apple from her little bundle. Maybe this would hold her until dinner. Perhaps the dining car would be some food that proved affordable. She was finishing her apple when Clara and Gage returned. The two women picked up where they had left off, chatting like long-lost friends. They talked all afternoon.

∞ ∞ ∞

Gage listened to the women, amused. From the things Megan was saying, he assumed she was a Christian.

He had known many people who claimed to be Christians, or who were religious, but none like her. He had seen those religious people all his life. Watched them turn on each other instead of helping each other. Most he found to be self-righteous and unkind.

Many years ago, he had watched his mother and sister suffer when their church ostracized his family. After seeing people who had known their family for years turn on her and her small children, Gage had decided if that was how Christians were supposed to act, he wanted nothing to do with any of it, including God.

He had run in the opposite direction as far and as fast as he could. His skill with a gun had given him every opportunity he could have wished for. It also brought along the respect he desired.

Most religious people had renewed his ill will for them with how they treated Clara. Never mind she was the sweetest, kindest woman alive, most so-called Christians behaved like the woman across the aisle had. Megan was different, though.

Gage glanced at the woman who had harangued Clara earlier. He caught her staring and their eyes met. Her lip curled, and she huffed as she made a show of deliberately turning her back to them. Gage chuckled and returned his attention to the girls. They were giggling like schoolmates.

"So where are you headed?" Megan asked Clara.

"Gage is going to be the new sheriff in Goodrich." Clara's voice rang with pride.

"The railway ends there, and the current sheriff is overwhelmed." Gage jumped into the conversation. "It is a stopover for a lot of cattle drives before they either board the train or cross the river and head north. They need a strong gun hand with the influx of people." He pointed to the gun on his hip. "That is where I come in," he said with a wink.

"We are going to be married there. The judge is an old friend of Gage's." The excitement in Clara's voice made him and Megan smile.

"How about you, Megan? What brings you West?" Gage asked.

"I am going to Coldville to meet my family." Megan smiled.

"I don't understand. You have never met your family? Your parents?" Clara blurted.

A shadow passed over Megan's face, and her hands trembled. A glance out the window at the fading light and pink-blue-and-gray-streaked sky told him it was time for dinner.

"Why don't we continue this conversation during dinner?" Gage proposed.

Megan's brow wrinkled as she glanced at her reticule. Gage understood her conundrum.

"I have an idea. Let's have a nice dinner to celebrate our upcoming wedding. My treat." He rose and gestured for the two women to precede him. Clara swept down the aisle, her bright skirts swirling. Megan hesitated, but Gage urged her on with a look.

"Thank you," she whispered as she followed her new friend.

The trio was soon seated in a nice private corner. Gage ordered dinner for everyone, and Megan told them her story. Their meal was nothing special, but one glance at the menu told Megan she wouldn't be able to afford food on this part of the journey. It was filling, though, and by the time they finished, Megan was yawning and ready to sleep again.

When they were back at their seats, Clara curled into Gage and fell asleep. Megan leaned against the window to take her own rest. The woman across the aisle was staring at them, disapproval written all over her craggy face. Megan sighed and closed her eyes. Her breathing slowed to an even, rhythmic cadence in a few minutes.

Gage stayed awake for a while and guarded the two women. Even the old bat across the aisle eventually fell asleep. He slid his gun partly out of the holster and rested his hand on the butt of the weapon. Pushing his Stetson down over his face, Gage finally leaned his head against the window and sought his own rest.

Chapter 7

Megan slowly stretched her stiff muscles and opened her eyes. Her head was throbbing again. The sun was peeking over the horizon as the train chugged along. Clara and Gage were still sleeping. Clara's head lay on Gage's shoulder, and Gage's head rested on top of her blond curls. His arm draped protectively around her shoulders. They were adorable.

Megan carefully stepped around Gage's outstretched legs to the aisle. She glanced across to the woman who had caused a scene the previous day and stifled a giggle. The woman's mouth was wide open, her chin was wet and shiny with drool, and her sensible bonnet was askew.

Megan hurried to the ladies' washroom to freshen up and smiled wryly at her reflection in the mirror. She had looked worse with better sleep than she had enjoyed in the last few days. Her eyes were slightly glazed and faint dark circles highlighted them, making them stand out even more in her pale face. It was too bad.

Megan shook out her hair to relieve the tension and massaged her scalp. She re-braided it, twisted it up again, pinned it tightly, and replaced her hat. She hoped she could leave her hair down around her brothers. Surely the rules in the West were more relaxed than in her grandmother's house. A few red curls had already worked their way out of her hat, but a person couldn't do much with naturally curly hair.

She was halfway back to her seat when someone gripped the back of her skirt and held her fast.

"Where is a pretty thing like you headed so early all by yer lonesome?" a slimy voice asked.

Fear jolted through Megan's veins, but she tamped it down. This wasn't the first time she had dealt with a bully. The city streets were full of them.

"Release me this instant!" she spoke loud enough to disturb those who were sleeping, and they began to stir. She turned toward the offensive speaker, but he still gripped her skirt in his meaty fist. The passengers' glares did not faze the rough man. The scowl he returned, discouraged any onlookers from helping her.

Megan took a deep breath to steady her nerves and twisted her head to get a better look of the man who sat holding her prisoner. The smell of whiskey told her that he was drunk. Mostly he was a dirty cowboy. She had read about them—men who spent months on the trail, drinking themselves into a stupor and chasing women when they were between drives.

"Let. Go. Of. Me." She could not back down. She would not back down.

"I jest want ter talk. Where ya headed all by yerself?" the man wheedled.

Megan refused to play his game. She stayed silent and still, looking him straight in the eye, waiting.

"Look. All I want is a little friendly conversation. Ya think yer too good fer me?" the man ground out. Releasing her skirt, he stood.

Megan backed away before he could catch hold again. No wonder everyone was frightened of the man; he was huge. Megan's head came to the middle of his chest. His red face and narrowed eyes evidenced his irritation. By now her bravery had fled, and she decided to try to retreat to the relative safety of her seat.

"Pretty little thing like you ought not be travlin' alone." He grinned.

"How I am traveling and who I am with is no concern of yours. Please leave me alone."

Anger glinted in his eyes, and experience told Megan she had only two choices left: fight or flight. Neither was good.

She turned to run and collided with something solid.

Solid and angry. Gage pushed Megan behind him with his left arm. His right hand rested lightly on the pistol on his hip.

"I believe the lady asked you to leave her alone. Nice-like. More than once." Gage's voice was like frosted steel.

Megan peeked around him. Everyone in the car was wide awake now watching the showdown between the two men.

"Who are you? What business is it of yers?" the bully sneered.

"My name... is Gage Reagen," Gage drew the words out. A murmur shuddered through the car, and the huge man shrank right before Megan's eyes.

"I thought that might get your attention." Gage's smile was humorless. Cold. Harsh. Frightening. "You owe this young lady an apology," he said pointedly.

The big man mumbled an apology, his puffy face now colorless. At Megan's nod of acceptance, he stumbled back to his seat. She was not sure what was going on, but she was glad the confrontation was over.

Gage turned to her, his gaze and smile warm once again, and escorted her back to their seat where Clara was waiting, wide-eyed.

"Are you okay?" she asked.

"Yes, thank you." Megan directed her thanks to Gage and interlocked her fingers to still her trembling hands in her lap. Her gaze traveled to the gun slung low on Gage's hip. "You must be exceptional." She nodded toward the imposing firearm.

"He is one of the best, and famous, at least around these parts." Clara beamed.

"I only use it when I have no other alternative. The gun, along with my reputation, is a good deterrent for those who are thinking about getting out of line." He patted the butt of the weapon.

"Well, thank you for coming to my rescue," Megan said.

"My pleasure." Gage tipped his hat to the ladies. "I am going to go get some breakfast. Do you want anything?"

"No thank y—"

"Oh yes, please. Tea and pastries. We would be ever so grateful if you could rustle up sugar for the tea as well." Clara grinned impishly.

Gage laughed at his fiancée's sassy grin, then leaned down to kiss her on the cheek before heading to search for nourishment. The woman across the aisle harrumphed, making a show of her displeasure, and Megan rolled her eyes.

He soon returned with a basket of pastries. The porter was right behind him with tea, and to their delight, an entire bowl of sugar cubes.

The cranky woman across the aisle got off at the train's next stop, for which Megan was thankful. Being kind to her all day long had been difficult when the woman kept glaring at her. The farther west the train traveled, the fewer passengers remained. By the time sundown came on the second day, the three were able to spread out and lie down on the seats and be more comfortable for the night.

∞ ∞ ∞

After two long days on the train, it was finally time for Megan to say goodbye to her new-found friends. Gage and Clara escorted her to the stagecoach.

"If you ever need anything, you know where we are. Please come visit if you get the chance, or if you ever come back this way, stop and see us." Clara hugged Megan tightly.

Gage helped Megan into the coach. "We mean what she says." He smiled.

Megan leaned out the window and waved to them as the stage took off with a lurch. She had barely known them for three days, and yet tears ran down her cheeks as they disappeared from sight. She had been safe with them and had not had to censor her thoughts or words to not offend or upset them.

Chapter 8

Only two other passengers were on the stage when it left Goodrich. Megan was nervous, being the only woman on board, but she soon discovered that her fellow passengers and the driver were kind. The man riding shotgun made her uneasy, but only because he was quiet.

The stage bumped and jostled and shook as the horses pulled it higher into the mountains, and Megan slid off her seat more than once. The air grew cooler as they traveled higher. She hugged herself to disguise her shivering, but the men both noticed.

"Would you like a blanket, miss?" the older of the two asked. At her nod, he pounded on the roof of the coach, calling for the driver to stop for a moment. They lurched to a halt, and the shotgun rider opened the coach door.

"This is a good time for a break. Everybody out; take a few minutes to stretch. Find a tree or do whatever you need to do. We won't likely stop again before we reach the Haven," the driver said. "Sorry, miss," he added as an aside to Megan.

Not until he apologized did she realize what he meant by "find a tree." Her face heated, and she hurried to find a place to relieve herself before the men were ready to go. As she stepped off the trail, her arm was caught in an iron grip.

"Let me check it first." The quiet shotgun rider was standing beside her. Megan nodded, not trusting herself to speak. The big man disappeared into the bushes, and Megan could hear him swishing about. He was back mere seconds later.

"It's clear," he said as he walked a few steps away. Megan scrutinized him for a moment. He was clearly waiting for her. She dashed into the bushes as quick as she could. Juggling the stiff taffeta dress, the bushes, and grass wasn't easy, but she managed and was soon safely back in the coach.

She flushed again. A woolen blanket was sitting on her seat. The door closed with a loud snap. She gazed through the window at the bearded man, and his cheeks turned bright red under his salt-and-pepper beard. She realized he might be as frightened of her as she was of him.

"Gets cold the higher we go in the mountains. Yer not dressed proper fer it." The shotgun rider's voice was gruff but his eyes were kind.

"Thank you." Megan shook out the blanket and spread it over her legs.

"Welcome, miss." He turned to take his seat on top of the coach.

"Megan. My name is Megan."

"Henry. Henry Mosely." He touched the brim of his wide-brimmed Stetson.

"Nice to meet you, Henry."

Henry climbed back onto the top of the stagecoach, and Megan tugged the blanket to her chin, snuggled into the corner, and did her best to make herself comfortable. The stage jerked forward once again, and the tumultuous ride continued until it was too dark to go on. They finally stopped, and the door was opened from the outside. A firm hand helped her out of the coach.

"Welcome to the Haven. Washing facilities in the back, folks. Wash up, dinner's on," a booming voice called.

It took a moment for Megan's legs to get used to solid ground again. She stepped aside to stretch, trying to alleviate her cramped muscles and breathed in deeply. The crisp mountain air and the scent of pine trees was refreshing. As she marched toward the small building the proprietor had pointed out, she caught sight of a man and woman standing behind the inn, at the tree line.

Indians. Megan watched them with curiosity. She had read dozens of stories about the savages of the West, but these two did not appear savage. Rather, they were a stunning couple. The man gave the impression he had been carved from bronze marble, so chiseled were his features. His buckskin breeches and long dark hair only accentuated the beautiful color of his skin. Megan could not help but stare.

She soon found herself gazing into a pair of chocolate-brown eyes. The young woman appeared to be curious about her too. She wore a supple buckskin dress adorned with colorful beads and shells. Her hair was raven-black and shone like brushed metal. Megan longed to touch it. The

Indian woman's face was softer than her partner's but still had the same high cheekbones.

Someone nudged her; it was her turn to use the washroom. She tore herself away and hurried inside to freshen up.

As she headed into the house after cleaning her face and hands, she saw Henry talking to the Indians, and she watched them until she was inside the warm inn. A young woman was standing at the door.

"Are you having dinner, miss? Staying in the rooms or in the coach?" the girl asked. One glance told Megan she was the innkeeper's daughter. They were so alike it was uncanny.

"I was planning to stay in the rooms and take dinner here as well. Please call me Megan."

"Miss Megan, my name is Rachael. You payin' in paper or coin?"

"I have coin. Ten dollars for the room, is that right?"

"Yep, ten dollars for the room, and one for dinner," Rachael said.

Megan carefully counted eleven dollars in coins. She only had a few pennies left.

"Dinner's gonna be right good tonight. Ma cooked us up a nice venison stew, and we even got a fresh-baked rhubarb pie." Rachael's smile was contagious. Megan smiled back at her.

"What is rhubarb?" she asked.

"I don' knows how ta describe it, but it sure is tasty. I reckon it is maybe the best thing I ever did eat," Rachael said over her shoulder as she showed Megan into the dining room. The room was mostly bare, with only a simple, long wood table in the center. Megan slid onto the end of one of the benches on either side of it. Metal bowls and crude wooden spoons sat at each place along with a tin cup.

The innkeeper's wife ladled a thick stew into Megan's bowl.

"Be ya wantin' coffee or milk, child?" the woman asked.

"I would love milk, please," Megan murmured. Her mouth watered at the sight of the rich broth. Rachael trailed along behind her mother and filled Megan's cup with rich, creamy milk. Megan took a moment to give silent thanks to God for her food before eagerly digging in. She couldn't identify some of the ingredients in her soup, but it was tasty. The meat and vegetables were tender and the broth rich and deep. It filled and warmed her from the inside out.

When everyone had devoured their fill of the stew, the innkeeper's wife served large wedges of pie. The buttery crust melded with the sweet and tart fruit to create the perfect taste. After only two bites Megan decided she loved rhubarb. She was delighted to learn it grew in abundance in the surrounding area.

"It is actually a weed." The hostess smiled at her. "But it tastes nigh unto heaven in pies and cakes. We use it in jams and soups as well. 'Tis a useful weed."

Megan began to droop as she finished her meal, and the innkeeper's wife showed her to her room after dinner. It was simply furnished with only a bed and small nightstand. A crackling fire warmed the small space, and Megan was asleep within seconds of lying down on the bed.

It seemed as though only a few moments had passed before a knock on the door awakened her. The driver wanted to leave. A storm had passed through in the night, and the roads were soggy. It would be slow going, and they needed to get an early start.

Her throat was dry and scratchy and her head ached. Her muscles protested as she crawled out of the warm bed and slid on her clothes. The taffeta dress had held up quite well, although it had a few soot stains and wrinkles. Her body felt like her dress looked—worn, and slightly battered.

Megan wrapped the blanket around her again as the coach started off. Spring in the mountains was even colder than in the city, she was finding. The day slowly warmed up, but at many places along the trail, they could still see snow. She had barely drifted off to sleep when the coach came to a sudden halt.

"Everybody out." The driver pounded on the side of the coach, then he and Henry climbed down.

"Sorry, folks, spring runoff has made the trail pretty narrow here. We are going to have to lead the team across, and you will have to follow on foot. We may come upon a few of these spots here. Take care and stay near the side of the mountain, away from the edge," Henry instructed the passengers as the driver led the horses along the narrowest part of the trail.

Everyone cringed as the wheels of the coach came incredibly close to the edge of the mountain. Megan followed close behind Henry as they slogged through the mud. Icy water seeped through her shoes, numbing her feet almost instantly.

Henry called them to a halt ten minutes later. The rear wheel of the coach had slid off the trail and was hanging over the edge of the mountain. Henry ordered Megan to stay put.

She obeyed his request and leaned into the mountainside, far away from the edge of the trail as the driver coaxed the horses forward, while Henry and the other passengers attempted to right the coach.

The men grunted and groaned as they pushed, their muscles straining. Megan breathed a sigh of relief as they finally got the stage safely back onto the trail.

Henry waved for Megan to catch up. She shifted to take a step and nearly landed on her face. Her feet were solidly encased in the mud. She wrapped both hands around one leg and yanked, but no matter how hard she tried, she could not budge an inch.

"Miss? Are you coming?" Henry called back to her.

"My name is Megan. I can't. I am stuck," Megan shouted back. She didn't know whether to laugh or cry. She was embarrassed, but it was still funny.

Henry and her fellow passengers came back to help but were no more successful at extricating her. One foot was ankle deep, and the other had sunk to midcalf. She was well and truly stuck. Her fellow passengers each took an arm and tugged but the patch of mud she was in threatened to suck them in too.

"We could tie her to one of the horses?" the older of the passengers asked.

"Don't be a fool. We can't do that to a girl," the other man retorted.

Henry leaned back, rubbing his chin.

"Well, I certainly can't stay here." Megan shivered and her teeth chattered.

"I have an idea. But 'tisn't zactly proper-like," Henry finally said, pulling at his collar and blushing. He glanced at Megan as though for permission.

She had barely finished nodding when he stepped forward, lowered his shoulder, and picked her up. Her waist rested on his shoulder, and one arm pressed across the back of her knees. With a grunt, the big man heaved, and she was free. He wallowed through the mud and deposited her gracefully next to the stagecoach.

Megan registered the other passengers' shocked expressions, glanced down at her wet and muddy dress, and up to Henry's face, which was now a dull red. She started to giggle. It was all completely ridiculous. She laughed so hard, no sound escaped her lips, but then a loud snort ripped from her throat as she gasped for air. Henry's deep laugh soon joined hers, and when the driver, who introduced himself as George, came back to see what was going on, the confusion etched on his face started the laughter going all over again.

Eventually the little group gathered themselves together and got moving. Three more times they repeated the process of disembarking and walking before they were past the narrow spaces on the trail.

Finally they made it out of the mountains and into the hill country. Megan was chilled to the bone by the time they stopped for the night. They set up camp beside a small stream, and the men bunked under the stars.

Henry insisted Megan sleep inside the coach, and she did not argue. Her whole body hurt and sleeping outside didn't appeal to her tonight. She removed the thin cushions from the seats and laid them on the floor to create a little bed. She covered herself with the blanket she had been given earlier, and was fast asleep before the sun was fully down.

∞ ∞ ∞

Henry checked on Megan when the stew was ready, but she did not stir, so he let her sleep. He quietly let down the leather curtains over the windows of the coach. Not being near the fire, he was concerned she would get cold, but she would be less likely to have to deal with critters crawling into bed with her if she were off the ground. Last trip he had come this way, he had shared his bed roll with no less than three field mice and four snakes.

She was a pretty little woman and a plucky thing too. With her red curls, freckle-sprinkled nose, and those expressive green eyes, Megan reminded him of a girl he had known many years ago. He had been a wrangler for her and her husband when they had first made the journey West. This young woman could have been her twin. He suspected strongly this was the same child he had put on the train East many years ago.

He watched Megan sleep for a few minutes. Her long eyelashes lay against her pale cheeks and she looked angelic in the flickering firelight. Watching her, he missed his own family. Henry lowered the last leather curtain on the stage and went to seek his own rest.

∞ ∞ ∞

The sound of dogs howling set Megan's heart racing. Dogs in the city were dangerous, wild, and vicious. She turned to run, but felt as if she were stuck to the ground. Her leg was vibrating. A dog had clamped its jaws around her boot and was shaking her leg back and forth. She screamed, kicking and lashing at the brute with every ounce of her strength.

"Oomph." A human grunt broke through her terror. Her eyes fluttered open when the grunt was repeated.

"Miss. Miss, are you okay?" Henry was leaning through the coach door, shaking her boot with one hand and holding his stomach with the other.

Megan sat up with a gasp. Realizing she had been having a nightmare, she slumped back against the cushions. "Oh Henry, I am sorry. Did I kick you? Oh no, I am so sorry. I just—"

Henry held up his hand with a chuckle. "I'm fine, miss. Are you all right? We need to get the stage packed up, and George has breakfast ready if you be wantin' to eat."

Megan took his offered hand and scrambled from the coach. Her head was pounding and her throat was burning and scratchy, but she chalked it up to screaming. Her fellow passengers and George were already eating their breakfast: coffee, passable biscuits, salted pork, and red-eye gravy. George was a fair cook, and Megan ate her food with gusto.

With precious little time to see to her needs, Megan was soon back on the stagecoach, and they were rattling down the road at breakneck speed. Now that they were out of the mountains, they would make good time.

The jolting and jouncing of the coach did little to settle Megan's head, and her throat continued to burn. By the time they stopped at the little shack along the road to switch horses, Megan was feeling unwell. The other passengers disembarked at the shack. One headed for his ranch farther north, the other to his brother's place a few miles south of the way station. Now alone, she stretched out. The rough ride kept her from sleeping but lying down helped lessen the pain in her head.

Megan needed to be feeling better when she met her brothers. She was a little afraid of what they would be like but was desperate to make a good impression.

∞ ∞ ∞

"We can't all go. Three horses need shoeing, the west fence needs mending, and the cattle in the north section need to be transferred to the west pasture." Riley, the eldest of the Carter men, leaned against the stone fireplace. He studied his brothers. All of them wanted to meet their little sister at the coach depot in Coldville. It was a good two hours' ride into town, so they had to decide who would go soon, or they would be late meeting the stage.

"What do you think she is like?" Logan asked no one in particular. He was the youngest. He had been only a small boy of six when their father had sent her away.

"I was wondering the same thing. According to Father, Grandmother is a wealthy woman. I am sure she has had the best money can buy: clothes, education, and the like," Caleb responded. "I sure wish she had written back to us. The telegram didn't tell us anything other than she was arriving today." He ran his hands through his thick, dark hair.

Riley nodded. They had been surprised and puzzled when the telegram had arrived, but no letter or further telegrams had followed.

"I think three of us should go to town. The other two had best stay here and get work done. The hired hands and the Hernandez brothers can take care of the fences and help us get the cattle into the pasture. But I would prefer to shoe the horses myself," Morgan spoke up. He was the second eldest, and the best on the ranch at the blacksmith forge. He had a quiet power to him. When he spoke, people listened, including his brothers.

"Morgan is staying. I will stay as well," Logan volunteered.

"That leaves Caleb, Sawyer, and myself to go to town." Riley knew how much it cost Morgan and Logan to volunteer to stay behind. Sawyer had not spoken a word during the exchange, but none of his brothers dreamed of asking him to stay home. He had been hit the hardest when Megan had been sent away. Sawyer had fed her, and held her during the night when she cried. He had been inconsolable for days after their father had sent her East.

"Should I hitch up the buggy?" Sawyer stood.

"She will probably have trunks. Best take the wagon," Caleb said as the three headed to the barn.

"Wagon's not real comfortable," Sawyer said.

"She has been traveling by stage for the last few days; she can handle the wagon seat for a couple hours." Riley had no intention of coddling Megan. They lived on a ranch, and she might as well get used to the idea this wasn't the big city anymore. If she chose to stay, they would be thrilled, but he wanted to start on the right foot.

Minutes later the men were on their way into town. Sawyer drove the wagon, while the other two rode alongside. They rode in silence. Memories many years past flooded Riley's mind. Their lives were about to change. He didn't know whether he was excited or nervous.

∞ ∞ ∞

Megan had woken up much sicker this morning. Her head pounded and throbbed as if it would fall off with every jolt of the coach. Her throat was burning, and waves of nausea threatened to overwhelm her. The heat was oppressive and stifling.

Helena's taffeta dress had held up, though. It was only slightly rumpled and dusty, despite her stint in the mud the day before. Her hat, however, was worse for the wear. It had gotten crushed more than once as she had slid of the seat and landed on it. She debated whether she should pin it on, but she couldn't bring herself to. The hat was too badly damaged, and it wouldn't do to step out of the coach with it askew and broken. She tugged on her gloves and sat back as the coach slowed to a crawl as they pulled up to the depot right on time.

With every breath, her throat felt as if she were breathing fire. Tears stung her eyes. Now that the moment was here, she was afraid, sick, and plain exhausted. Before she could compose herself, Henry opened the door.

"All out for Coldville," he said. Poking his head inside the coach, he continued, "We are here, miss. Can I help ya?" He offered her his large, calloused hand.

Megan took the assistance gratefully and stumbled into the sunlight. Her eyes closed of their own accord. The bright light hurt and intensified her already-throbbing headache.

She was aware of Henry letting go of her hand when she was securely on the boardwalk in front of the depot. She didn't know what to do now. What she wanted to do was sit down and have a good cry. Megan cracked her eyelids, but the pain was intense. She stumbled to a bench outside the stagecoach office and sat to wait for her brothers, hoping they knew where to search for her.

"Megan? Megan Carter?" a deep voice sounded from somewhere above her.

"Yes," she answered, turning her head toward the sound. She still couldn't get her eyes open.

"Megan?" this time a different man spoke.

"I-I am sorry. I am not feeling well." Megan's voice trembled as she thrust herself off the bench to stand.

The second man reached for her arm as she tipped forward. Megan flinched and jerked away automatically. She sighed when he froze. This was awkward. She forced her eyes open. The pain was intense, but she bit her lip and impelled herself to peer at the man in front of her. She wished she hadn't. Nausea churned her stomach.

Three tall, dark, and handsome men stood directly in front of her. At least she thought they were dark and handsome; she could only see their outlines. Their features were fuzzy.

"Megan, I am Riley, this is Caleb, and this is Sawyer." The tallest man shifted forward, his hat in his hand.

"We're your brothers," one of them blurted.

Megan struggled to keep each one straight in her head. She couldn't think. Her brain was foggy. This was not the first impression she wanted to make.

"Megan, do you have a headache?" Sawyer asked.

The effort of standing upright taxed every bit of her strength. "Yes," she whispered. Her knees buckled and the world tipped sideways. A strong arm slipped under her knees and another behind her shoulders. The world tipped again, and she closed her eyes and tried not to give in to nausea as she was carried swiftly down the street.

Sawyer was a few feet from his destination when Megan's head fell limply onto his chest. He would have known his sister anywhere; she was the spitting image of his mother. So close they could have been sisters. Same copper hair, same green eyes, even the same pained squint on her face that their mother used to get when she had one of her headaches.

"Doc! Anne!" Sawyer called as he strode up the steps to the local doctor's office.

"Sawyer, what on earth?" The doctor's beautiful blond daughter opened the door to let him in. His brothers were on his heels.

"It is my sister. I think she has fainted," Sawyer said.

Anne motioned for them to follow her into her father's office, where Doc Warren glanced up from his desk.

"Abigail," Doc called his wife. She appeared quickly, and the two women took charge of the unconscious Megan.

"Boys, you wait outside. We will let you know what is going on in a few minutes." Doc shooed them out the door.

Riley and Caleb paced the waiting room while Sawyer leaned by the door.

"Someone should go get her trunks," Caleb spoke up.

"I am not leaving her. Not again," Sawyer said. His brothers didn't argue.

"You stay here. We will go get the trunks and get them loaded into the wagon." Riley was always the one take charge of a situation. Sawyer was thankful his brothers understood. They left, leaving him to pace the waiting room alone.

A few minutes had passed before Anne entered the waiting room.

"How is she?" Sawyer asked.

Anne smiled at him. "She will be fine. She is suffering from a pretty severe cold, and between that, the headache, and her nerves, it simply got the better of her. Dad will be in with instructions later."

Sawyer sagged with relief.

"Maybe you had better sit down." She took his arm and led him to the settee. Sawyer sank down into it, putting his head in his hands as Anne sat next to him.

Sawyer turned to her, meeting her pale blue eyes. "She scared me."

"I can understand how her reaction frightened you." Anne smiled. "You Carter men are usually strong and in charge. It is interesting to see you all a little out of sorts."

Sawyer smiled back. He didn't take her words personally; most men he knew didn't do well with women fainting. Anne had opened her mouth to say something else when her father came into the room.

"Doc, is she really okay?" Sawyer was on his feet instantly.

The doctor stopped next to Anne. "She will be. I have given her a dose of headache powders, and Abigail will get some ready to send home with you. You should take her home and make her as comfortable as possible. She will need plenty of rest and sunshine." He hesitated before continuing, his brow furrowed. "How much do you know regarding your sister's situation?"

"Megan has been living with our wealthy grandmother back East. That is all I know. Why?"

"It appears she has had a difficult time of it... for a long time, probably years." Doc sounded as though he was measuring his words with care.

"What do you mean, a difficult time of it?" a sober voice interrupted.

Sawyer hadn't heard his brothers return. They were standing in the doorway looking grim.

"What's going on?" Sawyer swiveled his gaze between them and the doctor.

"She has no luggage. None. Not a single bag or trunk," Caleb said. "Unless you call this a bag." He held up a shawl tied around a small reticule.

"What did you mean difficult time, Doc?" Riley asked again.

"She is thin. Too thin. Her back is crisscrossed with scars, which makes me think she has been beaten. She has spent a lot of time on her hands and knees as well. I suspect she was a servant in someone's household." The older man rubbed the back of his neck and sighed.

"Her dress isn't hers, either. It doesn't fit her. It is a little too big. A well-made dress like this would be tailored perfectly," Anne said. "Her underthings and shoes are hers, though, and they are worn down to nothing."

"What do we do now?" Sawyer asked. "What does all this mean?"

"I will tell you what you do. You take her home. You love her. You care for her like she should have been cared for from the beginning. Jamison never should have sent that child away, and someone should have checked on her before now. But now that she is here, you boys make sure she is cared for. If you don't, you will have me to deal with." Abigail's voice cracked through the room like a whip. She filled the doorway, puffed up like a mother hen.

"Yes, ma'am." Sawyer had the good sense not to sass her. "Is she able to make the trip back to the ranch?" His mind was immediately working on a solution if she couldn't.

"They brought the wagon, Ma." Doc was rubbing his mustache, clearly amused at his wife's outburst, or more likely, at the Carter boys' reaction. Abigail Warren was a sweet, compassionate woman, but when she had a bee in her bonnet, look out.

"Well, then. Anne and I will round up quilts and such. One of you boys go to the livery and have clean hay put in the back. We will throw the quilts over the straw and create a nice bed for her to lie in on the way back to the ranch." The women didn't wait to see if the men agreed with the plan or not, they got right down to business.

Caleb volunteered to go get the hay, and Riley and Sawyer stayed to talk to the doctor.

"What do we need to do when we get her home?" Riley took charge again.

"My wife covered it pretty well. Plenty of good food, rest, and care is what she needs. Treat her with kindness, like you would a skittish horse. I don't know what happened back East; she isn't up to saying much. I do know she never read your letter. She told me a cousin, Titus, sent her West after he read it."

"Titus St. James. Aunt Amelia's boy." Sawyer recognized the name, but the Carters had never met any of the St. James family. They had never met Adelaide Carter, either. He rose, running a hand through his hair.

Not for the first time, a deep anger rose in his breast toward his father. He hadn't understood why they had never gone to visit Megan. Jamison Carter wasn't a cruel man, but after his wife's death he had lost some of his softness. Life was harsh on the range, and he had raised his boys to be tough.

Sawyer was so lost in his own thoughts, he didn't see the ladies return, and he almost jumped out of his skin when Anne put her hand on his arm. He relaxed into an easy grin as soon as he saw who was standing there. Both women got the giggles, and the tension in the room was broken. Caleb returned to find everyone laughing.

"Wagon's back," he said.

The ladies hurried to put the quilts in the wagon bed, still smiling, and Sawyer watched Anne as she moved gracefully to arrange a bed. His face flushed when his brother caught him staring. He was in love with Anne, and his brothers never missed an opportunity to tease him about it.

"I have given your sister a sleeping powder for now. She should sleep the rest of the day. I will send a few more with you, in case she needs them. The hope is with rest, and with good food when she wakes, her headache will go away. Take care to keep her warm, and feed her lots of fluids: broth, water, soups, and things along that line. Mrs. Hernandez will know what to do." Doc Warren handed Riley several small glassine envelopes with the sleeping powders and the headache powders.

Sawyer followed Doc and Abigail into the small examining room. Megan was fast asleep on the chaise. Abigail had taken the pins from Megan's hair, and her tresses spilled over the cushions, glinting like copper fire in

Helena remained rooted to the spot for a moment. Adelaide took it as a sign she would comply as usual.

Adelaide sat at her desk and took another glass of sherry. "You and I are alike, you know." The laudanum had relaxed her, and she couldn't stop the words spilling from her mouth. "We both like the nicer things. You know Megan isn't like us. Low-class, that is what she is. I should have made sure she disappeared in the asylum. Then my problems would have been over. Once I get her back here, I will make sure she is never found again, and you and I can go back to having things the way they should be, the way they used to be," she slurred.

"No." The word burst out of Helena. "I am nothing like you."

"You certainly have been putting on a good act if that is the case." Adelaide laughed.

"You are right. And I am ashamed of myself. I am ashamed of you. I am leaving. For good. Unless you get those men back here and tell them you have changed your mind. If you insist on following through with this hateful scheme, I don't ever want to see you again. Megan is my cousin, my uncle's daughter, your son's daughter. She has never been anything but kind toward me, despite my selfish behavior. I am going to pack my bag." Helena walked away, firmly shutting the door behind her.

Adelaide sat at her desk glaring at the door. How dare Helena speak to her in such a manner? She shouldn't be surprised, though. Helena was prone to temper tantrums. She would be back.

Several minutes later, Adelaide heard the telltale clip-clop of a horse pulling a carriage to the front door. Helena was taking this a little far. She went to her window and watched as Jenkins helped load Helena's trunk onto a hansom cab. It wasn't until Helena herself climbed into the coach that she realized—Helena was following through on her threat.

She turned away from the window swiftly. The action, combined with the recent dose of laudanum, made her head swim. Helena was leaving, and she wasn't coming back.

She couldn't lose Helena. She couldn't. Adelaide hurried to the parlor door and threw it open, then dashed down the hall. If she hurried she might be able to stop her, convince her to stay.

Adelaide's foot slipped on the wooden stair and she pitched forward. The next stair came rushing at her face, and her head hit it with a crack. Excruciating pain shot up her leg as her body hit the stairs again, and a scream echoed throughout the hall as the world went black.

Chapter 9

Megan stretched leisurely, basking in the sun streaming through her bedroom window. She had been here a week and a half and could barely believe this was her new life. She had her own bedroom—a beautiful room at the front of the house. Her bed was big, soft, and comfortable. The dark wood beams accented the Spanish flair of the room, and Megan loved it.

The scent of frying bacon wafted into the room, and her stomach growled at the decadent smell. She hadn't seen the main floor yet. Mrs. Hernandez cooked a huge feast for the ranch hands every morning and evening but still insisted on bringing meals to her in bed.

Megan was determined to get downstairs for breakfast today. She threw off her covers and slipped into a dark purple dress. Anne and several other girls from town had come to the ranch and thrown together an entire wardrobe for Megan. She had five dresses, all kinds of underthings, and even a beautiful red wool coat for when the cold weather returned. Anne was coming later today with what she called the crowning jewel of Megan's new wardrobe: her very first party dress.

Coldville was having a dance in a few days. According to Anne, the town held the shindig every spring after the calving was done. Megan had never been to a dance and was looking forward to it.   Sawyer and Logan had been teaching her the dances all week long.

Megan slid her feet into her soft moccasins and hurried down the stairs toward the kitchen. Mrs. Hernandez insisted she wear them. They were surprisingly comfortable.

"Can I help?" Megan slid into the kitchen, nearly bowling Mrs. Hernandez over. The tiny woman paused with her hands on her hips.

"You should let me bring you breakfast. You still need to rest," she said with a frown.

Megan smiled. "Nonsense. My cold is gone and I am feeling fantastic. I have spent close to a week in bed and am fit as a fiddle. Please, let me do something. In all honesty, I am going crazy sitting around doing nothing. I need to feel useful. Please."

Mrs. Hernandez grabbed Megan's shoulders and peered carefully into her face, her brown eyes searching Megan's. Finally, she let go with a nod.

"Yes, you look good. Take this plate of bacon to the table and come back for the biscuits. I will ring for the men to come and eat." She beamed at Megan.

The expression reminded Megan of Moriah, and for a moment she missed her old friend. She hurried to put the heaping platter of bacon on the table and returned for the biscuits. They were large and fluffy, and the platter was chock-full of them. It was heavier than Megan anticipated and she almost dropped it. She succeeded in setting it on the table just as a dozen men poured into the dining room.

Megan shrank back a little. They were each so tall and big that she was a little intimidated. She would have ducked into the kitchen and hidden except Mrs. Hernandez came and took her by the arm.

"Boys, look who has joined us for breakfast." The housekeeper led Megan to the table, and the men scooted down the bench to make room for her. She sat next to Riley, who was at the head of the table, with Sawyer on her other side. Glancing around, she noticed the others smiling at her. Her smile matched theirs, spreading across her face.

The Hernandez boys took after their mother: slim, with dark hair and eyes. Megan assumed the older man sitting beside Morgan must be their father.

Riley said grace and the whole table served themselves. It was organized chaos, with biscuits being passed one way, thick slabs of smoky bacon another, and talking all around.

Megan was mesmerized by it all as she passed the plates on, listening intently. She had never experienced so much noise at a meal before. Even the fancy dinner parties her grandmother adored had been muted, quiet affairs.

She sat gawking until the room quieted as everyone ate. Megan then realized she had no food on her plate. She stared at it for a moment, trying to decide whether she should ask for the bacon at the other end of the table. She still felt a little out of place and nervous with her brothers, and she was embarrassed by her lack of attention.

She settled for a biscuit.

Riley called out, "Pass the bacon, please."

Megan's gaze flew to his face, and she could barely suppress a giggle when he winked at her. She took several pieces of bacon, another biscuit, a heaping spoonful of jam, fried potatoes, and even a slice of ham. Sawyer insisted she try some porridge he called grits and told her to put butter and thick maple syrup on them.

The oldest of the Hernandez boys told her to try salsa on her potatoes and insisted she have eggs as well. Megan surprised herself by finishing everything on her plate. She even had a second helping of the grits, which were creamy and delicious.

As soon as breakfast was over, the men headed back onto the range, and the women cleaned the kitchen and got started on lunch.

"You don't have to help me, dear." Mrs. Hernandez was elbow-deep in a batch of bread dough.

"I like helping you." Megan smiled.

The two women worked on, chatting until Anne arrived.

"Go clean up, Megan, so you can try the dress on." Mrs. Hernandez shooed both girls out of the kitchen.

Megan washed her hands and face and hurried to her room, where Anne was waiting. A beautiful ivory-and-gold dress lay draped across her bed.

"Oh, Anne, it is beautiful." Megan reached out to her new friend. Anne took her hands and tugged her into the room.

"Everyone worked on it. It is your dress for the dance." Anne was practically jumping up and down. Megan could see the gown was a labor of love, and she was humbled. These women, who were essentially strangers, had done this for her.

"Thank you." Tears filled her eyes as she fingered the intricate lace.

"Mr. Jensen had this beautiful gold lace, and he was going to throw it out, but we took it, and see how pretty it is." Anne picked up the dress and twirled around. "Try it on." She shoved it into Megan's hands.

Megan needed no further urging to slip into the gorgeous dancing gown. The ivory satin was cool against her skin as it slid down her body. She held her arms out to inspect the dress. The gold lace peeked out of the sleeves, overlaid in a beautiful pattern down the length of the sleeve all the way to the wrist. The shoulders were puffed, but the sleeves were fitted.

She twirled, glancing at herself in the mirror. The gold lace covered the fitted bodice, and the square neckline accentuated Megan's slender neck and heart-shaped face. The pure, ivory satin flared at the hips, and the hem kissed the floor. The gold lace was repeated along the hem of the skirt in an elegant cutout pattern.

"Oh, Megan. You are gorgeous," Anne breathed, clasping her hands under her chin.

"It is a beautiful dress." Megan deflected the compliment. According to Adelaide, no one with pale, pasty skin and frizzy red hair could ever be pretty. She had come to believe those words years ago. Acquiescence was easier than hoping and dreaming.

Anne let the moment pass. "Are you going to wear your hair up or down?"

"I don't know, what do you think?" Megan twirled a red curl around her finger.

"I think we could do half up and half down. Something like this." Anne took a few strands of Megan's copper tresses and expertly twisted them into a pretty style in seconds. Anne eyed it critically in the mirror. After a moment, she nodded. "Yes, I like it."

"Me too." Megan smiled.

"I need to get back to town. Dad has errands for me to run. I will let the ladies know you like the dress, shall I?" Anne helped her out of it, Megan slipped the purple cotton dress back on, and the girls headed downstairs.

"Have the boys bring you to my house before the dance. I will help you with your hair if you want," Anne offered.

"I will ask them, although... somehow, I don't think Sawyer will have any trouble with our request." Megan laughed as Anne blushed. They giggled while Anne climbed into the buggy. Megan walked into the yard and waved as her friend drove away.

She walked around the yard for a few minutes. Megan hadn't seen much of the yard since she arrived, so she walked around it for a few minutes. The fenced in area was large, with the ranch house settled near the back. The landscape was fairly barren but still beautiful. She had turned to go back into the house when the sound of hooves caught her attention.

Megan watched as two of her brothers raced each other into the yard from the east pastures. Sawyer's horse leapt the fence easily, and Morgan's black stallion took the fence just as effortlessly. Horses made her nervous, but they were amazing animals: beautiful and smart.

Megan froze and her breath caught in her throat as a huge dog jumped the fence seconds behind them. She opened her mouth to shout a warning, but the words stuck and she couldn't get even a squeak out. She remained frozen in fear as the creature ran straight toward her. She turned to run, but stepped on her skirt and fell flat on her face. She threw her arms up to protect her head and curled into a ball.

"Rebel, heel." Sawyer's voice carried over the yard. The dog stopped immediately at his command. Megan carefully peeked out from her fetal position, shaking so hard she couldn't untangle herself from her dress to get to her feet. The enormous canine was mere inches from her face. His tongue lolled from his mouth, which was open in what seemed like a toothy grin.

Sawyer hauled her to her feet. "Megan, are you all right? What happened?" he asked, his face wrinkled in concern. Morgan was by her side the next instant, an identical expression furrowing his brow.

"Th-th...." Megan swallowed. "Is that a pet?" She pointed to the dog.

Morgan relaxed and smiled. "Yes, we have had Rebel since he was a puppy. He is great at helping us round up the cattle. Dad got him from an old trapper. He is part wolf." He patted the dog on the head.

Megan squeaked and hid her face in Sawyer's chest, trembling.

"Morgan." Sawyer's voice was low and sober.

Megan took a chance and looked through her fingers at her brothers.

Morgan peeked back at his sister, and she was relieved as understanding dawned on his face.

"Megan, Rebel won't hurt you. He is a well-trained working dog. He will protect you. He isn't wild or vicious." Morgan spoke, his voice gentle.

Megan gawped at him. Sawyer's hold was calm and steady, and she was starting to calm down. When she peeked at the dog, he had not budged from his spot as he had been commanded. The dark eyes stared back at her, and the shaggy head cocked to one side as if trying to tell her something. Megan clenched her hands together in an attempt to still her shaking.

"Would you like to pet him?" Morgan asked.

"I am afraid." Megan shrank back into Sawyer.

"I am not going to make you do anything you don't want to. Do you want to go back into the house?" Morgan was gentle.

Megan nodded, and Morgan gestured for Sawyer to take her inside. They had reached the steps when Mrs. Hernandez came outside to ring the bell for lunch. As it pealed across the ranch, the men once again flooded into the house for their meal. Megan begged off and went upstairs to lie down.

She slept through lunch and didn't come back downstairs until dinner, but by then she was feeling like her normal self again.

The next day, Megan went back outside. As she stepped onto the porch she saw Rebel sitting at the foot of the steps.

The dog stood on all fours, tail wagging. Megan wrinkled her nose. Her heart was racing. Morgan had told her the dog was safe, and each of her brothers had reiterated the assurance throughout the day.

Megan moved in front of the dog. She had second thoughts as she realized his head came to her elbow.

Once again, Rebel cocked his head to the side as if to say something. Megan gulped, took a deep breath, and slowly extended her shaking hand toward him. His wet nose sniffed her trembling fingers, and he huffed, then bumped his head against her hand as if to say, "Pet me."

Megan couldn't refuse his charms. "Okay, Tiny. Here goes nothing." She carefully ran her fingers over the top of his head and scratched behind his ear. When Rebel opened his mouth in a happy grin, Megan let out the breath she had been holding. She continued to pet the dog for a few minutes, then sat on the stairs, looking into the yard. Rebel sat and stared her in the eyes. From where she was sitting, the dog was taller than she was.

"Lie down, you tiny thing," Megan said, half joking. To her surprise Rebel obeyed immediately, putting his head right at her feet. This time, Megan cocked her head and looked into his brown eyes. When Rebel lifted his head, Megan broke the connection and stared toward the mountains.

"Oh, Rebel." She sighed. The dog didn't twitch. Megan turned back to him. His eyes were closed and he appeared to be sleeping. "Tiny," she said. Rebel's head popped up, and his tail swished back and forth in the dust. Megan grinned at him. "Tiny?" she tried again. This time the dog got on his feet and nuzzled her face with his cold nose. Megan flinched, but she stayed calm, realizing he was only being friendly. She knew instinctively that they would be fast friends for a long time.

Chapter 10

Mrs. Hernandez scooped several cups of flour from the barrel into a bowl. "Megan, can you run to the chicken coop for me and see if you can find half a dozen eggs? I need them for the cake I want to bake for dinner," she called over her shoulder.

Megan lifted her hands out of the bucket of soapy water and dried them on her apron. "Sure. You only need six?"

"Yes, but if you find more, bring them in too. My boys have been wanting me to make a custard." She smiled.

Megan nodded and headed out the kitchen door. The chicken coop was all the way at the far west end of the yard. She took a deep breath and turned her face toward the sunshine. Life had taken on a new normal for her in the last few weeks. She was feeling healthier than she could ever remember.

She worked as hard on the ranch as she had as a servant in Adelaide's home, but here everything was different. Mrs. Hernandez was in charge of the house, and Megan was her helper. They kept the house clean, did the laundry, the cooking and baking, and kept up with the chickens.

Mr. Hernandez and his three sons were in charge of the barn and the horses. The Carter boys and four other hired men worked the cattle, mended fences, and did everything else the huge ranch required.

Megan hadn't had much to do with most of the hired hands, although they came to meals in the main house. The Hernandez family were around more often, so she grew to know them much better. The boys were close to her brothers in age and temperament, and they treated her like their sister. The Carter men highly respected Carlos Hernandez. He had been like a second father to them and he now acted the same way to Megan.

She was lost in her thoughts and didn't notice Tiny had joined her until she nearly tripped over him. He pushed right in front of her, blocking her path to the chicken coop.

"Tiny." She sighed, exasperated with the huge canine. She wasn't afraid of the dog anymore and went to step around him.

To her surprise, he growled at her. Her heart fluttered and she stumbled back. As soon as she did, his ears perked up and his tail wagged. Megan's brow furrowed. What was going on? She took a step forward again, and Tiny lunged in front of her, growling. This time he snapped at her.

Megan was frightened, but she couldn't understand what was happening. She didn't think Tiny would bite her, but he was acting strangely. She timidly reached out to the dog, offering the back of her hand like Morgan had taught her. Tiny nuzzled her hand and licked her enthusiastically. Megan rested her hand on his head and inched toward the chicken coop. Tiny growled again, took hold of her skirt, and yanked her backward.

Megan fell, and Tiny barked in a frenzy. In sheer terror, Megan curled into a fetal position and covered her head and neck. The dog's barking faced away from her, and the attack she was expecting never came. After a moment, she carefully lifted her head to see what was going on. She froze, and her stomach knotted violently.

Coiled three feet away from her was a rattlesnake, poised to strike Tiny. She was terrified, both for Tiny and for herself. She was afraid if she stirred it would draw the reptile's attention or distract the dog.

The sharp retort of a gunshot echoed through the valley and silence followed. Tiny trotted to Megan and licked her face. Juan Hernandez ran to where Megan lay and helped her up.

"Are you all right?" he asked. His hands were shaking.

"I am not hurt. Is Tiny okay?"

Juan and Megan carefully ran their hands over every inch of the dog and found no evidence the snake had bitten him. Megan sagged with relief.

Mr. and Mrs. Hernandez ran toward them. The men disposed of the snake while Mrs. Hernandez took Megan back to the house for a cup of tea.

"I need to get you the eggs." Megan remembered when they were halfway across the yard.

"Never mind, Juan will get them," Mrs. Hernandez assured her.

Megan was still shaking when Mrs. Hernandez handed her a nice hot cup of chamomile tea. Tiny curled next to her feet, and his tail thumped on the floor every few minutes.

"I think you deserve a little treat too." Megan's laugh was shaky.

"I agree. You are a good dog." Mrs. Hernandez set a bowl with several pieces of raw meat in front of him.

Juan came in a few minutes later with the eggs, and the women set to work baking a chocolate cake, a creamy custard, and with a few leftover egg whites, Mrs. Hernandez showed Megan how to make a meringue for a tangy lemon meringue pie.

Megan had barely finished frosting the chocolate cake when the men started drifting in for lunch.

"Mrs. Hernandez, can we serve dessert first today?" Megan asked, only half-serious.

"I think that is a lovely idea. Life can be short, as we were reminded this morning. Let's celebrate life. Slice the cake and I will slice the pie," Mrs. Hernandez surprised Megan by saying.

Megan grinned at her.

The two women cut the desserts and set them onto two trays, and Megan carried the tray with chocolate cake to the men sitting at the table. She gave Juan his plate first, making sure to serve him the biggest slice of chocolate cake. She also kissed him on the cheek. "Thank you," she said.

Riley's eyebrows arched toward his hairline. "What did you do, Juan? I need to know so I can get the same treatment." Everyone at the table chuckled.

Megan served her eldest brother a piece of cake and kissed his cheek too.

His belly laugh echoed through the dining room. Megan sassily delivered a slice of cake and a kiss to every man at the table, and they roared with laughter.

"Seriously, why are we eating dessert first?" Paulo asked through a mouthful of the rich chocolate cake.

Megan and Juan told them what had happened that morning, with a few interjections from Mr. and Mrs. Hernandez. Lunch took longer than usual, but no one minded today. Tiny got more praise, and a few extra pieces of meat slipped to him under the table.

∞ ∞ ∞

"Where are those girls?" Sawyer paced the Warrens' living room. Doc laughed and shook his head. Everyone looked forward to the shindig every year, and Sawyer was anxious to spend time with Anne. The spring dance was one of the few times he could hold her in his arms without censure.

"Patience. They will be down in a minute." Abigail Warren smiled as she came down the stairs. She was dressed to the nines, in a dress that could have come from any shop back East. Doc was in his best duds, wearing an honest-to-goodness three-piece suit. He offered his arm to his wife as she reached the bottom stair.

"We will meet you at the dance. You boys wait. The girls were just finished when I came down. Both pretty as peaches," Abigail told Logan, who was lounging on the sofa as Sawyer paced. Sawyer would take Anne, while Logan officially escorted Megan.

"Ahem." Anne's discreet cough brought Logan to his feet. Sawyer turned toward the sound, and both men were rendered speechless for a moment. They were a beautiful pair: Megan in her golden dress, her copper hair shimmering in the lamplight, and Anne in a baby-blue gown with white lace trim, and her blonde curls piled high on top of her head. Sawyer was positive they were the two most beautiful women in town.

Megan self-consciously plucked at her skirt as the other occupants in the room stared up at them. No one was saying anything, and Abigail looked like she might cry.

"May I have the pleasure of escorting you to the ball, ma'am?" Logan was the first to speak. He winked at her.

Megan blushed and took his offered arm. Her brothers were especially handsome tonight in dark dress pants and crisp, colored shirts. Each brother wore a different color. Sawyer matched Anne, in a dark blue shirt. Riley wore red, Morgan sported yellow, and Logan, green. Caleb was debonair in a chocolate-brown shirt. Megan thought she must have the handsomest brothers in the whole world. They definitely took after their father, with dark blonde hair and deep blue eyes, except Caleb and Morgan. Caleb had green eyes and red hair like Megan, and Morgan was the dark one of the family. Dark hair and hazel eyes combined with a normally serious expression made him appear far more imposing than he truly was.

The dance was being held at the newly built schoolhouse and was already going strong when the little group arrived. Seconds after she stepped inside the door, a tall, gangly cowboy whisked Megan onto the dance floor. She didn't have time to take a breath before the next dance started, and yet another eager partner carted her in a different direction.

Despite having learned to dance merely days before, Megan was a whirl on the floor. Fortunately, few of her dance partners were experienced themselves, and no one seemed to notice or care.

Just when Megan thought she was going to have to be rude and excuse herself from the next dance, a familiar voice broke through her thoughts. "Excuse me. I think this dance was promised to me," Morgan said as he cut in. The young man Megan had been dancing with bowed out graciously with a smile, and Megan sagged with relief.

"Having fun?" Morgan smiled at her.

She caught a glimpse of herself in the window. Her eyes were bright, and her cheeks flushed.

"Oh yes, I am. Could we sit this one out? I need something to drink, and my poor feet," Megan breathed.

"Yes, Anne figured you might be needing a break. She enlisted my help. Come with me." Morgan put his arm around her waist and led her off the floor toward the punch table. Abigail Warren was taking a turn ladling the punch, and she had a large glassful for Megan.

"Aren't you the popular one?" She winked at Megan.

Megan had never felt so important before. She felt as though every man in the county had danced with her, and still more were waiting. But Morgan's deep scowl had scared off a few of them as he had escorted her to the punch table.

"Psst, Megan... over here." Anne's whisper reached Megan, but she could not see her friend.

"Where are you?" Megan whispered back.

Anne's head appeared, peeking above the windowsill behind Morgan. She waved at Megan.

"Take the side door. No one will bother you for a while if you are outside. Get a little break." Morgan winked.

Megan practically ran to the door. The cool evening air was a delicious change from the warmth of the schoolhouse. Anne had thrown a quilt on the ground outside the window so they could sit without soiling their dresses. Megan sank onto it with a sigh. She slid off her dancing slippers and massaged her feet.

"Goodness. Are all the dances going to be like this?" Megan asked.

"This is the West. There are ten to twenty men for one woman here. You are new, so everyone wants to dance with you. The fascination will taper off a little, but not much. It has been a long winter, and the dance is a much-needed diversion. It is all in good fun." Anne leaned against the building as she talked.

"I haven't even seen you since we got here."

"I know. I have been dancing too. Sawyer has danced with me three times already. So has Malachi Jones." Anne wrinkled her nose.

"Who is Malachi Jones?" Megan didn't remember being introduced to him.

"Malachi Jones is a nice old man, but he is also the town drunk." Anne sighed.

"And you dance with him?" Megan was aghast.

"Yes, he isn't drunk tonight. A little annoying maybe, but harmless, and I have known him since I was a little girl," Anne reassured her. "He has had a tough life, and it means so much to him to be able to dance a little."

The girls lapsed into comfortable silence for a few minutes. Megan had opened her mouth to say something when a loud voice interrupted her thoughts.

"Hey, Sheriff." The voice came from the window above them.

"Howdy, George. Enjoying the dance?" a new voice responded. It sounded vaguely familiar, but Megan could not place it.

"Shur am. I seen you ain't been doin' much dancing."

A pleasant chuckle sounded. Megan liked the sheriff's laugh. "No, I am not much for dancing. Would have to be a pretty special young lady who would put up with my two left feet"

Megan peeped at Anne, but she was listening to the conversation with an amused expression.

"What about that there Carter girl? I hear she come from back East where she has been living with the grandmother."

"No, thank you. I have dealt with girls from back East a few too many times. Can't stand them. Stuck-up snobs, most of them. Man hunters too. I prefer to not deal with the affected airs, and the deception and greed. Plenty of good women around here; don't need one from *back East*." The sheriff sounded bitter.

Megan's eyes widened. She didn't know whether to laugh or cry. His words would have had some truth if he had been talking about Helena, but Megan was nothing like what he had described. He hadn't even bothered to get to know her before passing judgment. She should be used to people having poor opinions of her by now, but they still stung a little.

"She seems like a right nice girl," George came to her defense.

"I wouldn't bet on it. We must seem like country bumpkins to her. Did you see her dress? Far nicer than any around here. I guess I shouldn't jump to conclusions, but I have met her kind before. Constantly pretending they don't know how to do something, usually to get you to show them how to do it. That kind of thing. I don't like lying in any form, and deceitful behavior doesn't sit well with me. I would rather not deal with it at all."

A loud cheer came from inside the building. Megan was too stunned by the words being spoken to even wonder what the crowd was excited about.

"I guess the short answer to your question is, no, I haven't danced with the Carter girl, and I probably won't," the man continued. "Besides, since she lived with her wealthy grandmother, I doubt she will be here long. Most society girls are coddled and spoiled. With the amount of money the Carters have, I am sure she has plenty of beaus back home."

The sheriff excused himself.

Anne pressed her hands against her mouth. "Oh, Megan. I am sorry you heard those terrible words." She breathed a heavy sigh.

"It isn't the worst thing to have been said about me." Megan smiled sadly.

"He shouldn't have said such things. He hasn't even met you," Anne huffed.

"To be fair, he didn't know we would be listening," Megan said to calm her, but secretly she agreed with Anne.

"Well, he isn't anywhere close to being right. You are the kindest, sweetest person I know." Anne put her hands on her hips, jutting her chin out, a fierce glare in her eyes.

Megan laughed and hugged her. "Thank you, Anne. Now. I think we had best get back to the dance."

They rose, slid on their dancing slippers, and headed back into the dance.

The rest of the evening passed in a whirl until the dance broke up in the wee hours. The Carters went to the Warrens' with a few other people and stayed up talking until dawn. At first light, they headed back to the ranch. Cattle and ranching didn't take a break for dances.

Chapter 11

Megan glared down at her dress in disgust. This was the third one Rebel had torn this week. Unless he was working the cattle or off with the boys, the huge canine was never far from her side. She had only one dress left unscathed in her wardrobe, her gold-lace one, and she was not going to give the dog a chance to tear it.

"Oh, Tiny. I love you, but you need to calm down." Megan ruffled his fur and hauled him out of the front hall and back onto the porch. "Go play," she instructed. Rebel huffed, as though he were insulted, but trotted off into the front yard.

Megan headed upstairs. Mrs. Hernandez had said she would mend the dresses tomorrow, but until then Megan would need something to wear. Her mother's trunks were in the attic, and according to the housekeeper, the dresses in them would most likely fit Megan.

The attic was a dusty mess full of trunks, portraits, lampshades, and other things piled haphazardly everywhere. Megan quickly found one of her mother's trunks and was delighted to find a lovely yellow cotton dress right on top when she opened it. She changed and brought her torn one to Mrs. Hernandez.

"I could mend them myself," Megan protested as she handed it over.

"Nonsense, I need to do a batch of sewing anyway. Your brothers have shirts that need mending; my boys too. I will have to go get thread to match this purple dress, and I have to pick up a few other things in town as well. I will get it done at the same time." Mrs. Hernandez dismissed her protestations with a smile.

"Do you think it would be all right if I poke around in the attic more?" Megan wanted to look in the trunks more closely to find more information about her mother.

"I don't see why not. You may be able to find more to wear. Your mother's yellow dress is pretty on you, and still stylish. It must be at least twenty years old, but it looks new. I remember helping her make it. It was the last one we sewed together before she was too big carrying you to wear it anymore." Mrs. Hernandez smiled wistfully, as if lost in her memories.

Not wanting to upset the woman, but desperate for answers, Megan watched her work in the kitchen for another half minute before dashing back up to the attic again. She went directly to the trunk she had opened. She found several other dresses inside and set them aside to look at more carefully later. Beneath them, she found a beautiful ivory shawl wrapped around something bulky.

Megan cautiously unwound the delicate, lacy wool and found two porcelain figurines. One was a little boy and a dog; the other, a little girl dancing. Megan wrapped them back in the shawl to take them down to her room. She would ask her brothers if she could have them.

In the bottom of the trunk was a set of miniatures. Megan inspected them carefully and recognized her father from his portrait back at Adelaide's. The woman in one of the small portraits could have been Megan's twin. Five more miniatures, clearly her brothers, completed the set.

Caleb's bright green eyes made his miniature stand out. She put the others in order of age and sat back. The paintings were so accurate and lifelike, they looked as if they might come alive any moment. She put them back in the bottom of the trunk, making a mental note of where they were for the future.

As Megan moved toward a pile of stuff in the corner, her foot caught on a box and she tripped. The avalanche of lampshades, curtains, and various bric-a-brac sent her sprawling. She lay on the floor for a moment until she was sure nothing else would come tumbling down, before picking herself up and trying to dust off her dress. She turned to the offending box and stopped. It wasn't a box she had tripped over. It was the leg of a harpsichord. The old quilt covering the instrument had slid off when everything fell.

Megan ran her fingers along the smooth walnut finish and stared at it for a moment. Looking around the cluttered room, she saw the four legs of a stool peeking out from near the window. She dragged the little bench from beneath another quilt and sat in front of the instrument. Reverently she opened the cover and ran her fingers over the keyboard. She pressed one of the keys, and a clear middle-C sang through the attic.

Megan loved all music. Adelaide had entertained many famous musicians at her home, and Megan had spent many hours sitting outside the doors of the music room, listening to them ply their craft. The piano in the ballroom had given Megan many hours of solace when Adelaide was off in Europe or to a society party. She would be forever grateful to old Mrs. Bixby for teaching her how to read music and play.

Adelaide had sent her to the sick woman's house as a punishment, or so she thought. Megan smiled remembering her friend. Mrs. Bixby had a cranky exterior but was a kind old soul who had hated Adelaide Carter and the kind of society woman she portrayed. The day Mrs. Bixby died had been one of the saddest in Megan's life.

Megan's eyes flooded with tears at the memory. She wiped her nose with the back of her hand and began to play. She let the music flow from her heart and soon lost track of time.

Sheriff Summers rode into the Circle C Ranch at a leisurely pace. Doc Warren had asked him to bring medicine for the new girl, along with the mail that had arrived for her. The two letters arriving in one day had just about caused a riot at the general store. No one got much mail out here.

He had agreed to bring them to the ranch, more out of curiosity than anything. Despite his protestations at the dance a few weeks ago, the Carter girl intrigued him. He had heard nothing but praise of her from everyone who had met her.

Jamison Carter had been a tough man; most would have called him strict, but not mean. The family name was respected in the entire country due to his hard work and character. They had lost a good man when he had died a few months ago. Andrew was good friends with the Carter brothers. There were few men he would want at his side in a fight more than they. Andrew doubted their sister was worthy of the Carter name.

Mrs. Hernandez usually met him on the porch, but she was nowhere to be seen and Rebel was also conspicuously missing. He checked his gun. It released easily. With all the strange happenings in the valley lately he didn't want to take any chances. He stepped on the porch and froze as the clear melody of "Amazing Grace" came from somewhere inside.

Music had never emanated from this house as far as he could recollect. Stories of wonderful sing-a-longs and parties at the Circle C were passed around by the locals, but no one had played a note on the piano since Mrs. Carter's death.

He pushed the door and it swung open easily. He proceeded into the foyer, his hand resting on his gun butt, and glanced around. The beautiful music was coming from somewhere upstairs, and Mrs. Hernandez was sitting at the foot of the stairs, dabbing her eyes with her handkerchief. Rebel was there, too, his head in her lap. The dog's ears twitched and he watched the sheriff but he didn't move.

Andrew halted. He could easily get lost in the melodies. "Mrs. Hernandez? Are you all right?"

"Yes, yes. It has been so long. So like her mother, she is."
Mrs. Hernandez sniffed as she got to her feet. "Why are you
here, Sheriff Summers? Is there something you need?"

"Doc sent me with more headache powders, and two
letters arrived for Miss Carter at the general store." He held
the envelopes up to show Mrs. Hernandez. He let her take
the envelope of headache powders but held the mail back. "I
would like to give them to her personally, if I may."

"Of course. As you can hear, she is in the attic," Mrs.
Hernandez said with a sly grin. Her tone made it clear she
thought something was afoot.

"Now, Estrella, the law requires I give them to whom
they are addressed." He felt as if his collar shrank three
sizes, and he ran his finger between his shirt and his neck,
pulling the fabric away from his throat.

Mrs. Hernandez laughed and shoved him up the stairs.
"Go on with you."

Andrew climbed the stairs and slowed as he reached the
attic door. The music had changed into a rousing rendition
of "Come Ye that Love the Lord." He cracked the door open
and peered beyond. Sitting with her profile to the attic door,
Megan was playing with her eyes closed, clearly unaware of
his presence. She still didn't notice him and he didn't want
to startle her, so he remained silent as he observed her.

Red curls had come loose from their braid and bounced
fetchingly around her face. Cobwebs and dust streaked her
hair and attractive yellow dress. Her fingers danced across
the keyboard with speed and grace.

The dust in the room tickled Andrew's nose. He scrubbed
at his face with his empty hand and tried not to sneeze. But

he couldn't stop the inevitable and let out a huge sneeze at the exact moment Megan finished the hymn.

Megan bolted out of her seat and held her arms in front of her in a defensive gesture. Her eyes nearly swallowed her face.

"Oh my, you frightened me."

Andrew sneezed again, this time so forcefully he knocked his hat off.

Megan covered her smile with her hand but did not come closer.

"I am Sheriff Summers. I came to deliver these letters. They arrived in town for you this morning." Andrew held out the two slim envelopes.

Megan took them eagerly. "Oh, thank you, sir." She curtsied.

Now it was the sheriff's turn to hide his amusement. He took a good look at the girl standing in front of him. She seemed oddly familiar, but he chalked it up to family resemblance. Still, something tugged at the corners of his memory. Perhaps there was more to this girl than he had originally thought. She had a smear of dirt on her nose and one cheek, and she seemed not the least bit aware of her appearance.

"I should go." Andrew picked up his hat and held it in both hands for a moment before putting it back on his head.

Megan was intimidated by the tall, dark stranger. The gun on his hip, while a normal sight here in the West, took getting used to. Perhaps he was a gunfighter. She pushed past her initial fear and stepped forward.

"Please allow me to show you to the door, Sheriff."

He motioned for Megan to lead the way and they headed down the stairs. Rebel bounded up the staircase when he saw Megan. He stopped short right in front of her, and Megan pitched forward. She would have taken a nasty tumble down the stairs if Andrew's strong arm hadn't caught her.

"Tiny, *sit*." Megan said. The dog obeyed instantly, a repentant look on his face.

"Tiny? I thought the dog's name was Rebel?" Andrew set Megan back on her feet.

"It is. But the silly mutt will only answer to Tiny for Megan." Riley's voice came from the bottom of the stairs. All five Carter men were standing there watching them. Andrew let Megan go as though his hands were burned.

Megan wasn't offended. He hadn't done anything inappropriate, but out here, it was best to err on the side of caution when dealing with a man's sister. She prayed her brothers wouldn't be upset with him, or be mad about her being in the attic. Sawyer took hold of the dog, and Logan took Megan's arm helping her to the bottom of the stairs.

"You all right, sis?" Logan asked.

"Yes, thanks to the sheriff." She blushed.

"We heard you playing. You play beautifully." Morgan's brow furrowed.

"I am sorry. I didn't think anyone would hear, or mind." Megan panicked, remembering how Adelaide had reacted the one time she had come home to find Megan at her piano. The look on Morgan's face sent chills down her spine. She was in trouble.

The temperature in the room seemed to rise twenty degrees as hot and cold flashes shot through her, and she gripped the banister, her knuckles white. Her grandmother had warned her of what her brothers would do to her when she angered them. She could stand anything except going back to that place. The memory of the horrible, vacant stares, and bone-chilling screams of the tortured minds in the asylum made bile rise in her throat. A tiny moan escaped her lips.

Morgan reached for her but stopped when she flinched. She was relieved when he opted for words instead of actions.

"Megan, it is all right. I remember Mother used to play like that. You like to play, don't you?"

"Yes. I do. It is a beautiful instrument." Megan studied her brothers. They smiled at her in reassurance and she smiled back, though she was still fearful. She could not explain the feeling to them; they could not possibly understand what living in fear every day had felt like.

"I think we should bring the harpsichord down and put it back where it belongs in the great room, where Mother used to play," Caleb said, his voice hoarse.

Megan could hear the tears he was choking back. Her heart softened, and her fear disappeared. She touched Caleb's arm, and her heart thrilled as he placed a large hand over her small one. Maybe having big brothers wasn't so scary.

∞ ∞ ∞

Andrew stood back, watching Megan Carter's reactions in confusion. He had written off her jumpiness in the attic as the result of him startling her, but this was even worse. He watched her expression run the gamut of fear as Megan paled and began to shake when Morgan spoke to her. Usually he could read people well, and he didn't think this was an act. She seemed legitimately frightened, but of what? Certainly not her brothers.

Andrew slipped out as the Carters discussed bringing the instrument down from the attic. He had barely mounted his horse when Megan's voice stopped him.

"Sherriff Summers. Sheriff Summers. Wait."

Andrew peered down to see her standing on the porch. For an instant, he had the most intense desire to pick her up and kiss her soundly. The feeling surprised him.

"Thank you, Sheriff, both for the letters and for keeping me from falling a moment ago. Tiny can be a bit... shall we say... enthusiastic?"

He touched the brim of his hat. "My pleasure, ma'am." He turned Ebony toward the road and spurred her into a fast canter. From back East or not, Megan Carter had intrigued him, and he definitely wanted to know more about her.

Chapter 12

"Who are your letters from?" Sawyer asked.

"I forgot about them." Megan tore the first envelope open and scanned the letter. "It is from Titus," she announced. She perused a little further. "Oh." She sank onto the steps.

"Bad news?" Riley drifted in closer.

"Not bad, just unexpected. Helena has gone to France with her father. She left two weeks ago. She sends her love to each of us." Megan fell silent as she continued to read. "Oh," This time Megan sat up a little straighter. Her brothers leaned in expectantly. "He got Tillie out. I am glad." A tear fell down Megan's cheek.

"Out? Out of where?" Sawyer asked.

"Blackwell's Island Asylum." Megan shuddered. She saw the look of shock that passed between her brothers, but she was still intent on reading her letter, and chose to ignore it.

"Titus contacted Tillie's husband. He had no idea what kind of place she was in and immediately came and had her released. Titus employed them to take care of his house in the country. Now Tillie is back with her little boy. She says she is so happy, and much healthier now.

"Titus says she will write soon. He is still working on getting Miss Nell out. It sounds like Dr. Kent is helping him.

159

I liked Dr. Kent. He showed kindness to me and to Tillie." Megan sighed and lapsed into silence, her gaze on the letter, though she wasn't reading.

A moment later, Megan folded it and put it back in the envelope. She tore open the other letter and read the words hungrily.

"It is from Moriah." She smiled. "They love the country. Rollins is a natural with growing things, and they are doing well. She has gone into town several times to check on the street children, someone has taken them in, and they are happy and healthy in their new home. Oh, I am glad. They deserve a family. Every child needs to be loved." She leaned back against the railing with a happy sigh.

Her brothers were watching her closely, with somber expressions, but Megan didn't know why. The letters had been good news.

"What is wrong?" she asked, twisting her hands.

"Where did you meet Tillie?" Riley asked.

"At Blackwell's."

Several emotions flickered over her brothers' faces.

"Why were you at Blackwell's?" he probed.

Megan studied the faces surrounding her and saw anger, grief, compassion, and confusion in her brothers' expressions. She took a deep breath to steady her nerves. "Grandmother had me committed after I had an argument with Helena over one of the street children."

She told them everything about those horrible weeks. From when tiny barefoot Davis had come to the kitchen to return a bottle of laudanum she had dropped all the way until she had first stepped off the stage in Coldville.

And then you were waiting for me on the platform. You were there for everything else," Megan finished her tale what seemed like an eternity later. She wouldn't look anywhere but at the floor, terrified her brothers would be ashamed of her behavior. Perhaps they would even send her back to her grandmother. Before she could stop it, a tear ran down her nose and dripped onto her dress.

"You say Uncle Henri and Cousin Titus got you released from the asylum?" Morgan asked.

The kindness in her brother's face gave her courage. "Yes. Titus said something about my committal being clandestine and somehow, they were able to get me released and take me home. I suspect money changed hands then too," Megan replied, twisting her hands again.

"And Helena helped you get to us?" Morgan probed.

She nodded. "Moriah and Rollins helped too. I am glad they are away from the city now. They always sought to live in the country."

"They were Adelaide's cook and butler?" Caleb asked. "When did they move to the country?"

"Titus wrote some details. Let me see...." Megan picked up the first letter and shuffled through the pages. "Yes, here. He says the day I left, they decided to move. In Moriah's letter...." She shuffled more paper. "She says her sister asked them to come help with the orchard the night before Grandmother dismissed them. It was perfect timing."

"They seem like nice people," Caleb said.

"Moriah and her husband were the kindest people I have ever known. If I had had parents, I imagine they would have been like those two." Megan glanced at her brothers as she spoke. Their shocked expressions registered too late; she couldn't take the words back.

"I am sorry, I didn't mean... I meant...." The desire to run to her room and hide was overwhelming.

"Megan." Riley reached for her, but she flinched and shrank back. "Megan," he tried again, speaking calmly but not trying to approach.

She peered at him through her tears. "I am sorry."

"It is all right. Speaking for myself, I guess I never realized it was like you really never had parents. We thought Grandmother was taking good care of you. We trusted you were going to the best schools and doing all kinds of things. I am sure if Father had known how you were being treated he would have come and taken you home."

A weight lifted off her heart as she saw the love and acceptance on the men's faces. Their expressions were open, and there was no anger there. She was their sister, and come what may, they would not abandon her.

"I think it would have helped if I had received word from Father even once. Or if I had gotten a single letter from you all." Megan's chin quivered.

The Carter brothers gawked at each other. Riley spoke first. "Megan, we sent letters. Father wrote two or three times a year. We assumed it was you who did not want to contact us."

Megan opened and closed her mouth in shock. For twenty years Adelaide had let her to believe her family hated her and was ashamed of her. She had been sure to tell Megan that every single day.

"You wrote me letters?" she whispered.

"Every year," Logan spoke up.

"On your birthday, Christmas, and usually once or twice besides. Each of us sent them at various points throughout the years." Sawyer wrapped his arm around her.

She leaned into his strength. All those years. Lost. Megan would have sunk to her knees except for her brother's strong arms. "How I wish I could read them." She bit her lip to stop the tears, but they leaked out. When they started, the dam burst and she covered her face with both hands and sobbed. Rebel shoved his wet nose under her elbow and whined.

"I am s-s-sorry." Megan hiccupped. Wrapping her arms around the dog's thick neck, she buried her face in his fur.

∞ ∞ ∞

Morgan's heart broke as his sister wept. Looking around at his brothers, he realized none of the Carter men knew what to do to comfort her. Logan moved toward her, but Morgan caught his arm, shaking his head. They let her cry, and watched, astonished, as their big cattle dog comforted Megan better than they could. Her sobs eventually subsided to shudders, then stopped altogether.

"I'm sor—"

"Please don't apologize," Morgan said. "Your feelings are more than justified. It is we who should apologize. We don't have a lot of experience with tears. You have to give us some leeway, and we will learn through this together. Yes?" He drew Megan into his arms and held her tight. She barely came to the middle of his chest. His heart ached, knowing how many years of each other's lives they had missed. The guilt for not pushing his father to bring Megan home sooner tightened around his chest, crushing the breath from his lungs.

"Family hug," Logan called out.

Megan pursed her lips and wrinkled her nose. "What is a family hug?"

Logan laughed and wrapped his arms around her. "This."

All five of her brothers engulfed her and each other in an enormous hug. Megan was in the middle and purposely squished. It took her a moment or two, but Morgan teared up when his sister relaxed and hugged them back.

"So this is what it is like having a family," she whispered.

The tears leaking from his brothers' eyes told him they had heard her too.

Yes, this is what it is like when our family is complete again. Morgan squeezed everyone a little tighter.

"Wait," Megan shouted as she ran across the yard.

Morgan stopped the wagon and waited for her to catch up.

"Can you take these letters into town and post them for me?" She was breathless from running.

"I can. Would you like to come with me?" He took the letters from her and extended his hand in an invitation to climb onto the wagon seat.

"Should I go tell Mrs. Hernandez so she doesn't worry?" Megan grasped his hand, clambering up beside him.

In response, he put his fingers to his lips and whistled loudly.

One of the Hernandez boys poked his head out of the barn. "Sí, señor?"

"Please make sure your mother knows that Megan is going with me into town," Morgan called.

The boy waved and ran toward the house as they drove away.

Megan enjoyed the scenery as they jostled along. The ranch was tucked away against the rolling hills, and the wagon had to climb to the plains. The summer sun was hot, but a nice breeze came from the west, making it pleasant. Megan turned her face to the sun, basking in the warmth.

"What are you thinking about?" Morgan was watching her.

"Back in the city, in the summer, it would be sweltering. You could cook eggs on the streets and the sidewalks. The sewers would be overflowing, and their reek was unbelievably potent. Dirty animals, people living on the streets, dark, damp stairwells, musty buildings, and death. Death was everywhere. Dead animals, dead and dying people. Here... here it is different." Megan took a deep breath.

"Here I smell life, grass baking in the sun, dirt and dust, water, wood." She took another breath. "And cattle." She wrinkled her face in disgust.

Morgan laughed. "Yes, there is that."

Megan dissolved into hearty laughter, and they were still chuckling as they arrived in town.

"I need to run to the livery. You can post your letters at the general store across the street. We ordered a few things for you and got word they came in the mail. Hats and things. Anne and Abigail said you needed them. If you need help carrying them, I will come give you a hand when I am done with the horses. Otherwise, you can put them in the wagon. I will leave it here." Morgan jumped down and lifted his sister onto the wooden walkway in front of the general store.

She hesitated for a moment before squaring her shoulders and walking into the store, then peeked back to see Morgan watching her with a smile. Giving him a wave, and a smile in return, she walked into the door.

Megan's heart was pounding. She had never been inside the general store before and didn't know where to go. It wasn't as though she was back in the city. The dangers were different here, but her brother was outside if there was any trouble.

Shuffling noises behind the counter almost convinced her to run back to Morgan. A man came from behind the curtain that led to the back room with an armful of paper-wrapped bolts of fabric. She broke into a relieved smile when she recognized him as Mr. Jensen, one of her favorite dancing partners from the ball.

"Well, Miss Megan Carter. How lovely to see you. How can I assist you today? Have you come for your packages?" His gravelly voice belied the twinkle in his eyes.

"I did. I also need to post these two letters, if you please." She handed the envelopes across the wooden counter.

Mr. Jensen took them and put on a pair of spectacles. "Mm–hm. Yes. I will get these on the next run. Henry will be in for the post tomorrow. I will put it onto your brother's account."

The elderly store clerk put his spectacles back into his vest pocket. "Come with me to the postal counter." He beckoned with one finger for her to follow.

He opened the wire cage surrounding the area behind the counter and dug around for a moment before bending down and pulling a large box from underneath it. He stacked two more on top. "Here are your packages. Do you need me to put them into the wagon for you?" His blue eyes twinkled merrily when he spoke.

Megan tentatively lifted them. They were tall and unwieldy but not too heavy. "No, thank you. I think I can get them." Megan slid them off the counter and peeked around the stack in her arms. She just needed to walk a straight line to the door and only a few more steps to the wagon.

The boxes were a little heavier than she had thought, and by the time she arrived at the door, her muscles were straining and her fingers were beginning to slip. She bit her lower lip in concentration, focusing on getting the bulky stack out the door without dropping it. She stepped over the threshold, taking care not to step on her skirts and trip herself up. Only a few more steps.

"Ugh." Megan's breath whooshed out in a huge grunt as she ran into something solid. The boxes went flying, and she found herself flat on her back on the walkway. Strong hands grasped her upper arms and lifted her to her feet before she discerned what was happening.

When she focused, she was looking into the stunning gray eyes of Sheriff Summers. She had made a note of their color at the house a few days ago; today they were a beautiful dusty blue gray, as if they reflected the blue in his shirt. Something about him felt vaguely familiar, but she couldn't place it.

"Are you all right?" the sheriff asked.

For a moment, Megan was tongue-tied. "Yes, I am sorry. I wasn't watching where I was going." She brushed off her skirt and bent to retrieve the boxes now scattered along the walkway. The sheriff helped her pick them up and put them into the wagon.

Andrew took off his hat and ran a hand through his hair. He didn't have time for this. Why was this girl always in his way? Guilt coursed through him at the thought. This was only the second time he had seen her. How had she gotten under his skin so fast? He smashed the hat back onto his head, irritated at how much he wanted to make a good impression.

He watched as the petite redhead nearly upset herself trying to set the last box down in the wagon bed. She was too short to reach and pitched forward.

Andrew put a hand on her back to keep her from falling in and tipped her back onto her feet. When she was steady on her feet, he jerked his hand away, flexing it as though it hurt.

Megan turned to him. "Thank you for your help. I do hope you are no worse for the wear after our encounter."

"No, I am unscathed. I hate to dash off, but I am on my way to the Golden Rose. One of the girls has been attacked by her inebriated customer." Andrew Summers kept his voice harsh.

Megan Carter was making a definite impression, but he wasn't letting her into his head any further. He was blunt concerning his mission on purpose, hoping to see her recoil or do something to validate his wariness of her.

Megan peered down the street to the Golden Rose. The saloon was alive with voices.

"That is terrible. Is she all right? Is there anything I can do to help? Does she need anything?" Megan's face showed her genuine concern.

Andrew took a moment to absorb what she had said. Was she actually offering to go with him to the saloon? "She is a little roughed up, but Hiram got to her in time. Hiram owns the saloon and Lacey is one of his special girls. He takes care of his girls. She will be fine. You should stay away from that place. It is pretty rowdy and can be dangerous, especially for a girl like you." His voice held a steely warning.

"Do you deal with these kinds of things often?"

"I go where I am needed. Sometimes it is chasing down a cattle thief, and sometimes it is helping a farmer drag a cow out of a mud hole." Andrew shrugged.

"Sheriffs here in the West are certainly nothing like the policemen back where I am from. Many of them are overgrown bullies with badges, at least the ones I have encountered."

"We're a different breed of men here. Most of us are good men who want to uphold justice and keep the peace, including some of us who are gunslingers. Take Gage Reagan, for example. He's the fastest gun in this part of the country and he's been hired as a sheriff, though I doubt he would be seen helping a farmer haul a cow out of the mud."

"I know Gage Reagan and his wife, Clara. I met them on the train coming here. He was nice. They both were," Megan said, her voice mild.

"I doubt he was really Gage Reagan. He is no gentleman." Andrew scoffed.

Megan laughed lightly. She apparently didn't feel the need to argue with him.

Her little laugh made him feel like a clod. It was the same little laugh that haunted his dreams. He wanted to lash out at the woman beside him, but he was far too much of a gentleman. He spotted her brother moving toward them and turned back to her to say goodbye. The sight of her petal-pink lips smiling at him stopped him in his tracks.

She was still laughing at him. He had to get away before he said something he would regret.

∞ ∞ ∞

"Megan, are you ready to go?" Morgan was by her side.

Megan turned to say goodbye to Sheriff Summers, but he was already halfway across the street, striding toward the saloon. Morgan hopped onto the seat and leaned down to help her up. She took his hand and scrambled into the wagon.

The back was full of supplies. She hadn't noticed her brother loading several other items into the wagon. A new saddle, some halters, a shovel, and several sacks of feed now sat in the bed of the wagon.

As Morgan guided the team out of town, Megan glanced toward the Golden Rose. Sheriff Summers was nowhere to be seen. She stared at the doors, hoping to catch a glimpse of him as they drove by. A familiar face peeped through the front window, staring right at her. Megan sat back with a gasp of fright.

"What is it? What is wrong?" Morgan took her hand.

She peered back at the window. The face was no longer there. Surely she was mistaken, although she was fairly certain she had just seen a petty criminal and neighborhood bully from back East.

"Nothing. I thought I saw someone I recognized." Her stomach clenched, and her heart pounded. Surely her imagination was working overtime. There was no way a poor bum like Michael O'Shea would be this far west.

Chapter 13

Megan was jumpy for the next few days. Her only relief came when Anne rode to the ranch with another letter. Megan ran upstairs to read it while Anne and Sawyer rode to a neighboring ranch. The owners and several hands were ill, and Anne was bringing them more medicine because Doc was busy with a ranch hand who had been trampled by cattle. He was going to lose a leg, and his life was touch-and-go.

Megan curled up on her bed and read the letter voraciously.

Dear Megan,

How can we ever thank you, my friend? Your cousin has been an absolute godsend. I am grateful for you asking him to investigate things for us. He may have told you already, but a few days after you left, he found my husband and told him about the things happening at Blackwell's. Stuart came and got me the same day, and Titus offered us a job here at his estate in the country.

It is a beautiful home. Stuart loves working in the gardens, and little Michael is happy being able to run and play in the sunshine. It has done us a world of good. If there is ever anything we can do for you, please do not hesitate to call on us.

You might be interested to know that Dr. Kent and Titus are working toward reform in the hospital. They have been putting pressure on the board to put measures in place to stop the mistreatment of patients. I enclosed a newspaper clipping talking about it and I hope change will be inspired by the revelations there.

I hope someday we will meet again. In the meantime, I am enclosing our address in case you wish to write. I would love to keep in touch.

Love,

Tillie

Megan plucked out the newspaper clipping and read it carefully. The article was scathing in its report on the conditions at the asylum. It was a clear call for change. She read through the rest of the missive, searching for information regarding Miss Nell, but found none in either Tillie's letter or the newspaper article.

"Megan? Are you there?" Mrs. Hernandez's voice floated up the stairs.

"Yes, ma'am. I will be right down." She hurried to see what the housekeeper needed.

"Can you do me a favor? I meant to bring the men their lunch, but I am elbow-deep in preserving those lovely raspberries the boys brought in, and I have two pies in the oven. Can you take the basket to them? The buggy is hitched and ready to go."

Megan hesitated. She had barely learned to drive the horses, and except for a gentle filly named Juniper, she was still frightened of most of them.

"Juan hooked Juniper to the buggy. I would send him, but he is in the middle of something as well." Mrs. Hernandez correctly guessed the cause of Megan's hesitation.

"Where are they?" Megan asked.

"Down by the river. I told them I would bring lunch to the bridge. They will be waiting there by now."

Megan agreed to go. They weren't too far away, and driving the buggy alone would be good practice. Caleb would be pleasantly surprised, as he was the one teaching her. She put on her bonnet and hurried to the wagon. If they were waiting for lunch, the boys would be hungry, and no one should be hungry for long. Megan remembered the feeling far too well.

She was at the edge of the yard when Sheriff Summers rode up. Megan drew Juniper to a stop as Andrew touched the brim of his Stetson.

"Miss Carter." He nodded.

"Sheriff." Megan nodded back.

"You headed toward town?"

"No, I am taking lunch to the men. They are down by the river." Megan tilted her head in the opposite direction.

"I happen to be headed in the same direction. May I join you?"

"Certainly."

Andrew dismounted and tied his horse to the back of the buggy, then climbed onto the seat with Megan and reached for the reins. She reluctantly handed them over and scooted farther away from the tall man.

"Where are the men?" Andrew asked.

"They should be waiting by the bridge."

Andrew flicked the reins and they were off. They rode along in silence for several minutes. The quiet made her feel uneasy, but she wasn't sure how to break it. She was about to say something when she spotted a horse galloping toward them on her side of the road.

"Look out!" she called to Andrew.

∞ ∞ ∞

The horse was on top of them. Andrew wrenched Juniper sharply to the right. The buggy heaved mightily as the right wheel struck a rock and came clean off the axle. The buggy lurched to a stop, pitching Megan forward, and Andrew threw his arm out to keep her from flying out of the vehicle.

When she dug her fingers into the side of the buggy and managed to stay on the seat, he grudgingly admired her quick thinking.

The other horse jumped and twisted, and took off running, and its rider flew off and hit the ground with a sickening thud. As soon as the saddle was empty, the horse calmed down and stopped several feet down the trail.

"Stay here," Andrew told her as he leapt from the buggy.

"No, he looks hurt. I can help."

"Wait until I get the horse under control." Andrew sighed. Pushy Eastern women. Thought they could handle everything.

Andrew slowly approached the horse, talking gently. In a few moments he found the cause of the horse's panic. A burr had been placed under the saddle. Andrew threw it into the bushes and turned to the rider, who was still lying prone in the road. Megan was already there. He sighed.

"I asked you to wait," he said.

"I did until you had control of the horse. This man is unconscious. I think his leg may be broken. He is going to need a doctor."

"Someone doesn't like this man, whoever he is. I haven't seen him in these parts before." Andrew checked him for injuries. Megan was right. His leg was definitely broken.

Andrew unhooked the horse from the buggy. Megan sat on the seat while he untangled Juniper and transferred the saddle from the runaway horse to the gentle filly.

"I need you to ride and go get help. Go down to the men at the bridge and send one of them for Doc. Someone else will have to come get the lunch." Andrew handed the reins to Megan.

She froze and stared at him.

"Don't tell me. You can't ride." Andrew's voice dripped with sarcasm. Who did she think he was, some rube who didn't know what happened outside of the valley? He was aware what wealthy women back East did. Riding lessons every week, fencing, needlepoint. He had been wrong about Megan. She was no different than Corrine. He glared at the girl in front of him, waiting for her to answer as his anger bubbled up.

"I have met her kind before. Constantly pretending they don't know how to do something, usually to get you to show them how

to do it. That kind of thing. I don't like lying in any form, and deceitful behavior doesn't sit well with me." The memory of the words she had overheard from below the window assailed her.

Megan stared at the stirrups, glanced at Andrew, and took a deep breath. He would never believe her if she told him the truth. She had seen the others ride often enough. How difficult could it be?

"Will you give me a hand up?" she asked. Judging by Andrew's body language, he was obviously disgusted with her. But he could not refuse without being rude, so he helped Megan into the saddle. Juniper skittered to the side a bit but calmed swiftly. It was as though she sensed Megan was new to riding. Megan tapped on Juniper's flank with her heel, like she had seen her brothers do many times.

Juniper started down the road. Megan was thankful she was pointed in the right direction at least. She glanced back at the sheriff.

"Move. This man needs a doctor, remember?" Andrew took off his hat and roughly smacked Juniper with it. The horse picked up speed and Megan concentrated on staying in the saddle.

"I said to hurry," Andrew shouted.

Megan dug her heels into Juniper, and the horse leapt forward. She relaxed her muscles, trying to follow the rhythm of the horse's body, but she bounced around a great deal.

"Go find Morgan, Juniper. Go to the bridge." Megan prayed the horse could understand her because she had no clue how to direct her. She was getting dizzy from being bounced around and wasn't sure how much longer she would be able to stay in the saddle.

A moment later, the bridge came into view. "Morgan, Caleb, help! Somebody, anybody!" Megan shouted. The echo of Juniper's hooves on the wooden planks filled the valley.

"Whoa, whoa, Juniper, whoa." Morgan jumped in front of the fast-moving horse. He snatched her reins and she slowed to a halt. Megan fell off the horse into Caleb's waiting arms, limp as a wet rag.

"What happened? What's wrong?" voices asked from every direction.

"Back on the road. Sheriff Summers, Andrew. Rider got thrown. Needs help." Megan was out of breath and hardly able to speak.

"Carlos, Logan, go help Andy. Take the wagon. You may need it," Morgan shouted to the others as Caleb set Megan on a large rock beside the bridge.

Riley held a canteen to her lips. "Here, drink this. It's only water. Drink."

Megan eagerly took the water. It was warm but still refreshing. After a few moments, she collected her thoughts and spoke clearly.

"The sheriff is back on the road. He stopped by as I was bringing you your lunch. He joined me. We were run off the road by a runaway horse. The rider was thrown and is unconscious. Someone needs to go get Doc, and someone needs to get the lunch too." Megan took another drink.

"Why were you riding Juniper?" Caleb asked.

Megan explained what had happened. "I am sorry, I should have told him I couldn't ride. I was more concerned about what he would think than what would happen. I should have thought it through a bit more."

"You could have been hurt or killed. You know that, right?" Caleb rubbed her back. He clenched and unclenched his jaw, as if working to regain control of himself.

"I know. It won't happen again." Megan hung her head. Her brothers were angry, and the anger resonated deeply with her fear. She had done a foolish thing. She opened her mouth to apologize again, but Riley reached for her before she could speak.

"We found you such a short time ago. We don't want to lose you." He pulled her into a tight hug.

She melted into his arms, relieved they understood.

Several minutes later, the wagon came into view, moving slowly down the road. The runaway horse was tied to the back, and Carlos was in the bed with the unconscious stranger. Sheriff Summers was guiding his horse to pull the Carters' buggy, the wheel of which had been replaced on the axle.

Logan waved at them as he drove across the bridge. "We are going to bring him into town to see Doc. Will meet you back at home later," he called as they passed. Riley waved him on.

∞ ∞ ∞

Andrew jumped down from the buggy and untied his horse. "I am going to go into town with them. I need to find out who the injured man is." He hauled his saddle from the back of the buggy and threw it on Ebony. He was cinching the belly band when Caleb wrenched him away from the stallion.

"What—" The big man punched him in the jaw, knocking him to the dirt.

"What did you do that for?" Andrew moved to get up, but his friend drove him back into the dirt with his foot.

"If you know what is good for you, you had best stay down. Morgan is coming, and he is angrier than I am," Caleb hissed.

Morgan was heading toward them, his face like a thundercloud. Andrew stayed where he was on the ground. Morgan would break his jaw.

"I get why you sent our sister to get help, but did it ever occur to you she couldn't ride? She has never even driven a buggy before." Morgan towered above him.

"How was I supposed to know?" Andrew scrambled to his feet, but his anger fled when he saw Megan. Even with the distance separating them, he could see she was pale and shaking. "Why didn't you tell me?" he asked her.

"I tried. But you were so irritated with me, I thought you wouldn't believe me. I know what you think of girls from back East. At the dance. Anne and I were sitting under the window." Megan's voice tapered to a whisper.

Andrew's face flamed with embarrassment and shame. He never meant for those words to get back to her. No wonder she hadn't told him she couldn't ride.

"She could have been killed, Andy." Morgan was still scowling, but his voice was calm.

"I am truly sorry. I never would have sent you if I had known. I am sorry you did not feel like you were able to tell me the truth. I am even sorrier it was my behavior that frightened you."

Megan nodded.

"I haven't made a good impression, have I? Can we start over?" Andrew asked.

"I think I would like to try again," she said.

Morgan cleared his throat, reminding the two they were not alone. "Allow me." He stepped forward. "Megan, I would like to introduce you to the sheriff of Coldville, Andrew Summers. He is also a good friend of the family. Andrew, this is my sister, Megan Carter, newly arrived from back East."

Megan smiled and clasped Andrew's offered hand. "It is a pleasure to meet you, Sheriff." She curtsied, hiding her laughter.

"The pleasure is mine, Miss Carter," he responded with a little bow.

"Megan. Please call me Megan."

"Thank you. Please call me Andrew." He tipped his hat. "I hate to run, but I need to check on the injured rider. Next time you are in town, Morgan, stop by if you would. We need to catch up." Andrew needed to get answers to some questions but didn't want to be rude or too inquisitive, especially in front of Megan. He mounted his horse and rode off after Morgan assured him they would talk soon.

When the sheriff was out of sight, Caleb lugged the basket of food from under the seat in the buggy.

"Might as well have lunch," he said.

"You hungry?" Morgan handed a piece of cold chicken to Megan.

"Yes," she said before taking a huge bite.

The men laughed.

The basket held not only chicken but thick slices of sourdough bread with butter, garden-fresh carrots, and a bucket of raspberries. There wasn't a single crumb of food left when they were done. Megan licked her fingers. She had never had fresh raspberries before. The sweet, tart berries might be her new favorite food. Although, she had thought the same thing about rhubarb pie a few weeks ago. She made a mental note to talk Mrs. Hernandez into making one soon.

Caleb hitched Juniper back to the buggy and helped Megan into the seat, then jumped up beside her. She stared at him in shock when he handed her the reins.

"You can do it, and when we get back to the ranch, I am going to saddle Juniper and you are going to start learning to ride."

"Oh, but I...."

"No arguing. You are going to get back on a horse as soon as we can. If you are going to live here, you have to learn to ride. It is not an option." Caleb's tone was sharp, and Megan blinked back tears. He immediately shot her a look of regret and put his hand on her arm.

"Sorry, Megan. I didn't mean to be harsh. I'm used to talking to greenhorns and cowboys, not women. You need to get back on the horse as soon as possible. I don't want you to be afraid of them. But you will need to be able to ride out here. This isn't the big city. We don't have trolleys or hansom cabs, and someone won't always be around to drive you in the wagon. Do you understand?" His voice was much gentler this time. "I know you are afraid, but I also know you can do this."

His explanation and faith in her did much to bolster Megan's own confidence. This was all so new, and she had so much to learn, that the scope of her ignorance was a tad daunting. She agreed to get back on Juniper that afternoon.

Anne and Sawyer were pulling back into the yard when Caleb and Megan drove in. Caleb asked Sawyer to help with Megan's riding lessons, explaining the reason behind the urgency.

Anne drew Megan aside. "You should consider wearing pants if you are going to be learning to ride astride."

"Pants?" Megan's eyes were wide.

"Well, yes. I wear them on occasion when I am doing a bit of riding. If you stop at the house next time you are in town, I will give you a pair." She laughed. "Although, I think we may have to hem them for you."

"Pants would be a good idea, sis." Caleb had overheard their conversation.

The more Megan thought about it, the more she warmed to the idea.

"I will be in town tomorrow. I have to get three of the horses reshod. Can we get them from you when we are there?" Sawyer joined the conversation.

"Of course. Take it easy on the riding lessons until you get them, though. Your legs won't be used to the saddle,"

Anne warned. She clucked and slapped the reins and was soon out of sight down the road.

Caleb let Juniper rest an hour, then turned her into the corral to warm up before he saddled her and had Megan start her riding lessons. Judging by the fact she had stayed on the horse earlier, he thought she would catch on quickly. He was right. With a little instruction, she was soon guiding the horse at a fast canter back and forth across the yard.

Over the next several days, Megan enjoyed her riding lessons. The pants made mounting the horse much easier. She had learned much since leaving her life back in the city, and while she missed her friends, she was genuinely happy for the first time she could remember.

Megan was excited; she and her brothers were going to her first barn raising. The Stantons had lost their barn after lightning had struck it during a violent spring storm. Etta Stanton was heavy with their fifth child, and Frank was unable to get the barn built on his own. The community was happy to get together to help their neighbor.

The way the event was organized fascinated Megan. The ladies brought their best dishes. Pies, casseroles, preserves, and pickles lined makeshift tables. Wagons rolled into the yard filled with planks the ranchers had hewn during the week. Children were already running around playing. It was organized chaos and she loved it.

Frank had obviously not been idle. The ruins of the burned barn were piled high at the tree line, leaving the original barn lot clear for the men to work.

Etta was busy trying to rein in their exuberant twins. Patience and Prudence were only a year old, but they were already walking and into everything. At five, Faith was the oldest, and Hope was next at three years old. Megan immediately went to help her wrangle the children. She could see that Etta was already worn to a frazzle, and the day was just beginning.

Megan tiptoed behind Faith and tapped her on the shoulder. "Tag, you are it," she said as she dashed away.

With a squeal of delight, the little girl chased Megan, and several of the other little girls joined in the game. Patience and Prudence toddled along, trying to keep up with their older sisters. Faith soon tagged Hope, and they were off again. Around the trees, down by the well, into the wide-open meadow, Megan and the girls ducked and dodged each other.

It was nearing lunchtime, so Megan stopped the game and helped the girls pick flowers until their mothers called them to eat. Faith and her sisters combined their flowers and handed their mother a large bouquet of the pretty blooms. Megan found a glass jar to use as a vase and insisted Etta stay sitting on the porch while she helped the girls get their food.

By the time lunch was over, the four girls were more than worn out. Despite their protestations, their mother insisted they lie down. She did compromise, however, and allowed them to rest on a blanket on the porch instead of inside the cabin. Megan joined her on the porch to take advantage of the shade.

"Thank you for your help, Miss Carter. I am plumb wore out with this coming baby. And the twins. They keep me right busy." Etta fanned herself with her hand.

The day was warm and sunny, and Megan was certain the pregnancy was not helping Etta keep cool. "Would you like a glass of lemonade, Mrs. Stanton?" she asked.

"Please call me Etta, Miss Carter, and if you wouldn't mind, I would certainly love some lemonade."

"It is Megan, and I will be right back, Etta."

She hurried to the refreshment table, which was sitting in the shade of the large oak tree in the front yard. Large pitchers of beverages were scattered along it. Megan poured a large glass of the sweet-tart lemonade and turned to go back to the porch, bumping into someone standing right beside her. She jumped back with a yelp of surprise and the lemonade sloshed down the front of his pants and onto his boots.

Megan froze with a horrified grimace. She cringed, not wanting to look at the man she had doused with the sticky, sweet liquid. She waited for him to yell at her, but instead, a muted chuckle sounded from somewhere above her, drawing her unwilling glance up.

The unfortunate victim of her clumsiness was Andrew, and he was highly amused. What a way to "start over."

"Sorry," she whispered.

"It is fine. I was wanting to cool off anyway," he said as he extracted a dripping-wet handkerchief from his pocket.

He wrung out the lemonade and mopped his brow. Megan smiled a little at his attempt to make her feel better.

At her smile, his chuckle turned into a full-blown laugh. It was contagious, and soon Megan was giggling along with him. Andrew used a dish towel to sop up what he could of the lemonade and walked with Megan back to where Etta was sitting.

"You take a bath in the lemonade, Sheriff?" Etta hid a smile behind her hand.

"Yes, Mrs. Stanton, it appears I did." His eyes twinkled, and a wide grin split his face.

"It was my fault." Megan smiled.

"You sure smell pretty, Sheriff," another of the ladies called. Megan was a little surprised to see he was such a good sport as the ladies teased him. She was also embarrassed they had seen the accident. She pulled out the square of linen she kept in her skirt pocket and handed it to Andrew as more lemonade ran in a rivulet down his face.

"Where did you get this?" His voice changed to a whisper, and the wonder on his face arrested her attention.

He was the man who had come to her rescue. She couldn't believe she hadn't seen it before. All those nights dreaming of the stranger on the docks and he had been right in front of her. Her fear had blinded her. She stared at him as he repeated the question.

"A kind stranger gave it to me on the worst day of my life," she managed to whisper.

"That was you?" Andrew's voice was incredulous.

"It was. I have been grateful for your kindness that day. It was a beacon of hope in the dark days after we met."

"I often wondered what had happened to you. I cannot believe I did not recognize you." Andrew held the handkerchief in front of him.

"I do look a little different, I hope." Megan chuckled self-consciously.

"You do. Although I found you beautiful on that day, today you are a hundred times more so." Andrew pressed the precious fabric back into her hand, wrapping his fingers around hers just as he had on the day he had given it to her.

Her heart did a little dance at his touch, and her smile widened.

Prudence wasn't settling in for her nap and toddled up to Megan lifting her tiny arms in a silent plea to be held. Though she was loath to turn her attention away from the handsome lawman, Megan could not resist her adorable hazel eyes and picked her up. Prudence lay her raven curls onto Megan's shoulder and was asleep in seconds.

"How are you feeling, Mrs. Stanton?" Andrew asked.

"I am doing well, Sheriff," Etta said, shifting in her chair. She leaned forward, lowering her voice as worry flickered across her face. "Did Frank talk to you about the drifters we had the other day?"

"He did. I will be making inquiries, and I will make sure the other ranchers are aware as well. Please don't worry."

A shout drew Andrew's attention to the yard. It was time for the barn to be built. "Excuse me, ladies, I must tend to my official duties as the judge and jury for this little competition." With an exaggerated bow, Andrew excused himself and hurried to join the men.

Anne and a few of the other women and children joined Megan and Etta on the porch to watch the competition.

"How does this work?" Megan asked no one in particular.

"The men will form four teams and compete to see who can get their side of the barn raised first. The first team to get their wall up, completely finished will win their choice of either a heifer or the four piglets from this year's weaning," Etta explained.

Megan watched, intrigued, as the men formed teams of seven to ten men each. She was excited to see her brothers and two of the Hernandez boys formed one of them. Andrew fired his gun, and the race was on. Friendly shouts, sawing, and the sharp crack of hammers striking nails echoed through the yard.

Megan was amazed at how swiftly the men built the frames for the walls on the ground next to its corresponding side. Megan's brothers had the front wall, with the barn doors and the window for the loft. It was the most difficult one to complete.

The teams were running neck and neck as they lifted the four frames into place by hand. They used two-by-fours to prop them up as they walked the frames to an upright position. The sound of nails being hammered in to them was deafening. Some of the women cheered their men on.

Boards flew onto the frames, and men were soon on top of the wall helping secure the beams for the hay loft and the roof.

Megan shifted Prudence in her arms. The little girl was still fast asleep despite the noise. She smiled down at her, burying her face in the toddler's silky curls. The sweet smell of lavender and baby skin sat heavy on her, making her heart ache. She missed the little ones back East. Those children had never smelled of lavender, but they were sweet just the same.

Her little friends back in the city were beautiful souls, aged far beyond their years by the harsh life of living on the streets. Megan missed Davis and the others.

Megan let her gaze wander from the builders. Frank Stanton and Andrew had positioned themselves off to the side to watch the men building the barn. Andrew's pants had dried already, Megan noted.

The sheriff cut a handsome figure with his broad shoulders and long, lean legs. His Stetson was shoved back on his head, and the way he stood with his hands on his hips accentuated the breadth of his shoulders.

Megan blushed when he caught her staring. She couldn't stifle her gasp when he winked at her. Burying her grin in Prudence's curls, she turned her gaze back to her brothers. In the few minutes she had been watching Andrew, the men had completed the walls and had started building the floor of the loft, and the roof.

"I can't believe how fast they are getting this barn finished," Megan told Etta, impressed.

"Yes, you should have seen them when they built the schoolhouse. I think it took the men all of an hour to put the whole building up. Of course, it didn't have a loft."

"They seem to be having a good time."

"The men do enjoy the friendly competition." Etta laughed. "My Frank was a little disappointed he couldn't join in on this one."

A shout from the barn drew the women's attention. The Carter team had finished their side. After a quick hug and celebratory cheer, they kept working, helping the other teams finish. Within a few minutes, the last wooden shingle was nailed onto the roof.

Andrew fired another shot to officially end the competition, and a cheer rippled through the spectators. Etta's face lit up with a smile that wiped ten years off her age. She and Frank shared a special glance across the yard.

Frank and Etta didn't have the wild, crazy kind of love Megan had read about in the novels Helena had left lying about. Instead, they had the steady, constant kind of love Megan longed for; the kind that bore itself out in small kindnesses and commitment to one another day after grueling day. Through sickness and health, and famine and drought. Love was the same no matter where one lived, whether East, West, North, or South.

Andrew's voice pulled Megan from her thoughts. "The winners are the team from the Circle C. Riley, I see your team has elected you to speak for them. Which of the livestock prizes would you like?"

The crowd hushed, waiting for his answer.

"Frank, everyone here is aware of your generous heart and work ethic. You have had a rough year, and we were glad to give back to you today a fraction of what you and Etta bring to the community. There is not a single family here who hasn't been touched by you folks. Not one." Riley paused as several men shouted their agreement.

Etta was crying, and Megan put her free arm around the woman's shaking shoulders, juggling the still-sleeping toddler.

"My brothers and I have had several good years on our ranch, and we would like to pass Frank's generosity forward to another family who needs the prize more than we do. We have talked it over with the other teams as well, and we would all like for the prize to go to Lem and Jenny Heath," Riley finished.

Megan was certain her heart would burst with pride. A few of the men shoved a stunned blond man forward, and Frank caught him when he stumbled toward Riley.

"All right, Lem. Which do you choose? The heifer or the piglets?" Andrew asked.

Megan felt sorry for the small man standing next to Andrew. He looked like he wanted to disappear. Jenny was even smaller than her husband, but she was beaming. Megan hid a smile as Jenny kept mouthing, "Piglets, piglets, piglets." Lem squinted in his wife's direction but it appeared he couldn't see her.

Megan wanted to shout the answer at the shy man, but she didn't dare. Riley glanced her direction, and Megan motioned to Jenny with her head. Her brother nodded and leaned down slightly to whisper in Lem's ear.

"We would be delighted to take the piglets, and thanks, folks." Lem turned several shades of red as he uttered those few words. Many of the men came forward and clapped him on the shoulders.

Megan hid a smile as Jenny clapped her hands in delight. Her pride and her pleasure in her husband were clear to see.

Megan fell a little more in love with the community of Coldville watching them support each other. As a whole, life in the big city was much less community-minded. Most people were out for what was best for them, at least the wealthier members of society were. She was so proud of her brothers at that moment that she could cry.

The men drifted toward the food tables again. Building a barn apparently worked up a powerful appetite. Prudence finally stirred, and began to cry. Megan handed the sleepy girl to her mother and slipped off the porch.

The afternoon had turned extraordinarily warm. The little body resting against her had been like a furnace, and now she was nauseated with the heat. If she didn't cool off soon, she might faint. The men were busy eating, and Etta was busy with her fussy one-year-old, so this was the perfect time to slip away.

Megan wound her way down to the creek and slipped off her shoes and stockings. She waded knee-deep into the water, lifting her skirts to keep them from getting wet. She bent down, she scooped up a little cool water with her hand, and splashed it onto her face and the back of her neck. It helped a little, but Megan was still far too warm.

Her neck and arms screamed at her. Holding a baby for two and a half hours had not done her any favors. She was stiff and sore, but it had been worth it to cuddle with the adorable tot.

Glancing around to make sure no one was watching, she flipped her skirts over her shoulders in the back, wrapped the extra fabric around her left arm, and walked into the water until it came to her waist. Before long she was standing in the middle of the creek.

Within a few seconds, the cool rushing water had cooled her enough for the nausea to dissipate. She wandered down the creek a little ways, but did not want to get too far away from the party.

A tree growing over the water blocked her view of the homestead and the people celebrating there. Several branches dipped down into the slow-moving creek, creating a fun pattern of ripples. She enjoyed a few minutes of privacy before turning and heading back to where she had left her shoes.

Megan rounded the branches in the stream and froze. Andrew was standing beside her shoes on the bank. She blushed furiously as he smiled at the spectacle in front of him.

Megan was mortified. Not only was she standing awkwardly in the middle of the creek, in water up to her waist, but her skirt was also lifted above her head in the back, and she was barefoot. It was at least, a very undignified picture.

"Hello." Andrew smiled wider.

"Hello, Sheriff." Megan kept her voice formal. She wasn't sure what he would think of her now.

"Are you in need of assistance?" His eyebrow rose quizzically.

"No, thank you, I am fine."

"Why don't you come out of there?"

Megan was a little miffed at the amused note in his voice. "I can't. I am barefooted," she admitted after a lengthy pause.

"Is that all? Come on out. I don't mind," he coaxed.

Megan shook her head and shuffled backward, almost falling as she did.

"Please come out. I would like to talk to you," Andrew tried again. He coughed, trying to cover a laugh, but Megan wasn't fooled for one minute.

"No. I am too big a girl to be running around barefooted. It isn't proper for you to see me like that." Megan was feeling warm again. She closed her eyes and wished she could sink under the water and disappear.

"We are not in the big city. It is not going to create a scandal for you to come out of the water and put your shoes and stockings back on." Andrew's smile was kind this time.

Megan still shook her head.

"Come out, or I will come in after you."

She wasn't sure if Andrew was joking or not, but his words frightened her enough that she hurried toward the shore.

Andrew turned his head, looking away, and extended a large hand to help her. Megan dropped her skirts off her shoulders and scrambled out of the creek, grasping his offered hand. She was pleased to see only the hem of her skirt had gotten wet. She carefully sat on the grass and slipped her shoes and stockings back on. Andrew was a gentleman and turned his back so she could do so in privacy.

"I hope I wasn't too forceful getting you out of the water, but there has been rain in the mountains. Flash flooding is something we watch for this time of year, and we wouldn't have any warning. You could be swept away in minutes. This time of year we also have to be watchful for snakes, both in the grass and in the water," Andrew explained.

Megan's heart skipped a beat. "Snakes?" Instinctively she tucked her feet under her skirts, her last encounter with a snake still far too fresh in her mind.

"Yes, especially in places like that tree in the water." Andrew was still facing away from her, so he missed her shocked look.

Megan stood and straightened her skirts. Her wet underthings would help keep her cool for a few minutes, and she was pleased that sitting on the grass had not caused them to soak through her dress.

Andrew glanced over his shoulder and smiled at her.

"Better?" he asked.

"Yes, thank you." Megan smiled back at him this time.

"I wondered where you went. Mrs. Stanton suggested you might be a mite warm, and she had seen you headed this direction. I think your brothers are ready to head back to the ranch. I wanted to ask you if it would be all right if I stopped by sometime this week so we could talk. I meant what I said about starting over, if that is all right with you."

"I would be pleased to get to know you better, Andrew. As my brothers' friend, you are always welcome at the ranch." Megan smiled at him. She was curious about the expression that flickered across his face, but he didn't say anything other than "Thank you, Megan. Shall we rejoin the others?"

Megan took his offered arm, and they walked back to the party. Andrew had been right; Morgan and Logan were searching for her. The wagon was hooked up, and the men were ready to head back to the ranch. The Hernandez family were already on their way. Evening chores wouldn't wait. Megan hugged Etta Stanton and her girls goodbye, with a promise to seek them out soon. She said a hurried goodbye to Anne, and then the Carters were on their way back to the Circle C.

Chapter 14

Andrew came to the ranch often throughout the next few weeks. He and Megan were soon fast friends, their misunderstanding forgotten. They took walks around the ranch with Tiny, who was never far from Megan's side if he wasn't working the cattle. Sometimes Mrs. Hernandez would send the two to bring lunch to the men.

Andrew soon learned Megan was a sweet, kind, and compassionate woman, nothing like he had first assumed. He was thankful both she and her brothers had forgiven him his earlier rudeness.

Andrew never talked about his past with anyone, but Megan drew him out like no one else. He found himself frequently sharing his frustrations, the burdens of the job, and even sometimes, bits and pieces of his years before he became the sheriff of Coldville.

"I grew up not too far from where you lived, I think," Andrew admitted one day.

"I didn't know you lived back East." Megan pulled Juniper to a halt near the brook. The weather was hot, and the horses needed to drink. So did they. Andrew helped her dismount, and they led the horses to the edge of the water. Megan took a drink from the canteen Andrew offered to her, then wiped her mouth with her sleeve. She waited patiently for her companion to continue his story.

"I lived with my parents near Five Points in New York City. At least until I was sixteen. The same year a couple of the gangs got into a donnybrook, and more than a dozen people were killed, including my father. Because my mother was terrified I would get enticed into the gangs, she sent me to live with an uncle in Texas for a while. I came back to the city a few years later and spent some time with my mother there until something happened."

Andrew clenched his jaw as the familiar anger boiled up. He needed a few minutes to gain control before he could continue.

"I became a Texas Ranger, then eventually made my way north and became the sheriff here in Coldville."

"What were you doing in the city that day when you helped me?" Megan asked.

Andrew stopped and looked at her earnest face. She was kind and beautiful, but oh so fearful. He wished he could wipe all her fears away. "I received word my mother was ill, and I traveled back and stayed with her until she passed away."

"Both your parents are gone too?" Megan's face was forlorn.

Andrew wanted to hug her. Time had dulled the ache over his parents, although he still missed his father's laugh and the sweet way his mother kissed his head every morning when he had come to breakfast. He would always miss them.

"Yes, Mother died the morning I met you. I was out for a walk, clearing my head. I have no love for the city and wanted to get home as soon as possible. I did not want to run into... well.... There is someone there who...." Andrew paused, not wanting to finish his thought. This pain was still fresh and raw.

"You don't have to tell me if you don't want to." Megan placed her hand on his arm. "I can see whatever happened hurt you deeply, even more than your mother's death."

Andrew was surprised Megan could so accurately read how he was feeling. She was right. He had held on to the pain of Corrine's rejection far more than he should have.

"If anyone deserves to hear this, it is you. I am not making excuses for my behavior when we first met. If I tell you this, it may explain why I was prejudiced against you." Andrew motioned for her to sit on the grass under a nearby tree. The horses were content to graze nearby, and he let them wander a bit on their own.

Andrew searched for a place to begin and finally spoke as he paced in front of the tree. "A few months after I returned to the city, a bad epidemic of influenza hit. Mother survived, but her lungs were weakened. She couldn't handle another winter where we lived, so we moved to a better area. Still not the Hill, but better than the neighborhood I had grown up in.

"I made friends in the new area, and I even went to a few society parties thrown by friends of a friend. I met Corrine at one of them. She was the daughter of one of the hosts. She was vivacious and lovely, and I had never met anyone like her.

"Corrine had a way of making me feel capable and strong. I was nineteen, and the world was my oyster. I had a good job, money in my pocket, and a good group of friends. Nothing could stop me from achieving my goals and dreams."

Andrew kicked at a rock, sending it skittering into the bubbling brook. The sounds of the water gurgling over the rocks mocked him like his heart did any time he thought about Corrine.

"I was a fool," he said, savagely kicking at another rock.

"No, you were not a fool. You are not a fool." Megan's soft words broke through his dark mood.

Her face was pinched and vexed. Any outburst of anger terrified her. Andrew understood why and worked to calm himself. The years had done little to dull the rage. It had simply festered, shoved in a corner of his mind to never be spoken of or dealt with. He took a deep breath and continued.

"Corrine said I was. I aspired and worked hard to give her everything. When I asked her to marry me, she laughed at me. I was from the wrong side of the tracks and would never make enough money to make her happy. I was only a fun diversion from the day-to-day dullness of living on the Hill. She told me every detail of how she and her friends had lured me in and set me up for the fall." Andrew sank down in the grass next to Megan.

"I left the city a few days later and returned to Texas. I never went back. I learned later Corrine married one of her school chums a short time after I left. I wandered for a bit and eventually ended here." Andrew shrugged. He could still hear Corrine's mocking laugh as he had walked away that day. Sometimes he was convinced the sound would haunt him forever.

"I am sorry she said those terrible things to you. Truly. She was wrong. You are not a fool." Megan laid a hand on his arm and waited until his gaze met hers. "I think I do understand why you acted the way you did. Thank you for sharing your story with me. I know it was difficult for you to do."

Andrew sighed. Her kindness only made him feel even guiltier for the way he had treated her. He prayed silently that the Lord would help him remember to leave the judgment of people to Him.

It was getting to be lunchtime. Megan and Andrew gathered the horses and continued on to deliver the delicious fried pasties and pies Mrs. Hernandez had cooked for the men's lunch.

Chapter 15

On their walk one sweltering afternoon, Megan was a little jumpy. Andrew watched her for a while, hoping she would open up to him. Finally he took it upon himself to probe a little.

"What is wrong, Megan?"

"Nothing, I am fine," she said, not lifting her gaze from the path in front of her.

"You don't seem fine," Andrew pressed.

"I'm sorry."

The immediate apology was an automatic response, and that bothered Andrew. "You don't need to apologize, but please tell me what is wrong." He stopped walking and waited for her to answer.

Megan sighed. "I think someone from back East followed me here."

"What makes you say that?" Andrew was skeptical. He knew about her grandmother, and her interment in the asylum, but he couldn't fathom anyone coming after her.

Megan tripped over her skirts.

Andrew led her to a large rock and they sat. "Please, go on," he encouraged.

"Several weeks ago, when Morgan and I went to town, I thought I saw a familiar face peering at me from the saloon.

Something else happened too. Last week, Tiny kept barking at the barn, and I am pretty sure I saw him darting away in the shadows."

"I am sure it was nothing, merely some drifter who looked similar. Who would be following you? Why?"

"It is the same man. I am sure of it. A local hood from back in the city. As to why, well, I suspect Adelaide has something to do with it." Megan sat on her hands, hiding them from Andrew so he wouldn't see them shaking, but he did.

"I doubt a woman as well-off and respected as Mrs. Carter would have anything to do with a low street thug."

She sighed again, and the terror in her eyes nearly caused Andrew to rethink his conclusion, but she stood and continued on down the path without another word on the subject. She was back to her old self the next time he saw her, and he did not think a thing about it.

∞ ∞ ∞

"Megan, are you coming?" Sawyer was already in the wagon.

She flew out the door, trying to tie on her bonnet as she scrambled into the wagon.

"Sorry... Tiny got in the way again, and I had to change my dress."

"That dog. Somedays I don't know about him." Sawyer chuckled. "Did Mrs. Hernandez give you a list of what she needs?"

"Yes, and if it is okay, I have a list of a few things I want to pick up too. I have a few pennies left over from my trip here, and I would like to purchase a little gift for Anne's birthday next week."

"You don't need to use your money. Anything you want, you put it on the tab for the ranch."

"I thought you would say that, but I wanted to be sure. I didn't want to assume." Megan smiled.

The siblings rode along in comfortable silence for a time. It was the middle of the summer, and the sun had burned much of the surrounding countryside to a dull brown. The landscape was still beautiful to Megan.

The grasses rustled in the slight breeze, like golden waves. Here and there a blue or purple flower stood out from among the pale reeds. Megan sighed, basking in the sunshine. She glanced over at Sawyer and he grinned at her.

She smiled back. Having five older brothers watching over her took getting used to, but she loved it. Being part of a family was nice, and she smiled much more these days. The wagon rolled into town at the same time as the stage rattled in.

"Can we stop by the shipping office? I would like to say hello and thank Henry. He was more than kind to me on the trip here, and I never got to thank him." Megan craned her neck to watch the stage.

"Sure. Tell you what, I will check and see if he is able to join us for lunch at Sadie's Dining Room, and maybe Andrew can join us too. If you want to go ahead and get your shopping done, I will meet you in the general store," Sawyer suggested.

Megan agreed as Sawyer slowed the wagon to a stop outside the general store. He jumped down and came around the box to Megan's side. His large hands spanned her waist as he helped her off it. He studied her for a moment, and she wondered what he was thinking, then he bent down and kissed the top of her head.

"Love you, sis," he said as he climbed back up onto the seat.

"Love you too," Megan said without hesitation.

Sawyer flicked the reins, and Juniper and Jax headed for the livery.

Megan stilled as he drove away. His casual declaration had taken her breath away. She was amazed at how easily love had come. For years, she had struggled to make Adelaide love her, but no matter how earnestly she tried, her grandmother still hated her.

She cared immensely for her uncle and cousins, but the love she had for her brothers was deeper and more solid. This was better than anything she could ever have imagined during the many long, cold nights she had spent dreaming in the attic.

Megan shook her head to bring herself back to the present. She had a birthday gift to buy. Anne had commented on something a few days ago, and Megan was hoping it was still in the store. She made a beeline for the counter and grinned. Perfect. It was still there.

Mr. Jenson finished with his customer at the dry-goods counter and shuffled to the glass case where Megan waited.

"Hello, Miss Carter. Do you have another letter to post?" He peered at her over his spectacles.

"Actually I am wanting to peek at this cameo, here." Megan pointed to the little pin under the glass.

"Ah... yes... I have had this jewel for some time now. She is beautiful, isn't she?" Mr. Jenson slid the piece from the black-velvet-lined box and handed it to Megan.

It was heavier than she had expected. The cameo was unusual; instead of being white, or white and coral, this was pieced together with several different colors and layers. The cameo itself was white stone carved in an intricate and beautiful profile of a young woman, silhouetted against a dark green marbled stone. The cameo was set into a fancy-scrolled gold backing, inset with more of the green stone.

Megan turned the piece over and was delighted to see it had both a pin and a small metal loop so it could be worn as a pendant. The brooch was exceptionally detailed, and at only two inches, was small enough for Anne to wear every day if she chose.

"How much is this, Mr. Jensen?" Megan cringed, worried she would not be able to afford it.

The price he quoted her was reasonable, but still more than she was comfortable spending without asking Sawyer first.

"Can you hold this for me for a few minutes?" she asked.

"I have had it for nigh on to four years, I 'spect I can hold on to it for a few more minutes." Mr. Jenson winked at her.

Megan could not contain her excitement and did a little dance. She moved on to the list Mrs. Hernandez had given her, and Mr. Jensen helped her find the thread, sugar, corn meal, a length of gray flannel, several tins of spices, a large bag of broken crackers, forty pounds of flour, and a set of purple ribbons.

The ribbons were for one of her mother's hats, which Megan was repairing. She had found several of them in the attic, and they would be lovely after they had a new ribbon or two.

Megan and Mr. Jenson had barely crossed the last item off the list when Sawyer entered the store.

"Did you find what you needed?" he asked, wrapping one arm around her shoulders.

"I found what I want for Anne, but I need to show it to you." She seized his hand and tugged him over to the counter, where the brooch was still sitting in its velvet box.

"It is pretty," Sawyer said.

Megan could tell he didn't share her excitement yet.

"It is gorgeous. See the detail in the necklace and headpiece?" Megan pointed to the floral crown and a tiny floral necklace on the image of the woman. Tiny sparkling stones were inset into the necklace, and her headpiece was delicately wrought gold. "But that isn't the only reason I think it is perfect. Anne and I were in here the other day picking up peppermint sticks for her dad. He gives them to the kids who come into his office."

Megan smiled. She and Anne had split one of the striped candies, much to Doc Warren's amusement. "Anyway, Anne saw this piece and commented on it. She has always wanted one; her mother had one when she was little."

"I don't remember Abigail ever having a cameo." Sawyer's brow wrinkled in confusion as he searched his memory.

"Not Abigail. Anne's mother."

Sawyer's eyebrows rose. "I forget Abigail is not Anne's mother. Anne was so little when her mother died, how does she remember the cameo?"

"She was five when her mother passed away. Abigail married Doc the next spring," Megan reminded him. "I need you to see it. I know you said I could charge whatever I fancied to the ranch account, but it is somewhat costly, and I needed to double-check. If it is too much, I can give you the money I have like we discussed earlier, and I can earn the rest somehow."

"How much is it?" Sawyer asked.

Megan held her breath as Mr. Jenson told him the cost.

"If you are sure the cameo is the gift you want for her, you should get it." Sawyer smiled.

"Mr. Jenson, we will take the brooch. Please wrap it for us as well," Sawyer said.

Megan squealed with delight and threw her arms around her brother's neck, giving him a peck on the cheek. "Thank you, thank you, thank you."

Sawyer laughed as he paid for the purchases. "Megan and I will come back for these after lunch."

They left the store and headed to Sadie's. She was the owner of the local boarding house, and her dining room was open to the public for lunch and dinner. Megan had never eaten there, but her brothers had raved about Sadie's onion soup and apple pie, so she was excited to try them.

"Hey, Carter," a voice boomed across the street. Megan recognized Henry's deep drawl. He ambled over to them.

"Henry." Sawyer clasped the stage rider's hand.

"Hello, Miss Carter," Henry said as he removed his hat.

"Are you coming to lunch with us, Henry?" she asked.

"I was headin' over to Sadie's now. Lookin' forward to a nice slab o' her pie. Apple, with a good wedge of cheddar on the side." He rubbed his tummy.

The trio crossed the dusty street and entered the busy dining room of the boarding house. Andrew already had a table and waved them over.

Sawyer and Henry waited as Andrew pulled out the chair for Megan to sit. After she was seated, the men took their seats. Sadie came to take their orders, and a few minutes later, they were enjoying a lovely lunch.

Henry was true to his word and ordered a double slice of pie, and a large chunk of cheddar cheese, with a cup of coffee. Andrew enjoyed a plate full of chicken and homemade noodles, and Sawyer equally enjoyed the beef stew. Megan had ordered the soup and sandwich, with a small slice of pie and a glass of iced tea.

The french onion soup was as good as any she had had in the city—better if her memory could be trusted. The sandwich of the day was sliced beef with a spicy white sauce, and the melted cheese on the soup was mirrored in the sandwich. The food was so good, conversation stopped until everyone was done eating.

Megan glanced over to find Andrew watching her and blushed when he winked. Her cheeks heated further when she caught Sawyer grinning at them both. Ever since the incident with the horse, Andrew had been a different person toward her. She found herself looking forward to his company. It didn't hurt that he had turned out to be her handsome stranger with the sad eyes.

"I am glad you asked me to lunch today, Miss Megan." Henry leaned back and patted his protruding belly.

"I am happy to see you again, Henry. I wanted to say thank you for your help when I came here. You were a blessing to me. Without you, I might still be stuck in the mud on the mountainside." She grinned at the big man.

Half the dining room turned to stare when Henry broke into a loud belly laugh. Sawyer and Andrew's confused looks sparked Megan to break into giggles as well. She explained how Henry had gotten her unstuck from the mud so the others could join in on the fun.

"I recognized who you were the minute I set eyes on you." Henry's smile slipped a little.

"Because I look like my mother?" Megan asked.

"Yes. Eileen Carter was a good woman. I used ta work for your father as a cowhand years ago. She was kind to me from the start. Not many women would be nice to a dirty cowboy. The world lost an angel the day your mama died."

"I didn't realize you knew our mother," Sawyer said.

"I worked on the ranch before you were born. I was working on the stage the day your papa sent this little one East. In fact, it was me who carried your sister and put her on the train." Henry paused. "You haven't grown much," he teased with a chuckle.

Now it was Megan's turn to draw everyone's attention. She laughed so hard she squeaked. Andrew tipped his hat back and laughed long and hard.

"Mama used to say good things come in small packages," Sawyer remembered.

"She used to play that harpsichord every Sunday. We'd sit around the table and sing songs. Yer pa would read the Good Book and say some words. That's before the preachers come up this way."

"I remember that." Sawyer leaned forward, his eyes bright.

"I remember when you come to Coldville too, Sheriff. First time you came here, you were green as green could be, must have been all of seventeen years old, trying to act twice that." He smiled.

"I have no idea what you are talking about," Andrew said, but a grin split his face.

"Sheriff Summers here, he came ridin' into town with a bunch of Texas Rangers. They were after a group of men who had stolen a shipment of gold. Thought they were plenty tough. Old Malachi outshot every one of 'em, and he were drunk as a skunk."

"I learned I had a lot of growing up to do that day. But I loved the area and came back a few years later, and here I am," Andrew finished the story. "Speaking of here I am, I have things I need to attend to. I hate to leave this fun little party, but I need to relieve my deputy so he can get lunch too. See you around?" He tipped his hat and dug in his pockets for the coins to pay for his lunch.

Sawyer waved him away. "Lunch is my treat today. For everyone."

"I wasn't expecting ya to pay fer my lunch," Henry protested.

"Nonsense. Let's call it a thank-you for taking such good care of my sister on the stage. Both times," Sawyer insisted. "Andrew, see you at the ranch soon?" he asked.

"I have things to take care of around the area, but as we discussed earlier, I will be by," Andrew said.

His expression was serious, and Megan feared something was wrong, but one glance at Sawyer dispelled the idea. He hid a smile behind a cough and his eyebrows were arched to his hairline.

Andrew shook Henry's hand and said goodbye. When Henry stood, he nearly took the entire table with him. The table cloth had gotten hooked onto his belt, and it took several seconds for him to disentangle himself.

When Megan finally looked up, the handsome sheriff was headed for the door.

Andrew slipped away with a wave to Megan. She returned the gesture with a smile before turning her attention back to Henry, who was still trying to dissuade Sawyer from treating him to lunch.

"Henry. Please. Can we just call it a thank-you? From my family to you?" Megan interjected, ducking her head to meet his gaze.

His face relaxed into a smile. "Sure, Miss Megan. I never could refuse your mama, neither. I won't deny I was plumb worried about you that day when I brought you back into town. You didn't look too well."

"I was feeling a bit under the weather, but I have been much better ever since. My brothers have been taking care of me very well." She smiled at Sawyer across the table.

"Abigail Warren threatened us within an inch of our lives if we didn't." Sawyer laughed. Megan hadn't heard that part of the story and her brother was only too happy to fill in the details.

Henry, Megan, and Sawyer spent another hour in the dining room chatting before everyone got back to their work for the day. The siblings stopped back at Jenson's store for their purchases before starting home.

On their way back to the ranch, they headed to the Warren's house to collect salve for Mrs. Hernandez and deliver Anne's birthday gift.

Anne burst into tears when she opened the package. She threw her arms around Megan and hugged her tightly. "You shouldn't have, but I am glad you did. Thank you so much," she cried. She released Megan and tearfully showed her parents the cause of her excitement.

"Where did you find this? It is beautiful," Abigail asked.

"In the glass case at Jensen's," Doc answered for them. "It reminded me of the one I buried Frances with." He rewarded Megan and Sawyer with a genuine smile. "I am glad Anne has one now too. It isn't the same, though; Anne's is much nicer. What do you think, Abigail?"

His wife smiled. "I think it is a wonderful reminder of your mother. It will be lovely on you, Anne, and it was nice of you to think of our girl, Megan."

Megan flushed. She hadn't been expecting praise; she was simply happy her friend liked the gift.

Doc disappeared into his office to mix the salve. Then after another round of hugs, Megan and Sawyer left, ointment in hand, and headed back to the ranch.

∞ ∞ ∞

Andrew directed his horse to a stop outside the Circle C. This was the third time this week he had found himself at the Carter ranch for no real reason other than to see Megan. The girl was fascinating. Speaking to her brothers had been the scariest thing he had ever done, and that included his time in the Texas Rangers. Each of them had wholeheartedly given him their blessing to pursue their sister, and his relief was palpable.

After several weeks, he believed he had been clear in his intentions, but from Megan's behavior, he wasn't sure she understood why he spent every spare minute of his time with her. He'd lifted his hand to knock on the door just as it swung open and Megan came onto the porch. She was beautiful in a white cotton dress with lavender flowers. Andrew normally did not notice such things, but this particular dress brought out her bright eyes more than usual.

He could drown in those emerald eyes.

Megan stopped and closed the door behind her. Andrew leaned in, placing his hands on either side of the door frame, trapping her. Fear flickered across her face. He stayed still, not wanting to frighten her further, but knowing she had nothing to be afraid of with him.

Megan took a deep breath, struggling to gain control. Andrew could see her heartbeat pounding in her neck.

"Sometimes you confuse me, Megan. How can the girl who volunteered to walk into a saloon with me, and who met one of the most infamous gunslingers in the West, be so frightened of people she knows?" Andrew kept his voice neutral, but tears still appeared in her eyes.

"I know, I'm sorry."

"You don't need to apologize. I am simply trying to understand." Andrew straightened and moved toward the swing on the far end of the shaded porch.

Megan followed him and sat on one end of the swing, tucking her feet under her dress. Andrew joined her, keeping some space between them. He craved nothing more than to hug her tightly, but that would not do. Not yet, anyway. He waited patiently for her to speak.

"I think part of it is, the more I know someone, the more I care for them, the more power they have to hurt me," Megan said after several minutes.

"I would never hurt you, and your brothers would never hurt you. They love you so much, why would you be frightened of them?"

"For the last twenty years, the people who hurt me the most were supposed to love me. Grandmother Adelaide has made it difficult for me to accept that others could love me and treat me right." Megan stared at her hands. "Father sent me to her. How could he have sent me away if he loved me?

His silence, or what I thought was his silence, hurt me deeply."

A single tear trickled down her pale cheek. He knew most of Megan's story. Her brothers had shared some of it, while Megan had told him more on their walks. It was challenging for her to share even a little bit of it.

"Yet you are willing to jump right in to defend Clara Reagan, or to help a woman you have never met in a saloon," Andrew pressed.

"I think it is because they needed me. I am usually able to ignore my fears when others need help. I don't know why, I just can." Megan shrugged.

"You were not afraid of Gage Reagan." A touch of bitterness crept into Andrew's voice. "He is one of the most dangerous men in this part of the country." He regretted both his words and tone the moment they were past his lips.

"Excuse me?" Megan's voice had gone soft. Andrew hid a smile as her chin jutted out and her eyes flashed with anger. He hadn't seen her angry before. If he were honest, she was adorable when she was.

"Well, he is a gunslinger. And many tough ranch hands and other gunslingers are afraid of him," Andrew insisted.

"You don't like him much, do you? What did he do to you?" Megan put her finger on the problem nicely.

"It is obvious?" Andrew laughed.

Megan didn't even crack a smile.

"I don't agree with how he got his badge," Andrew finally admitted, backpedaling a little. She really was angry with him.

"Why? What did he do?" Megan pushed.

Andrew shot to his feet, running a hand through his hair in frustration. How had this turned around so quickly? "He is arrogant, and I don't appreciate how freely he uses his gun. He is young and rash, and hotheaded in general. He is a rough guy and doesn't exactly live an exemplary life. His new wife is an ex-saloon girl. How can I agree?"

"How interesting, I found him to be a fair and honest man, and willing to champion those weaker than himself. I saw no hotheadedness. Indeed, he was exceedingly calm when dealing with a volatile situation on the train.

"Clara is a lovely woman and will make a wonderful wife. Do you know how she came to be a 'saloon girl,' as you called her? Do you have any idea the horrible indignities she has seen, what Gage has seen, what they both have suffered?"

Megan was standing toe-to-toe with him, her eyes flashing defiantly. She wasn't afraid of him anymore. Her words gave him pause, though. He was about to comment when she continued.

"Besides, is it your place to agree with his life? You do not need to make the same choices, you do not need to agree with his actions, but it is not your place to tell him how to live. That is his business, not yours." Megan turned away from Andrew in a cloud of red hair and purple-and-white skirts.

Andrew grasped her arm to stop her retreat. He was vaguely aware his hands wrapped around her upper arm. He dropped her arm as though he were burned when she glared at him.

"Forgive me, please, but don't leave. I did not mean to offend you. I am sorry."

Megan continued to glower at him, her hand on her hip.

"You like him, don't you?" Andrew asked, sitting back down on the swing.

Megan joined him again, her features softening. "I do."

"How can you justify his lifestyle and past with your beliefs? I share those same beliefs, and I cannot reconcile the two as easily as you have done."

"Firstly, it is not my place to 'justify' anything. God is the only one who can judge or justify. Second, I have enough to do keeping myself on the path God has set for me, without trying to herd anyone else." Megan sat back with a laugh.

"I don't think I understand."

"Have you read Matthew?" Megan waited for Andrew's nod. "Everyone remembers the 'judge not lest you be judged' part, but few apply the 'cast the beam from your own eye, before getting the speck out of your fellow man's.'"

Megan sat forward, her face a mask of earnestness. "That is what I mean. I have far more than enough to do to make sure I am right with God and doing what he wants me to do, both personally, and in my interactions with other people, to worry about trying to make other people follow my path."

Andrew's brow wrinkled as he considered Megan's words. He was startled when she put her hand on his arm.

"Not everyone believes in God, Andrew. Gage has many reasons he does not, and it is my job, as a Christian, to show him God does indeed exist, by both my words and my actions. Constant censure or condemnation will not accomplish any good at all." She peered into his face, her gaze searching his.

Andrew could not help but smile at her. He sighed. "I guess I never thought of it in that way, all I could see was... what he was doing was not something I would ever do. I certainly did not think to put myself out as better than anyone or as perfect. I have been judgmental. Again. Haven't I?" Andrew was disheartened once again. He desired to do the right thing, yet he seemed to keep failing in front of this special woman.

"I do hope I have not offended you."

"No, no. Not at all, I assure you. I am grateful for your honest answer, and the opportunity to learn and grow. I fear I have offended you, however, by my actions, both regarding Mr. Reagan, and when we met again here in Coldville. I am afraid I must ask you to forgive me, yet again."

"Of course I forgive you, Andrew." Megan took his hands. "We each have our own issues. As you said, you struggle with being judgmental. I struggle with fear. Fear that is justified, but I let it take hold too often, and that is also a sin. I must ask you to be patient with me, and I would ask you to pray for me in this matter, if you would."

Andrew was once again humbled by her kindness. "I would be honored to pray for you, and would ask you to pray for me as well."

Megan nodded, a pretty blush coloring her cheeks. Andrew shifted the conversation on to lighter things, and soon they were laughing as they rode out of the yard together for an afternoon of riding. Her brothers were busy with ranch duties, so today the two rode unchaperoned. Andrew was aware of the trust they placed in him and took the responsibility seriously.

Normally they rode down along the creek, near the road, or over toward one of the closer ranches. But today Andrew intended to take Megan to a special spot he had found a few years ago while he was exploring with the boys.

"Where are we going?" Megan twisted around in her saddle as they veered off their usual path.

"There is a place up near your north pasture I want to show you. It will mean a bit longer of a ride than normal, but I have plenty of water, and Mrs. Hernandez packed us some food." Andrew patted his saddlebag. "I think you will like it."

"The lunch, or the view?" Megan teased.

"Both, but mostly the view." Andrew shook his head in amusement. He loved it when she was cheeky.

"You know, I haven't seen much of the actual ranch. I have yet to see a cow up close." She laughed.

"Are you *serious*? You live on a cattle ranch."

"I grew up in the city, and know very little about animals. You know we don't have cattle in the city. Not live ones, anyway. I never saw one growing up, and we have one milk cow at the ranch, but she is in the small barn next to the bunk house and I never go there." Megan shrugged. "I have seen them in the pasture or when we ride by on the way to town."

"I am certain we can remedy that today if you would like," Andrew said.

"Is it dangerous?"

"Working with any animal can be dangerous, but I do know a thing or two about them, and we will be careful."

"Are they mean?" Megan said with a quaver of trepidation.

"They are big and curious. Most of them are not mean, but they are skittish. Once in a while, you will get one that is grumpy. Stay on your horse and listen to what I say and you will be fine."

Not for the first time, Andrew was reminded how enormous The Circle C was. Jamison Carter had been one of the first settlers in the valley, and they had kept the ranch free of most fencing. Andrew and Megan rode easily along, the summer sun warm on their shoulders. A light breeze from the north kept them comfortable as they chatted and ambled to their destination.

"I wonder what Adelaide would think of this?" Andrew commented.

"I think at one time, she lived on a farm, before she married my grandfather. But I cannot imagine her taking the route I did to get here. She likes her comforts too much to take a stage." Megan fell silent.

Andrew feared the memory of her grandmother was distressing her until a musical peal of laughter burst from her lips. This time he realized she was not mocking him. He sat back in the saddle watching her laugh.

Her head was thrown back and the sun behind her glinted off her curls, creating a halo of coppery fire around her beautiful features. Her face had filled into nothing short of stunning. She was short and rounding out in all the right places. Spunky and sassy, she was the bravest woman he knew. Her cheeks flushed pink with her laughter. Her emerald eyes twinkled merrily.

Andrew could feel his own smile spreading across his face. Her laughter was contagious, and he joined her in merriment. If only every moment could be this way. Andrew could not remember the last time he'd laughed this much.

Megan could not stop laughing for several minutes, and each time she would start giggling, Andrew would get caught up again. When they finally gained control, Andrew's stomach and face hurt.

He watched her face carefully as they rode over the hill. He was rewarded with a brilliant smile as Megan saw the landscape in front of them. An untouched meadow full of wildflowers blanketed the little valley tucked between the low hills. The small brook that branched throughout the entire ranch snaked through the meadow like a blue ribbon. The little waterfall at the far end sparkled like diamonds as the sun glinted off the water rushing over the rocks.

"Oh, Andrew. Is this what you planned to show me?" Megan pressed her hands to her cheeks. "It is beautiful. I never would have imagined places like this existed outside of fairy tales."

Andrew helped her down from her horse. She let her hands rest on his shoulders for a moment. When he peered down at her, she smiled at him, and it took his breath away.

"Thank you," she whispered.

He wanted to kiss her. Instead, he settled for grinning at her like a fool. "You are most welcome," he finally managed.

Megan released him and bent down to inspect the flowers around her skirts. He led the horses to the brook to drink.

He watched Megan as she lifted her face to the sun, flung her arms out, and twirled around several times before falling down in the tall grass. Andrew took the canteen from the saddlebag and plopped next to her. The sweet smell of the grass and wildflowers was intoxicating.

"Look at that cloud. I think it looks like a rabbit." Megan pointed to a big fluffy blob of white in the sky.

Andrew tipped his head, but he couldn't see it.

"No, you have to lie down. Look at it from this angle." Megan tugged on his arm, pulling him onto his back.

The earth was warm as he nestled his head into the grass and stared at the blue sky. He found the cloud Megan was talking about.

"Now it looks like a turtle." She giggled.

He could see the turtle. The cloud next to it resembled a horse. They lay in the grass for several minutes discussing the clouds.

Andrew sat up regretfully. He didn't want to leave, but they needed to get going. He stood, brushed the grass and dirt off his pants, and held a hand out to help Megan up. Her warm fingers slid into his, and with a gentle tug, she was on her feet. He accidentally pulled a little more than he needed to and she pitched forward into his arms.

Her breathless gasp matched his as they collided.

"Sorry," she whispered, but she didn't pull away.

"I am not," he said, lowering his head.

He was a breath away from kissing her when a low grunt startled him. Megan flinched in his arms and shook. When he glanced down at her, she buried her face in his chest. It wasn't until a squeak escaped that he realized she was laughing. For a brief moment, anger surged through him until the sound brought his attention to their surroundings.

A cow stood two feet away, considering them, nonchalantly chewing, mooing every few moments. His tension released in an instant and he chuckled.

"I–I can't believe my first kiss was interrupted... by... by... a... *cow*." Megan was laughing so hard tears streamed down her face.

Andrew hugged her tightly and laughed with her. He was encouraged when she hugged him back. The void that was left when she stepped back caused him a physical ache.

"We should get back."

He could hear the regret in her tone, but she was right. Things were getting cozier than propriety would allow. While her brothers were his best friends, he did not want to test the limits of that friendship with their sister. It took every bit of his control to pull back and offer Megan his hand.

Together they walked over to the horses, and Andrew helped her into the saddle.

"Would you like to see the interloper up close?" Andrew asked as he swung up onto his own mount.

"I think I saw her just fine, but sure." Megan turned Juniper around, and they approached the cow.

"She is bigger than I expected, but she certainly does not appear dangerous."

"They are an almost unstoppable force when they stampede. That is when they are the most dangerous. Cows are not usually a problem if there is only one or two. Bulls, on the other hand, can be cantankerous."

Andrew heeled Ebony into a gentle canter. Megan followed suit.

"What would make a herd stampede?" Megan asked.

"A gunshot, a snake, a fire. Many things. You should ask your brothers about the big stampede they had a few years ago. Thank God no one died. I don't know how everyone escaped that one. I happened to come upon it after it was over, and they cut a swath of damage for over three miles."

Andrew adjusted his hat. The wind was picking up, and the ominous darkening clouds indicated a storm was coming. They were riding through the middle of a large herd of cattle now. If a storm whipped up, it could easily spook the animals. He picked up the pace, not wanting to be caught in the open.

He nudged his horse closer to Megan and kept a close eye on the landscape, scanning for any trouble.

"Andrew, is something wrong?"

"No, I—"

A loud crack interrupted his reply. Juniper skittered sideways, and thunder filled the valley.

That wasn't thunder, Andrew realized. He searched frantically for something to shelter behind. Five hundred yards away was a stand of trees and rocks in the middle of the range.

He snatched Megan from the saddle. There was no time to pull her onto his horse, so he just held her close and heeled his mount hard. They leaped forward and covered the distance in a few seconds.

The thundering sound was coming closer. Juniper raced by them, her reins flying loose. Andrew still had one arm around Megan's waist as he slid down from the saddle.

"Go!" he shouted to his horse. The big animal did not need to be told twice, and raced off.

Andrew yanked Megan around to the opposite side of the biggest boulder and pressed her into the corner provided by a second boulder.

"Stay down. Keep your head down." He hoped she could hear him, the noise was deafening. He could barely hear himself.

The first of the stampeding cattle raced by the rocks. Andrew flattened himself into Megan, making them as low and small as he could. He caught a glimpse of her face, white and frightened. If she panicked and tried to get away, it could get them both killed.

Please, Lord, help us both to stay calm. Keep us safe.

The thunderous roll of the cattle's hooves striking the earth made even the rocks tremble. Andrew could feel the cattle brushing by, but he could not get any closer to the rock for fear of crushing Megan. He was just plain scared, and fear was not a feeling he enjoyed.

The minutes crawled as the cattle galloped by and the sound of their hooves died away. Andrew took a deep breath and peeled himself off Megan. He took a step back and scanned around to make sure all was safe before turning his attention back to her.

"Well, that was an adventure."

Her words shocked him into silence. He had expected her to completely fall apart. Instead, she was straightening her skirt, brushing her disheveled hair from her face, and looking at him with a small smile.

His respect for her grew even more in that instant. She was pale and shaking, but calm.

"You were asking about a stampede." He shrugged.

"You didn't have to show me. Your explanation was satisfactory."

For a half a second he couldn't tell if she was joking or not, but she couldn't keep a straight face. He threw his head back and laughed until he cried. Now that the danger was over, the tension released in their laughter.

"Do you think the horses got away?" Megan's brow was wrinkled in concern.

"I am certain they did. They can outrun the cattle easily. We are now stuck walking back to the ranch." Andrew smacked some of the dust off his pants with his hat.

"I am glad I wore sensible shoes." Megan scrunched her face.

He wanted to kiss that adorable nose.

Andrew gazed up at the sky. The clouds were turning blacker by the minute, and the warm summer afternoon was turning cool. A storm was imminent, and it had all the signs of a bad one.

"We are going to get wet, aren't we?" Megan sighed.

"Looks like it." Andrew offered her his arm to get over the rougher rocks until they reached flatter ground.

"Andrew?"

"What is it?" The tone of her voice concerned him.

"Please don't laugh at me when my hair gets wet. I am going to look like a drowned rat."

He stopped walking and stared at her. Her chagrined frown drove home the fact she was serious.

"Megan, nothing can make you remotely resemble a drowned rat. You are beautiful."

She snorted. "You haven't seen this carrot hair of mine get wet. It is a disaster. I am going to be quite hideous."

They went back to walking in silence. Andrew didn't understand why she was saying such things and didn't know how to respond at all to her self-deprecation. A few weeks ago, he would have thought she was fishing for a compliment, but now he had no doubt she truly believed what she was saying.

The first drops of rain splatted against the packed, dry earth, leaving dark stains wherever they fell. They were going to get very wet. Within minutes, the heavens opened and the rain came down in sheets. There was no place to shelter from it.

Andrew caught Megan as she tripped over her soggy skirts.

"They get heavy when they are wet." Megan tugged at the fullness, trying to untangle herself. "My boot is caught. Can you help me?" She flushed a bright red as she flailed her arms, trying to keep her balance.

Andrew stared at her for a moment until understanding dawned. For once, he could feel his own face flushing as he knelt in front of her and lifted the hem of her skirt. The buttons of her boot had caught on the muddy lace of her petticoat. He didn't want to tear the delicate fabric, and his fingers were fat and unwieldy as he worked the threads loose from the metal.

Time seemed to crawl until he finally got the offending shoe untangled. He straightened and peered down at Megan.

Water was running in rivulets down her face, and her coppery hair had turned a dark auburn. She was still beautiful. He'd opened his mouth to tell her when the sound of hooves distracted him.

"Are the cattle coming back?"

This time he could hear the panic in her voice.

"I think not. I think these are horses." Andrew peered into the rain. The sound was not loud enough to be cattle, and they were not in any danger of flash flooding. Even if the brook flooded, they were far enough away now that they should be safe. Sure enough, a large, dark shape loomed out of the gray curtain of rain.

"Over here." He cupped his hands around his mouth and shouted again.

The rider turned toward them, his hand lifted in a wave. Andrew recognized the silhouette astride the horse

"It's Riley," he said to Megan, who was hiding behind him. She put her head in the middle of his shoulder blades as she sagged in relief.

"Thank you, God," she whispered.

He silently echoed the sentiment. They had been walking for some time, and the lightning was getting closer every minute.

"You two all right?" Riley leaped off his horse, his boots smacking into the muddy ground with a splat.

"Yes," Andrew said.

Megan shot him a baleful look.

"What?" He was confused.

"That all depends on your definition of all right. I am cold, I am hungry, I resemble a drowned rat, and my dress weighs twenty pounds. I am tired, and we nearly got killed by a herd of stampeding cattle. And he says we are all right." Megan put her hands on her hips, glaring at the two men in front of her.

A ghost of a smile twitched at the corners of her mouth, and Andrew relaxed a little. She was teasing. Mostly. She was shivering.

"Let me signal the boys." Riley smiled at them and shot his rifle into the air. He shrugged his rain slicker off and wrapped it around his sister's shoulders.

"You okay, sis?" he asked again.

"Yes. I was only joking. Although I am tired, and we did survive a rather panicked mob of cattle intent on running us over."

"When Juniper came riding hard into the ranch, we realized something was wrong. Cattle stopped down by the east fences. Saw them when we started this way. They took out the fence on that end of the section, but we can fix that tomorrow. We need to get out of this storm." Riley gestured toward the lowering sky.

Logan came riding out of the rain. "You two okay?"

"Oh." Megan started to giggle.

It wasn't an amused giggle, but sounded forced and hysterical. Andrew saw she was close to losing the tight control she was holding over her emotions.

"We can tell you more when we get back to the ranch. Logan, can I ride with you? Riley, you take Megan. I don't like the looks of this storm."

Truthfully, Andrew wanted to be the one to ride with Megan, but he couldn't ask one of her brothers to let him ride their horse with their sister. It would be safer if they rode their own horses.

"Megan." Andrew waited until she met his gaze. "You look nothing like a drowned rat."

She rewarded him with a teary smile. At least he assumed they were tears; the rain was still coming down hard. A sharp crack of thunder reminded them all they needed to get out of the weather.

Riley swung astride his horse, and Andrew lifted Megan easily up to her brother. Riley tucked her in front of him.

Andrew knew she would be safe. He swung up easily behind Logan, and the four of them took off at a fast clip for the ranch house. The lightning streaked and flashed, and the thunder rolled as the storm chased them across the valley. Morgan joined them halfway back, and they finished the ride together.

Mrs. Hernandez was waiting with hot tea and soup and whisked Megan upstairs before anyone could blink. She was back in minutes with stern instructions for the men.

"You boys go change into dry clothes, this instant. Andrew, I think Morgan has a shirt you can wear. You can't be wet like that. Come sit by the kitchen stove and eat a bowl of this soup when you get dry. Quick, move." She snapped her fingers at him impatiently.

Andrew followed his friend into the bedroom behind the stairs and dressed in the pants and shirt Morgan handed him. Estrella Hernandez was right. He couldn't chance getting sick.

He needed to get back to town. He had been gone too long already. But Estrella insisted he sit and eat before he left. He hoped to get another glimpse of Megan before he left, but Estrella said she had eaten in her room and fallen asleep.

Andrew's horse had followed Juniper to the ranch, and the ranch hands had him brushed, fed, and watered by the time he was ready to head back to town. The storm moved through rapidly, with a lot of noise and rain, but not much damage. Andrew took stock of the surrounding landscape as he rode swiftly back to his home.

The next day Andrew rode to the ranch to bring back the clothes he had borrowed and to bring news—a traveling preacher was in the area, and the town was having an enormous picnic and service to hear him speak. He was on his way to the area ranches, spreading the news, and checking up on things after the storm. He'd also received a few reports of rustling on nearby ranches he needed to investigate.

"Will I see you there?" His question was directed at everyone, but his eyes were for Megan only.

"Yes, we will *all* be there," Riley answered. His eyebrow arched and the look on his face telegraphed his amusement.

Andrew smiled unrepentantly and winked at Megan, causing her to blush. Her brothers' wide grins only deepened it. Andrew chuckled as he mounted his horse. Life had become much more fun with her around.

Megan was so excited about the picnic she was ready before her brothers. As soon as she arrived, she found Anne and the two of them took off to find the other girls. A rush of pleasure skittered through Megan's heart when she saw the cameo nestled beautifully at the base of her throat. Anne had strung it on a piece of green satin ribbon and was wearing it as a necklace.

Most of the local ranchers had taken the day to come into town for the services and picnic. Everyone settled in on quilts, blankets, logs, and in the grass to listen to the preacher. He preached for two hours, keeping his audience in rapt attention. Megan found his sermon to be full of content and applicable to life, unlike many of the sermons she had sat through in Adelaide's church.

After the preacher had finished, each family brought food to share. Vegetables from gardens, salads, pickles, venison, beef, chicken, cakes, and pies galore filled the tables. Megan and her friends went down the line of tables, picking a little of whatever they desired.

After lunch, some of the men got together to play horseshoes and other games while the women chatted. Three-legged races, sack races, and several other games had been put together for the children.

Anne and Megan were soon joined by two young women.

"Megan, please allow me to introduce Elisabeth. She is the new schoolteacher, who just arrived for the next term. This is Lydia, the blacksmith's sister," Anne said. "Elisabeth, Lydia, this is Megan Carter, recently arrived from back East." Anne finished the introductions by flopping back down onto the blanket.

Lydia hugged Megan tightly before throwing herself onto the blanket in a giggling heap. Elisabeth was more reserved and sank slowly down. Megan sat between Lydia and Elisabeth. They made a stunning quartet. Anne with her golden hair and willowy figure, Elisabeth with her gorgeous chestnut curls, Lydia's raven-black tresses, and Megan's coppery curls. Many heads turned their way as they walked that afternoon, and Megan enjoyed every minute of it.

Megan hit it off with both women right away. She and Elisabeth bonded over being the new girls in town, while Lydia was witty and fun and had them in giggles much of the time. The four women were soon fast friends, and Megan knew the bonds formed this sunny afternoon would last for many years.

A cry of pain from the three-legged-race area arrested Anne and Megan's attention. Little Sally Samson and her sister, Louise, were in a heap at the finish line. The two women hurried to see if they could help. Anne examined the little girls while Megan helped untie their legs.

"It looks like Sally may have sprained her ankle. My father should examine it to be sure. Would you like me to take her to his office?" Anne asked the little girl's mother.

Sarah Samson picked up the still-crying Louise and held her tight. "If you could, that would be a big help. The baby is napping on the blanket. Warren is getting ready for the sack race, and the other boys are off who knows where. I can head over to check on her once my husband is done with the horseshoe tournament if that is all right."

Anne nodded and smiled at the frazzled woman.

"Can you be brave and go with Miss Anne to let Doc check on your ankle, Sally?" Sarah asked her.

Sally was still sniffling, but at the prospect of going with Anne, she smiled. "Yes, Mama, I like Doc. He gives me a peppermint stick if I am good."

The women laughed. "You be sure to only have one, you hear," Sarah admonished her.

Megan volunteered to help Anne take Sally to her father's office; they linked their arms and created a game of carrying the little girl down the street. She was soon laughing and having fun, and her tears were gone.

∞　∞　∞

"Sheriff!"

Andrew turned to see Sarah Samson running down the street toward him. The conversations around him stopped as the woman raced to his side.

"What is it, Mrs. Samson?" Andrew asked.

"Sarah, what is it?" Clark Samson, her husband, asked, reaching Andrew's side at the same moment.

"Anne and Miss Carter took Sally to see Doc earlier this afternoon. I went to go check on them since they had not come back yet, and Doc's office is locked. I knocked, but no one answered. Doc never locks his office, and Sally isn't anywhere. I can't find Anne or Miss Carter, either." Sarah dissolved into tears.

Andrew was immediately concerned. Sarah was right. Doc never locked his office, even when he was gone. It was open then, with a note telling where to find him. He searched around and spotted Abigail under a tree, quilting with several other ladies.

"I will look into it. You stay here in case the girls come back. If you see them, send one of them to Doc's."

Clark nodded, his face a mask of worry.

Andrew calmly made his way to the horseshoe tournament, where Morgan and Riley were pitching. He didn't want to cause any alarm by rushing. Instead of breaking up the game to talk to the older brothers, he pulled Logan aside.

"Have you seen your sister lately?" he asked in a low voice.

"She was with Anne a little while ago. Why?"

"She and Anne took a little one to Doc's a little while ago and they haven't returned. The office is locked."

Logan's head whipped around to look at the crowd. "Locked?" His brow furrowed. "Let's go check with Sawyer. Maybe he has seen Anne." Logan strode off toward the food with Andrew following. Sawyer was standing near the pie table, talking with Jacob Jasper, the blacksmith.

"Sorry to interrupt you, boys, have you seen Anne or Megan lately?" Andrew asked.

"No, I haven't seen either of them for over an hour now," Sawyer said.

"Is anything wrong?" Jacob asked.

"I don't know. Keep an eye out for them, will you, Jacob?" Andrew made a beeline for Abigail with Logan and Sawyer following close behind.

"Abigail, may I speak to you for a moment?" he asked.

She set down her quilting and joined Andrew and the two Carter brothers. "What can I do for you, Sheriff?" she asked with a smile. It faded as Andrew explained the problem.

"No, Doc should be there. I can think of no reason the door should be locked. I have a spare key here with me. I carry one in case of an emergency." Abigail headed down the street to her husband's office before Andrew could say another word.

"Abigail, you should wait here. Let me go in first." Andrew didn't want to tell her what he was thinking, but he didn't have to. Her expression told him she was thinking the same thing. She handed him the key.

Andrew unlocked the door and drew his gun as Logan and Sawyer silently slid theirs out of their holsters. Carefully they entered the waiting room, which was empty and still.

"Doc?" Andrew called.

A muffled thump came from the office. Then another, followed by an equally muffled groan.

Andrew threw the office door open. "Abigail," he shouted.

Doc, Anne, and little Sally Samson were bound and gagged on the floor. The adults were unconscious, and Sally had tears streaming down her cheeks. Andrew picked her up and brought her into the waiting room, where he untied her and removed the gag.

Abigail was there in an instant. "There now, sweetheart, it is all right. Someone will go get your mama in a minute. Let me look at you. You are such a brave little girl," Abigail crooned.

"Those bad men came and hurt us and tied us up." Sally was inconsolable.

"Andrew, help me with Doc." Logan called from the office.

Behind Andrew, Sawyer carried Anne into the waiting room. She was coming around, and Abigail pointed Sawyer to the smelling salts. When he opened them Anne jerked her head trying to get away from the sharp, acrid smell. Her eyes fluttered open as Sawyer removed the gag. He rubbed her wrists to return the circulation to her hands.

"Dad? How is Dad?" Anne's voice was slurred and groggy.

"He has a nasty bump on the head, but he will be all right." Doc's grumpy voice came from the doorway. Abigail sighed in relief.

"Megan. They took her. Those men took Megan."

Chapter 16

Anne's frantic words chilled Andrew's blood. Logan and Sawyer froze, his fear mirrored in their faces.

"Logan, get Sarah. Let her know we found Sally. Then sound the alarm. I want every man you can round up for a posse here as soon as you can get them. I will talk to them after I get the full story. Don't sound the alarm until Sarah knows we have found her daughter," Andrew repeated, wanting to spare Sarah the fright.

Logan ran for the door as fast as his legs could carry him.

Andrew helped Doc sit in a chair. "What happened?"

Anne and Doc pieced the story together with a few interjections from Sally. Sarah arrived as the alarm bell sounded. Logan was ringing it for all he was worth, and the clear metallic peal echoed through the town. Sally flew into her mother's arms the instant she walked through the door.

Seeing that the little girl was safe with her mother, Andrew hurried to his own office, Sawyer following close behind.

"What are we going to do?" Sawyer asked him.

"I am going to deputize you and a few others. We are going to go hunt down those men and rescue your sister." Andrew snatched a few deputy badges, several rifles, and a good supply of ammunition, then he and Sawyer headed to the alarm, where almost the entire town had gathered. Despite its name, it wasn't actually a bell but a huge metal circle that could be struck with a hammer.

Logan was waiting by the alarm with Riley, Morgan, and Caleb. Andrew knew at a glance that Logan had told them their sister was missing.

"A little while ago two men attacked Doc and Anne Warren in Doc's office. They were knocked unconscious, bound, and gagged. Little Sally Samson was bound and gagged as well. Those men kidnapped Megan Carter. We are not sure exactly when. She could have been taken a few minutes ago, or it could be an hour or more. I need men to mount up and form a posse to go after the girl."

Voices chorused from the crowd.

"I'll go."

"Me too."

"Count me in."

"You know I will go, Andrew." Ben Wheelwright, Andrew's young deputy, strode from the crowd.

"They attacked my daughter. I am going," Clark Samson ground out.

"Clark, I need you and Ben to stay here. Someone needs to take care of the town and make sure those scoundrels don't double back," Andrew said.

Andrew deputized Clark, the five Carter brothers, Jacob Jasper, and Mr. Jensen. He was humbled by the number of men who volunteered for the posse. A few men could not leave their families, or their ranches, but offered any other help they could give.

"Sheriff, any of the men on the posse that need them a horse, you have 'em come see me." Andrew turned to see Luther, the livery owner, standing behind him.

"Thank you, Luther."

Within a few moments, a posse of forty men followed him out of town. Andrew looked at the sky. There were still four or five hours of daylight left, and they would need every bit of it.

He fell back to let Jacob take the lead. Jacob was not only the town blacksmith, but he was the best tracker in four counties. A few miles outside of town he called the posse to a halt. He dismounted and examined the road.

"Two horses. One is riding double. They went off the road here. My guess is they are going to try to lose us by riding in the river for a while," he called back.

Sure enough, as the men followed the tracks, they led straight into the river.

"We had best split up. Jake, you take twenty men and ride on the other side of the river. Logan, you are a decent tracker; you stay on this side with me. First one who sees any sign of our quarry leaving the water, fire three shots. Keep your eyes open, men," Andrew said.

The posse split into two groups and rode along both sides of the river. They traveled in silence, occasionally shouting Megan's name, for two hours before the sound of rifle shots split the air.

"Here, they left the water here." Jacob was down by the water's edge. He pointed to a set of clear hoof marks in the mud. He mounted his horse again, and the posse continued on. Another hour had passed before Andrew called for a halt.

"Men, it is getting late. Those of you who need to turn back had best do so now. If you ride hard, you can get back to town before dark. If you want to stay, we will ride on until dusk. We will make camp and continue on in the morning."

"I am sorry, boys, I have to go back," Aaron Johnson, the Carters' nearest neighbor, said. "I know you are not going to go back 'til you find your sister. I will make sure the Hernandezes know what happened, and me and my boys will make sure to help them in any way we can while you are gone."

Several other ranchers echoed Aaron's words, volunteering to help keep the ranch running while the Carters searched for their sister.

"Thank you all. We cannot express how much your kindness means to us," Riley spoke to the volunteers.

"I mean to stay with the Carters and see this through," Andrew spoke up. "Ben is more than capable, and he will be in charge until I return."

Most of the men returned to their homes. The three who stayed were single ranch hands with no families. Andrew led them on, heading east, while the others turned back west to go home. The nine men rode until dusk, but with little sign of their prey. They set up camp and pretended to sleep.

Andrew tossed and turned. The guilt lay like a lead curtain on his heart. His job was to keep people safe, and he couldn't even keep the one he loved safe.

His eyes flew open. He loved her. He didn't know when it had happened exactly, but he loved Megan Carter. He lay back, resting his head on his saddle.

All he could see was Megan's trusting expression when she'd told him of the danger a few days ago on their walk. The guilt hit his gut like a hammer. It was going to be a long night.

Chapter 17

Consciousness came slowly to Megan. At first, she thought she was back on the stage, bouncing and flouncing along. Soon, though, she realized she was lying face down, draped over a horse. Her wrists were tied together and hanging above her head. A thick fog had invaded her brain, and it took her several minutes to remember what had happened.

Michael O'Shea had been waiting in Doc Warren's office when she and Anne had come in. Another man had been there too: a filthy, bearded man Megan had never seen before. He had snatched Sally the moment they walked in the door, and O'Shea had threatened to kill them if Megan ran or made any move to escape.

Tears welled in Megan's eyes as she remembered the sickening thwack of the gun barrel against her friends' heads. Much to her relief, the little girl had fainted. She remembered a cloth being put over her mouth and nose, a sickly-sweet smell, and then nothing. She had recognized the odor of chloroform an instant before she lost consciousness.

Megan opened her eyes a crack and peeked at her surroundings. She was definitely on a horse in front of the saddle. Her hands dangled down the animal's right flank.

Her sleeves were wet. She slowly turned her head, trying to catch sight of her captor. His legs were wet as well. She realized they must have crossed a river recently.

"Yer awake." The deep voice startled her. She started to struggle and found herself sliding off the horse, feet first. She hit the ground hard, but rolled to a sitting position and fumbled, trying to untie her feet. She had to get away.

Before she could get very far in untying the wet rope around her ankles, she was hauled roughly to her feet.

"Goin' somewhere, missy?" The dirty vagabond grabbed a fistful of her hair and pulled her face to his. His breath stank of whisky and tobacco. Megan gagged. "Get this through yer pretty little head. Yer coming with us. If anyone tries to rescue you, we'll shoot them. If you try to get away, we'll do worse to you than tie you up, you understand?" His voice was cold and hard.

Megan did her best to nod that she understood. The man slid a knife from the sheath on his hip. He traced the tip down the side of her face, down her neck, and across the bodice of her dress before bending down and with one swift slice, cutting the ropes off her ankles.

"Now git on that horse." He leered at her as he shoved her toward the animal.

After a few tries, Megan mounted the huge beast. The vile man swung into the saddle behind her. She leaned as far forward as she could, but he wrapped one arm around her waist and pulled her close. He grasped the reins with the other and urged the horse forward at a fast pace. Her face burned with anger and shame as she was forced to ride pressed against him. He cackled at her discomfort and continued to hold her close.

They rode until dark. Finally he directed his mount to stop and dismounted. He jerked Megan off the horse and threw her to the ground.

Without a word, he tied her ankles together tightly, then yanked her into a sitting position, then tied her to the trunk of a tree. For good measure, he tied her hands above her head.

"She won't be going anywhere trussed up like that. We can sleep tonight. No fire. Sleep in your bedroll," the greasy man said over his shoulder.

"Her grandmother wants her alive, and she will need to be able to walk on board the train by herself." From Michael's tone of voice, Megan could tell he wasn't in agreement with how the other captor was treating her.

∞ ∞ ∞

Michael didn't particularly care for his partner, but their employer had insisted, and he had been paid well. TJ Crenshaw knew what he was doing. He had been bounty hunting runaway slaves for years before that no-account Lincoln feller had set them free. He had always brought them back. A little used and worse for the wear maybe, but alive. Crenshaw had made sure to say so a hundred times on their journey.

247

Michael sighed but didn't say anything further. He removed his bedroll from his pack and lay down to rest. He would be glad to get back to civilization, with real beds and real food. They had had nothing but jerky and dried fruit today. He drank deeply from his canteen. As he did, he realized Megan had been given no food or water since they had left Coldville.

It wouldn't do to have her die of thirst before he could get paid. He walked over and held the canteen to her lips, and she took several swallows before he pulled it away. She never said a word, but the pleading in her green eyes nearly did him in.

Think of the money, all that beautiful money. He lay back down and was asleep in minutes. He had long since deadened his heart to the pricking of his conscience.

Megan was exhausted. With her arms tied above her head, and her feet straight out in front of her she could not get comfortable. The greasy man lurked about the campsite for a few hours, leering at her and drinking whisky. He didn't come near her until his bottle of whisky was gone. Megan shrank back as he leaned down as he leaned in, inches from her face. His rotten breath was hot and foul. She gagged.

"I do like me a redhead." Megan jerked her head away as he fingered her curls. Crenshaw dropped his bottle and grabbed her face with his hand, forcing her to look at him. "What's wrong, missy? You don't like ol' Crenshaw? Maybe it is time you learn your place, you little bogger." He ran his free hand down her neck and paused over her bodice before continuing down. He slowly lifted the skirt of her dress, leering at her the entire time.

Megan kicked and squirmed and screamed as much as she could. She fought like a tiger, albeit a restrained one. Crenshaw only laughed and pawed at her more. He covered her mouth with his hand and she bit him hard. Her face burned like fire where he struck her. He ran his hand up her skirt, and Megan fought to stay conscious.

"Crenshaw." Michael's voice carried to her foggy brain.

Crenshaw stopped his assault to stare at his partner.

"I's only messing with her. I ain't gonna damage the goods," he grumbled.

Michael did not appear pacified. "Get away from her, and stay away. I don't want her grandmother to refuse payment. This isn't one of your slave bounties. Get that through your thick skull."

Crenshaw stumbled away from Megan toward the fire and lay down, still grumbling. Within seconds his snores rumbled through the camp.

"I am sorry," Michael said.

He wet his handkerchief and wiped her face, holding the cool cloth to the place where Crenshaw had hit her. Megan could not bring herself to say thank you. She merely gazed at him, working to keep her disgust from showing.

"Please let me go."

"Crenshaw would easily find you again. Or your grandmother would send someone else." Michael shook his head.

"Why are you doing this?"

"Your grandmother pays well, and I need the money."

"My brothers would pay you whatever Adelaide is paying you. More even," Megan pleaded.

"I would never be able to go home. Adelaide Carter has more than a few people in her pocket. I don't want to argue with you. I don't have a choice. Try to get some sleep. It's going to be a brutal day traveling through the mountains tomorrow." Michael turned his back to her and lay on his bedroll again.

Soon the only sounds were those of a few bugs, a few nocturnal animals roaming the woods, the crackling of the fire, and Crenshaw's snoring. Megan finally succumbed and fell into a fitful sleep.

Chapter 18

Megan was slightly relieved to be riding in front of Michael the next day. He was no gentleman, but he was not the lecherous Crenshaw, either. They pushed relentlessly through the mountain trails, and her face bore many scratches from the brush. She held on to a little hope that they would come close to the Haven, but they did not. Crenshaw knew the trails, and he kept them far from the main path.

The trio rested long enough to give the horses water and eat a few bites of food at noon. The farther away from home they got, the less chance she had of being rescued. She had a fleeting moment of hope when the stage passed by in the distance, but Michael held his gun to her ribs.

"Remember what I told you in Coldville. Anyone who comes near us will get a bullet. Right between the eyes."

Megan had no doubt he would kill if tested. She stayed quiet, and the small flame of hope died.

The three of them made good time through the mountains and were soon on the outskirts of Goodrich. Crenshaw led them to a small clearing outside of town. "Stay here. I am going into town to get our tickets for the train. You keep her quiet."

Michael hauled Megan from the saddle and set her on the ground. He tied her hands behind her back and bound her ankles securely. He didn't gag her, though, for which Megan was thankful. He offered her another drink of water, and they waited in uncomfortable silence until Crenshaw returned.

He dismounted, clearly unhappy.

"An orphan train arrived a few minutes ago. Lots of people on the platform. But if we don't get on the train here, we have to go to Denver, and the chances of drawing attention and getting caught are much higher. Especially if anyone telegraphed ahead."

Crenshaw ran a hand through his hair. "You get this straight, beautiful. We are going into town and getting on board that train." His eyes were hard. "If anyone talks to you, you tell them we are your brothers. You have decided to go back East to live with your grandmother, and we are escorting you. Understand?" He leaned in close to her face.

Megan nodded.

Michael untied her and threaded her arm through his. "Crenshaw will get rid of the horses. You and I are going to mosey on down right to the train. No funny business," he warned, patting his gun with his free hand.

She and Michael walked down the dusty main street arm in arm. Megan didn't know what to do. She didn't want anyone to get hurt, but she had to get help somehow. If they got her back to Adelaide, she would never see her brothers again. Her heart sank even further when Crenshaw joined them, walking on the other side, sandwiching her between her captors.

As they arrived at the train station, Megan was distracted by the line of children standing against the wall of the station. Most were looking around curiously. Megan did a double take when she spotted one of the little boys who used to sell papers with Davis. She ducked her head, hoping he didn't recognize her.

"Miss Megan." His little voice rang above the crowd. The whole platform turned to gawk as he ran forward, ducking the arm of the stylish lady who appeared to be in charge of the children. He ran straight into Megan's arms and she hugged him tightly.

"Megan, I am so glad to see you." Another familiar voice startled Megan. Clara was standing next to her.

"H-Hi, Mrs. Reagan, how are you today?" Megan's voice sounded stilted even to her own ears. Guilt struck her heart as a pained expression flashed across Clara's face. She prayed her formality would clue the woman in to the fact something was wrong.

"Megan."

Megan's heart skipped a beat as Gage walked up to them. For a moment, her vision blurred, and she took a deep breath to keep from fainting. Michael's hand was resting on his gun, and Crenshaw had shifted sideways, his eyes boring into Megan.

"Sam, I am happy to see you. I think you should probably get back in line, though, huh?" Megan hugged the small boy as tight as she could before sending him back to the smiling woman waiting for him. The lady directed him to a kind-looking couple standing nearby.

"That is Mr. and Mrs. Griggs. He runs the livery. They are a nice family," Clara answered Megan's unasked question.

Megan relaxed a little. Sam was such a nice little boy. She hoped his new family would be as sweet.

"What brings you to Goodrich?" Gage's question brought her back to her predicament.

Michael's grip tightened on her arm, and Megan could hardly keep from wincing. "I am going back East. I decided I want to live with my grandmother. My brothers are taking me back on this train. I am sorry, Sheriff Reagan, but we need to go." Megan walked away from her friends, shaking like a leaf.

Clara and Gage looked after her in confusion.

"Gage, something must be wrong. Why would she act like that?" Clara clutched her husband's arm, tears filling her bright blue eyes. We are friends. There is no way she would treat us in this manner, so cold and formal. She would also never go back to her grandmother." Panic threaded through her words.

Gage was inclined to agree. His eyes narrowed as he glared down the platform at the two men. They flanked Megan, both keeping their hands on their guns. The younger man had a tight hold on her arm.

A commotion at the opposite end of the street caught Gage's attention. A dozen men were riding hard toward the station. Gage recognized the stone-faced man leading them.

"Clara, get the children off the platform." Gage's voice was low, hard. Clara did not ask questions but hurried to do his bidding.

"Megan, drop," Gage shouted.

The two men turned, drawing their guns.

His hands dove like lightning toward the gun on his hip. Before the men could sight in on him, he cleared the leather of the holster and fired one shot, the dirty bearded man went down in a heap.

Megan lay flat on the platform. With his free hand, Gage pulled back the hammer on the pistol and continued to fire rapidly. One. Two. Three more shots rang out. Both men lay motionless on the rigid wooden planks as the townspeople panicked in the background.

Gage ran to Megan and helped her up. Blood was splattered on one cheek and smeared along the side of her dress. He looked her up and down. The blood was not hers. Gage let out the breath he had been holding.

He turned to the first man who had fallen and recognized the face that had been staring at him from a wanted poster for weeks: TJ Crenshaw. The bounty hunter was dead, and the other man was alive, but barely. Gage collected the two kidnapper's guns. Neither man had gotten off a single shot.

The riders had reacted to the gunfire and were riding even harder and would be there in seconds. Gage assumed they were the posse sent to find Megan. Megan was not too steady on her feet, so Gage kept an arm around her. He turned her away from the gruesome scene as the riders joined them and leapt from their horses.

"Megan." One of the men reached for her, and she fell, sobbing, into his arms.

"Gage," the lead rider said in a terse tone.

"Andrew," Gage returned Andrew's greeting coolly. "This one is still alive. Maybe he has something to say."

He and Andrew knelt beside the other man.

"Who paid you to kidnap Miss Carter?" Andrew asked the man.

The dying man's lips formed words but no sound came out. The two lawmen bent down close to hear his answer. They asked a few more questions, but he was too far gone. A moment later he was dead.

Gage directed the men to take Megan to his office; he and Clara would join them in a moment.

∞　∞　∞

Megan clung to Sawyer as they walked down the street to the jail, which also housed Gage's office. She wasn't crying anymore, but she was glad to have her brother's strong arms around her. She loved Sawyer, but she craved Andrew's embrace even more. The thought made her blush. She peeked over her shoulder to make sure he was behind them.

Soon she was sitting in a wooden chair inside the small brick building. A glass of liquid was pressed to her lips. She could smell the alcohol and pushed it away.

"Drink this. It will help." Andrew was kneeling in front of her, holding the glass.

Megan took a sip of the amber liquid. It burned her throat but helped clear her head. She handed the glass back to Andrew, who passed it off to one of her brothers and took both her hands in his.

"Are you truly all right?" he asked, his gaze searching her face.

"Yes, truly. I am not able to express how thankful I am that you caught up with us. Also for Gage and Clara." Megan fought back tears as she looked around at her friends and family.

"Megan, I had time to think while we were searching for you. I know I was unforgivably rude when we first met. I am sorry. I know how different you are from what I first thought, and as we were searching for you, I realized I may have lost you forever. I don't want to spend another minute without you. I want to marry you. Spend my life with you. I love you. I promise you no one will ever hurt you again. I will keep you safe. I have a nice house in town; you wouldn't be far from your brothers, and it sure could use a woman's touch. Red gingham curtains, maybe. There is plenty of room for children when we get around to them." Andrew paused to take a breath.

"Andrew. I am honored you want me to be your wife," Megan interjected before he could continue. "And I love you too. At least, I think I do. But I can't marry you right now. I only recently found my family. I need more time to get to know them. To get to know who I am. Can you give me that time? Please?" Megan pleaded.

The room was so silent Megan could hear her blood pounding in her ears. Andrew took a deep breath and sighed. In those few seconds, Megan suffered terrible guilt. The last thing in the world she wanted was to hurt him. She turned her attention back to the man on his knees in front of her. He did not drop his gaze away as she peered into his gray eyes.

"I will wait, Megan. For as long as you need. I told you, I love you. I will protect you. I want what is best for you. I won't say I am not disappointed, but I do understand." Andrew squeezed her hands.

The others in the room sighed in relief. Megan had been unaware she had been holding her breath and let it out in a huff. "Thank you," she whispered, leaning forward to kiss Andrew on the cheek.

Someone cleared their throat. Megan looked up to see Clara and Gage. They must have slipped into the room a few minutes ago. Clara rushed forward to hug her, and Megan returned the embrace warmly. She introduced Gage and Clara to her brothers, and Clara insisted they stay for supper, then spend the night in their home. Riley accepted the invitation gratefully.

Megan was thankful to have something to take her mind off of the last few days. She would have to relive the events soon enough. She had overheard Andrew and Gage discussing whether they should ask her any questions. She would tell them everything in the morning. Something had to be done about Adelaide. For now, Megan was happy to spend time with her friends and share a fun evening full of stories and laughter.

Chapter 19

Madam Carter, there is a policeman here who wishes to see you."

Adelaide glanced up from her bed when Jeffries spoke from the doorway. She motioned for her butler to show the man up, then fluttered her hands about her head, making sure her hair was in place.

It wouldn't do for the policeman to think just because she was confined to this bed that she wasn't still *the* Adelaide Carter. She straightened her dressing gown and sat a little taller as the door opened and Jeffries ushered in the uniformed officer.

Officer Wainwright removed his hat when he entered the room. Adelaide smiled at him. A young man with manners.

"What can I do for you, Officer?" Adelaide asked, motioning for him to sit.

He sat in the chair she indicated and withdrew a small notepad. "I am terribly sorry to bother you, Mrs. Carter, but we have received a report I need to check on."

"It is fine, young man. How can I help the New York City Police Department?" She beamed at the handsome officer. It had been a long time since she had any visitors, and she wasn't about ready to let this one get away quickly.

∞ ∞ ∞

Officer Wainwright looked at Adelaide Carter. This frail woman could not possibly have ordered a kidnapping. She was dressed in a simple but high-quality blue dressing gown, a beautiful jeweled broach at her throat. Her hair was pure white, and her face thin and drawn. He was beginning to worry his visit would overtax her. As the butler had shown him upstairs, he had been concerned to see only a few pieces of furniture in the rooms downstairs and even less in the hallways. This room was lavishly decorated, further validating his suspicions.

"Officer?" Adelaide's voice brought him back to what he was supposed to be doing.

"Yes, apologies, ma'am. We received a telegram saying you were involved in something, but seeing you now, and your current condition, I am sure we were given the wrong information. I am certain a lady like yourself would never be involved in anything so underhanded." He rose to leave.

"Oh, you are too kind. You remind me a little of my son, Jamison. He was a kind boy too. Exactly like his father. They gave me this brooch." Adelaide fingered the shimmering jewels pinned to her gown. "There is a wonderful story behind these little jewels. Would you do an old woman a favor and sit for a few moments? I don't get many visitors, and it would mean so much to me."

Officer Wainwright couldn't refuse, despite needing to get back to his patrol. He closed his notepad and sat back down in the chair.

"My Joseph and I were married for thirty years before he passed away. We were utterly destitute on our first anniversary. The only thing he could get me were pretty little purple wildflowers from the side of the road. Honesty. That is what the flowers are called. Nineteen years later, he and my children gave me these." Adelaide unpinned the broach and handed it to him.

He turned the jeweled pin in his hands, examining it carefully. The pin was a small bouquet of four-petal flowers. Each petal was a purple jewel. The stems were emeralds, and a bow of diamonds tied the bouquet together.

"What are the purple stones?" he asked as he handed it back.

"Amethysts. Joseph had the piece commissioned in Paris. It is the only thing I have from all three of my loves. They are gone now. Joseph and Amelia died many years ago. Jamison died only recently, although I lost him a long time ago." Tears filled Adelaide's eyes and she dabbed at them with a delicate lace handkerchief.

"I am sorry for your loss, ma'am. Please accept my condolences. I am sorry, but I must leave now. I need to get back to my patrol. I am leaving my card. If you need anything at all, please do not hesitate to send for me."

He hurried downstairs, finding his own way. The halls were bare; even the rugs had been removed. The wallpaper showed faded outlines of where paintings and decorations had hung for years. He had to get a telegram sent to Mrs. Carter's grandchildren right away. Something was not right.

∞ ∞ ∞

Andrew could hear the music as he rode up to the ranch house. He smiled. Since the kidnapping, Megan had played the piano every single day. It seemed to be healing for her. The letter and telegram he was bringing would be another balm to her heart, of that he was certain. He didn't knock but walked right into the chaos that was becoming normal in the Carter home. Megan jumped up to give him a hug the moment she spotted him.

"I am so happy to see you. What brings you here today?"

Andrew laughed. "Since when do I need a reason?"

"You said you wouldn't be back until next week." Riley raised an eyebrow.

"You are right. I did have a reason for coming early. I got a telegram at the office addressed to you from the New York Police Department. A letter also came addressed to Megan. I thought I should bring them right out." Andrew held out the envelopes. Megan snatched the letter but didn't take the telegram, as if unsure that she wanted to read it. Riley took it instead.

"Well?" Caleb asked as Riley read it.

"I am not sure. It says, 'No evidence to support accusation. Stop. Carter household bare. Stop. Mrs. Carter bedridden. Stop. Advise if further investigation warranted. Stop.'"

"Bedridden?" Megan asked as she tore her letter open. "Perhaps this letter from Helena will say more." She sat on the steps and perused it. "Helena is getting married," she squealed. "And she wants me to be in the wedding."

"She wants you to go to France?" Andrew asked.

"No, she is getting married in New York," Megan clarified. "She was in Paris with Uncle Henri, and she met a New York businessman at the university. They hit it off, and are back now and planning an autumn wedding. Autumn in the city is gorgeous. I am certain it will be beautiful. She wants me to tell you she would love to meet her other cousins and hopes the entire family will be able to travel." Megan turned to her brothers. "Will we be able to go? The wedding is at the end of October."

"I think by then we should be able to arrange something. I don't want to make any promises, and I don't know if we can all go, but at least some of us will. Send a telegram back to her and let her know you can be in the wedding," Riley spoke for his brothers.

Megan threw her arms around him with a grin.

"The ranch should be settled for the winter by the middle of October, and the Hernandez boys can keep it going for a few weeks, I think. We should be able to go. I think we need to meet the rest of our family," Morgan chimed in.

The whole family started to talk at once, making plans. Andrew leaned back observing the chaos. He would miss Megan while she was gone, but he was glad she was going. It would be good for her to confront her grandmother.

Megan walked up next to him and wrapped her arms around his waist. He returned the embrace, and the two rested there in silence. Andrew wondered, not for the first time, how long he would have to wait to make this woman his wife.

He tore himself away after a few moments. He needed to get back to his circuit. The local saloon owner two towns over had been on a binge again, and Andrew was concerned. Hector Gonzalez was a mean drunk, and his young niece and nephew were usually on the receiving end of his rage. With a goodbye kiss on the cheek from Megan to tide him over until his next visit, Andrew was off.

Megan stretched, basking in the sun. The warmth was intense, and the road ahead shimmered with the heat. She didn't mind, though. Here in the open, with the slight breeze and fresh air, the heat was preferable to the heat in the city.

The city was closed, dark, and rank, even on the sunniest of summer days. Where she had lived, the streets were kept clean, and the parks were landscaped and green, but a few blocks away, sewage ran down the road, people lived and died crammed into tenement housing, and the smell of suffering hung thick in the air.

"Do you think Andrew will be surprised?" Megan asked.

"I think so. I don't believe we have ever done anything like this. Not for anyone. Yes, he will be surprised," Riley answered. He was driving the buggy, while the rest of her brothers trailed behind on horseback.

"How will we get him there?" Megan asked.

"Jacob has that covered. He is going to tell him there is trouble at the schoolhouse. Andy will likely be so concerned with getting there, he won't notice half the town is missing," Riley responded.

Megan sat back, satisfied. It had taken them the better part of a month to plan this party for Andrew's birthday. She had never had a birthday party herself, but she had seen many of them. Adelaide had thrown lavish parties for Helena. Anne had helped Megan plan this one, and half the town was going to celebrate with them.

Instead of driving into Coldville, they went directly to the schoolhouse on the outskirts of town. Anne and Abigail were already there, and Megan hurried inside to help them with the decorating while her brothers hid the horses and the buggy in the tree line nearby.

Megan and her friends hung paper chains all over the schoolroom. Several of the women and children in town had made them from colorful wrapping paper, brown packaging paper, even the labels from cans. They were bright and cheerful.

A few chairs were lined against the wall for those who didn't want to dance, and the desks had all been moved outside to the woodshed to make room. It was going to be warm inside, but fun. All the food was being set up outside in a large tent that had been pitched a few days earlier.

"How are we keeping the tent a secret? Won't that ruin the surprise?"

Megan stretched on her tiptoes on top of the bench trying to get the end of the paper chain to stick to the wall. The gum paste was not working very well. She was going to have to resort to a hammer and nails in a minute.

"Andrew helped take the desks outside." Abigail grinned.

"What?"

"Yes, we told him the tent was to keep the rain off the desks and that we were doing a full cleaning of the schoolhouse, desks, everything." Anne laughed.

"Which we did. We did not want to tell him a falsehood." Abigail winked at them.

Megan dissolved into laughter and had to sit before she fell off the bench.

People from town and the neighboring ranches trickled in, and soon the tables were heaped with food, the paper chains all hung, and the lumbering blacksmith headed off to fetch the unsuspecting sheriff.

Nerves hit Megan, gnawing at her stomach. What if Andrew got angry? What if he didn't want his birthday celebrated? What if he couldn't come? The questions flew though her brain with intense fury.

"Hey, Squirt, it will be all right."

Megan's heart lurched when Sawyer used Titus's nickname for her. She had not told anyone he used that endearment. She was looking forward to seeing her suave cousin in the autumn. She reached back, squeezed her brother's arm, and smiled. She smiled a lot lately. Sometimes her cheeks hurt from it.

"Here he comes," a lookout at the front window hissed.

Everyone fell silent as they waited for their guest of honor to join them. Boots pounded on the wooden steps, and the door flung open.

"Surprise!" a hundred voices chorused.

"What in the...?" Andrew's face relaxed into an enormous grin.

Megan walked up to him and wrapped her arms around his waist.

"We all wanted to tell you how much we appreciate you, and since I happened to know that today is your birthday, I thought today would be perfect," she said.

Andrew stared at her for a moment. When his head started to lower, she knew he was about to kiss her. The fact they were being scrutinized by everyone barely crossed her mind.

"No cows here," Andrew murmured.

"My brothers are here, though," Megan reminded him with a tiny grin.

"It will be worth it." The words were scarcely out of his mouth before his lips covered hers.

Time and space faded away as a delightful tingling rushed from her lips down through to her toes. She moved her hands up his arms to grasp the back of his neck as she pressed his face a little closer to hers, deepening the kiss.

The onlookers' whistles and cheers reminded them they were not alone. Megan shrank back, knowing her face was flaming red. She sent a fearful glance toward her brothers, but they were all proud as peacocks. If they could have puffed their chests any more, they would have popped a button. She laughed.

Her big, strong brothers were adorable and complete mushes. Andrew laughed and hugged her close as people came to offer their congratulations on his birthday. Only a few mentioned the kiss, for which Megan was thankful.

Lem and Clint got the party started with a fun reel on their fiddle and guitar. Andrew enticed Megan onto the floor to dance. He was a good dance partner, and Megan felt a twinge of regret that she had not been able to enjoy his company during the last dance.

They were in the middle of their third dance when the doors to the school flung open with a crash. The room fell silent as Hiram and the girls from the Golden Rose sashayed into the party.

The girls were wearing low-cut brazen dresses in an array of bright colors. With their painted faces, they appeared shameless, but their eyes darted about, and a few clung to each other. As bold as they were in the safety of the saloon, here they were anxious and afraid.

Angry murmurs resonated throughout the room, and several of the women tugged their men out of the girls' path. A few of the men whistled and catcalled. They were shushed and pushed out the back door.

"What are *they* doing here?" someone shouted from the back of the room.

Megan sighed and pressed her lips together. Why were people so self-righteous?

Hiram's jaw clenched and his shoulders stiffened as he towed the girl on his arm farther into the room. Megan recognized the girl in the red dress as Lacey, the girl who had been injured in the spring. The stark fear on her face propelled Megan forward. She reached out with both hands and grasped one of Lacey's.

"Welcome, I am glad you could come celebrate with us. I am certain Andrew will be delighted you could make it as well. Are any of you girls hungry? There is lots of food in the tent out back. If you prefer to be indoors, we are having a lovely dance in here, or there are chairs if sitting is what you would prefer at the moment." Megan linked arms with both Lacey and another girl who introduced herself as Tina when asked. She drew them, and Hiram, who was still attached to Lacey's other arm, into the middle of the dance floor.

∞ ∞ ∞

Andrew sucked in a deep breath as Megan led the two women and the sullen saloon owner toward him. She was in her element, defending someone from the pride and prejudice of others. Her color was high, and her eyes glinted with suppressed anger. She had never been more beautiful.

Several women in the room stiffened and whispered among themselves. Anne and Abigail reached out to two of the women who trailed behind Megan and welcomed them to the party. Lydia and Elisabeth followed suit.

Andrew smiled and grasped Hiram's hand as he approached. "Good to see you. I am honored to see you here. You must have closed up shop because everyone is here." The significance of that fact did not escape Andrew. Hiram was all about money, and the loss of revenue was significant, if not in actuality, at least in the owner's mind.

"You done a lot for us, Sheriff. Figgered we could come say thanks. I know you don't care for my place of business, or what we do there, but you never let that stop you from helpin'. Me and the girls are all grateful." Hiram said his piece in his usual gruff fashion.

"I am awfully hungry," Lacey whispered to the saloon owner.

Hiram's expression softened. Despite Andrew's disagreement with the work the women at the Golden Rose performed, Hiram treated them all well, and none of them were forced to work if they objected. It had been one point on which he and Andrew had agreed upon.

"Why don't you and the ladies follow Anne and Abigail to the lawn? We have pies and cakes and many delicious treats outside. Andrew and I will be out in a moment."

Andrew was surprised at Megan's statement, but he backed her up with a smile and a nod. Each of the women made sure to talk to him personally as they filed past. Some nodded and murmured a simple thank you.

Others were more specific. The youngest of the girls tugged at his heartstrings. She was perhaps seventeen years old. He wished he could get her away from the saloon and into a good solid family to take care of her a little while longer, but that was not likely.

He was intrigued by Megan's reaction to the girl. She kept looking between her and the crowd, and a slow smile crept across her face. He couldn't wait to hear what she was thinking.

The door swung shut behind them, and the volume in the room ratcheted up.

"How could they welcome those people?"

"Really, such trollops."

Anger bubbled up inside Andrew and threatened to overflow. A small hand on his arm stopped the words that threatened to explode from his mouth. Megan was beside him, her chin held high, eyes flashing. She presented such a fierce picture that he took a step away from her. So did the entire crowd.

"How could we welcome those people? How could we not?" Her voice was hushed, trembling with suppressed anger.

"But they are whores." One of the women marched out of the crowd, her hands on her hips.

"They are women. Young women. The same as many of you," Andrew called out. The smile Megan flashed him sent his heart skittering.

"You, Leona Jorgenson, when you lost your husband four years ago, tell the truth. What options did you have to keep you and your children alive and fed?" Megan turned back to the crowd.

"Why... I married Pete here," Leona stuttered, her face turning bright red.

"And if he had not married you? What would you have done?" Megan pressed.

Leona had no reply. She shook her head and slunk farther back into the crowd.

"And you, since you are so vocal, Missy, what skills do you have that would keep a roof over your head if Christopher died tomorrow?" Megan shifted her attention to the woman who had been the loudest.

"I certainly would not work at a saloon." Missy was adamant.

"Are you sure? Have you ever been so exhausted you could not see straight? So hungry you are certain your stomach is eating you from the inside out? So cold you cannot feel anymore, but are shaking so violently your bones might break? Can you honestly say you wouldn't do anything for a scrap of food, a bit of warmth and sleep, a bit of safety and respect?" Megan's voice had dropped to a whisper.

Andrew put an arm around her shoulder as the Carter men, Doc Warren, and Jacob flanked her. He met the gazes of several of the men, who had the good grace to break eye contact in shame. A few of them were frequent visitors to both the saloon and its women.

"No, but what would you know about cold and hunger? You lived in a fancy house back East and now live with the wealthiest men in the valley. How would you know?" Missy asked.

"That is enough." Her husband plucked at her arm. The fear in his eyes was justified. Andrew sensed the Carter brothers bristling. They were too gentlemanly to act on their anger, but tensions were rising rapidly.

"I know." Megan's dignified answer rippled through the crowd. The whispers stopped and silence hung over the room. "My grandmother hated me so much that she sent the men who kidnapped me and attacked Anne and little Sally Samson. I was beaten, starved, even sent to a mental asylum as punishment. I know what it is like to fear for your life, and be desperate for the smallest human kindness."

Missy's face drained of color. Her mouth opened in a silent O, but she didn't speak.

"I don't wish to be harsh, and I know you want to do what is right. Consider the women who walked in here tonight. Why would they leave the warmth and safety of their jobs, demeaning as they are, when all they face outside of the saloon is coldness and censure?" Megan put her hand over her heart, tears welling in her eyes.

Missy responded to those tears with her own. Apologies flowed freely between many of the women. Andrew had a feeling their little town would be a kinder, better place because of the little spitfire he yearned to call his wife. She was worth waiting for.

People soon fell back into the rhythm of the party, and the atmosphere was jovial once again. Andrew offered Megan his arm, which she took with a small smile, but her eyes did not reflect it. The shadow of sadness and worry still hung in her expression.

"What is wrong?" Andrew asked, pulling her aside.

"I am sad at how the girls were treated today. I worry about the young ones especially." Megan swiped at her eyes, dashing the tears away.

"Yes, I saw you watching Lettie. Who else were you looking at earlier?"

Her eyes brightened, and she perked up. "Oh, I was going to talk to you about that. And you." She seized hold of Riley's arm and dragged him into their circle.

"Who? What? Me? What did I do?" Riley sounded so guilty that Andrew and Megan laughed.

"Gunnar, our ranch hand. He is in love with Lettie. You should have seen him the other day in the general store. He caught a glimpse of her out the window and lit up like a beacon. And today – the minute she walked in the door – he looked like a love sick calf. We should help them somehow."

"I have never seen him in the Golden Rose," Andrew commented when Riley's brow lowered. The men of the Circle C were not encouraged to frequent the saloon.

"I think he has seen her from a distance. You know how shy he is. I highly doubt he would have approached her. Perhaps we can get them to dance together." Megan assured her brother.

Megan's scheming amused Andrew. The cheeky grin she flashed him was his undoing. He threw his head back and laughed, a great hearty laugh. Riley joined him in his laughter, and they had to take a moment to gain control before heading outside to fulfill Megan's promise to join the others.

The party was a phenomenal success, and it was late when the Carters headed home full of good food, merriment, and good memories.

Chapter 20

S ummer passed, and soon the intense heat lessened to warm days and cool evenings. Letters passed fast and furious from New York to the ranch, and Megan was excited to participate in Helena's wedding.

They took the stage, with Riley and Morgan riding horseback alongside the coach. The nights were cold, but unlike her trip West, there was no rain in the mountains. Megan was ecstatic to spend the evening with Clara again before they boarded the train East. She wasn't looking forward to the arduous trip or seeing her grandmother again, but she was excited to see her cousins, Uncle Henri, and all her friends.

Gage and Clara escorted them to the train early in the morning, and Clara hugged her tightly. "Megan, I am happy we met. Your kindness on the train meant more to me than I was able to express at the time. You are the closest friend I have ever had, other than Gage. I want you to be the first to know. Gage and I are going to have a baby," Clara whispered as she held her tight.

Gage laughed at Megan's squeal of excitement. Clara blushed as he explained to the Carter men the cause of their joy. A round of hugs and congratulations intermingled with the conductor's call to board. They lingered so long, Caleb had to jump on board the moving train as it pulled away.

The conductor led the way through the first-class car and onto the small balcony. Megan gasped as she peered down and saw the tracks zipping along beneath them. The conductor stayed inside the first-class car but motioned the Carters on to the next car.

"There is the car you requested, Mr. Carter. Everything is arranged precisely as you ordered."

Riley thanked the conductor, pressing a few bills into the man's hand. The little man thanked him profusely before returning to the passengers inside the car. Morgan easily crossed the gap between the two cars and held his hand out to help Megan. She hesitated for a moment.

The track flashed underneath them so fast it was making her dizzy. Riley joined Morgan, and they both reached for her. She grasped both their hands. With Caleb and Sawyer behind her, she trusted they wouldn't let her fall. Her legs were quite a bit shorter than theirs, and her skirts complicated things, but she traversed easily with their help.

The new car had a nice little balcony on it. There were even benches if they chose to sit outside. The wind blew steadily, keeping the soot and smoke away from the area, and spending time there would be enjoyable and pleasant. Riley opened the door to the car and led the way in. Megan stopped in awe inside the doorway.

It was like a little house on wheels. There was a sitting area with plush mahogany chairs and benches upholstered in red velvet. Gilt-edged mirrors hung on the walls between windows, and rich velvet curtains were tied on either side of the window.

"Oh, my," Megan breathed.

"It is beautiful," Logan agreed.

"We shall have to thank Mr. Corbin when we reach the city. Mr. Corbin was one of Father's schoolmates back east. He wrote after Father's funeral and told me if we ever needed anything, to let him know. I thought after hearing Megan's description of the trip West, perhaps we could make things a little easier going back East for the wedding," Riley said.

"Where will we sleep?" Megan asked, dreading the answer. To her surprise, Riley motioned her forward.

"Here. There are four separate sleeping compartments in the middle of the car. Mr. Corbin often travels with guests, so he has plenty of space." Riley took her hand and led her to the other end of the sitting area.

What Megan had assumed was the wall of the car, was in reality, the wall of one of the compartments. A sliding door with a little window led from the hallway into the compartment. Megan opened the door and peeked inside.

The bed was tucked into the far wall, complete with pillows, a real mattress, and even a luxurious coverlet. A small dressing area and a washbasin completed the little bedroom. There was even a small closet for her clothes. Megan was stunned.

"This is your compartment," Riley said.

"Do they all look like this?" Megan was doing the math in her head. Four rooms, and six travelers.

"Yes, but it will be fine. We will take turns sleeping in the sitting area." Morgan gestured to the plush couches.

"Mr. Corbin has given us the use of his car for the entire trip, both there and back again," Riley said. "I think we will be comfortable."

The Carters went back to the sitting room and made themselves at home. Within a few minutes, two porters came in and dressed the tables for dinner, a pristine white tablecloth was draped over the dark wood.

The porters drew real crystal from the cabinets above the benches and set bone china with gilded edges on the table, along with real silverware. Megan was impressed. One of the porters was the poor gentleman who had been helpful to her before.

"Hello, do you remember me?" she asked.

"I do, miss." He smiled at her. "I do hope we won't be having to put you back together as much on this trip."

Megan laughed. "Me too."

"If you and the gentlemen would please have a seat, we will bring in your breakfast," he instructed, still smiling.

Megan was ravenous. She sat in the chair Riley held for her as several white-coated porters brought in covered silver trays. The smells wafting through the car were mouthwatering. They set four trays in the middle of each table and whisked the covers away.

On one tray there were sweet-and-tart cinnamon fried apples, and another held fluffy biscuits. A third tray held a bowl of delightfully creamy sausage gravy, and the last contained dreamy scrambled eggs. Megan and her brothers helped themselves, and she sighed with pleasure as she ate a bite of the sweet-and-spicy apples.

When breakfast was finished, the porters showed the Carters where the magazines and games were kept.

"Mr. Corbin said to be sure you were comfortable, and he sent along a wide assortment of things. If you need anything at all, let us know. We will check on you periodically as well," one of the porters said as they whisked away the breakfast dishes.

∞ ∞ ∞

The week of travel flew by. The men had been so busy on the ranch, they had not gotten a chance to get to know Megan well. The time spent on the train was good for all of them. Megan was somewhat sorry when it reached the station in New York until she spotted Titus, Uncle Henri, and Helena waiting for them.

She threw the window of the palace car open and waved wildly. "Titus. Helena." Her cousins waved back just as energetically.

The train had barely come to a stop before Megan flung herself into Titus's arms.

"It is good to see you, Squirt." He hugged her tight, kissing the top of her head.

"Helena. Uncle Henri." Megan hugged her uncle and cousin next. Helena was gorgeous as usual. Her face had a softness, however, Megan had never seen before. Helena hugged her, then reached back to a man hiding in the shadows. A tall, thin man with a handlebar mustache walked into her embrace.

"Megan, this is my fiancé, Carlton Edwards the Third. Carlton, this is my cousin, Megan. The one I told you about. And these strapping gentlemen behind her, I assume are my other cousins."

"Yes. Allow me to introduce Riley, Morgan, Logan, Caleb, and Sawyer Carter. My brothers." Megan's chest puffed with pride. Handshakes, hugs, and how-do-you-dos were exchanged while the Carters waited for their trunks to be unloaded.

Helena pulled her aside. "Megan, do you think you will be free tomorrow? I should very much like to go dress shopping with you. We should pick a dress for you to wear as my bridesmaid."

"I should think so. I don't believe we have much planned. Although I think we are going to go see Grandmother one day while we are here. Have you seen her?" Megan asked.

"No, I have not. I did write to her and tell her I was getting married and sent an invitation, but I received no response." Helena hung her head. Megan could see Adelaide's silence had hurt her.

"That doesn't sound like her at all. She lived and breathed for your visits. You remember I wrote you what the police telegraphed us?"

"I remember, but I thought you must be mistaken. Megan, I overheard her make arrangements to have you taken care of. I never dreamed she would follow through, or

I would have told you. Do you think I should tell the police now?" Helena's voice trembled.

"I think we should go shopping tomorrow, and worry about Adelaide later, ladies." Henri St. James put his arms around the girls' shoulders. "If it will make you feel more at ease, we can plan to visit her on the day after tomorrow." He guided the girls to the waiting carriage.

Two gorgeous open carriages waited for them. The two women climbed into them while Henri arranged for their trunks to be brought to his home in the city. Carlton, Logan, and Sawyer joined the girls in their carriage, while the others piled into the second vehicle. Megan soon recognized where she was and delighted in being able to point out various landmarks from her life to her brothers.

"A little way down this block is Tony the grocer. He and his wife had given birth to their first child when I left. Is there any way we could stop?" Megan pleaded.

"Megan, if you want to stop, tell the driver. You have as much to say about what we do, and when, as the rest of us. I certainly do not mind spending a few minutes in the gorgeous fresh air while you visit a friend," Carlton spoke.

"We would love to meet them if they are willing," Helena said.

Megan needed no further encouragement. "Please take the next street to the little grocer's on the corner. I would like to stop there for a few moments," she told the driver.

"Yes, miss." He turned the carriage down the street Megan had indicated. The other carriage followed their lead. The elegant horses and the gilt carriages with their well-dressed passengers were out of place on this street.

Adelaide had never known where Megan had gotten the groceries from, but Megan had preferred the little grocery store to the higher-end market. Prices were better, and Moriah had told her any money she saved could be given to the street children.

The driver helped Megan out of the carriage, and she was surprised to find she was a little nervous. She straightened her hat, brushed a few imaginary wrinkles from her dress, and walked into the little shop. Tears rushed to her eyes when she saw the jolly Italian man behind the counter. She waited off to the side for him to finish with his customer.

"*Ciao, amico.*" Megan said hello to her friend as she hurried to greet him.

"Hello, madam. I am most sorry, but do I know you?" the grocer asked, confusion etched on his face.

"Tony, it is me, Megan. Megan Carter. Do you not recognize me?"

"*Che non può essere. Sei così bello.*" It is not possible, you are beautiful. He came around the corner and took her hands. Peering into her face, he nodded. "Yes, I cannot mistake those Irish eyes of yours, little one."

Tony wrapped his arms around her in a fierce hug. He leaned back and shouted upstairs, "Maria, come and see the elegant lady who has come to our shop." He winked at Megan. "Bring Geno too," he called.

Maria came down the stairs. "Antonio, for shame, shouting in front of a lady, what must she think of us...?" She stopped talking and stared at Megan. "Megan, is that you? You look well, your cheeks are rosy, and your clothes, so pretty. Such a lady you are. I am so happy to see you."

Tears coursed down her cheeks. The curly-haired baby in her arms touched a pudgy finger to one as it dripped off her nose.

Megan threw her arms around both of them, hugging them tightly. She had missed her friends. They had been good to her, and she planned to repay their kindness somehow.

"We wondered where you had gone. I am glad to find you were in a good place. We worried." Maria cried into her hands.

"I am sorry to have upset you. I did not have a chance to let you know what was happening. I didn't know myself until it was too late. My grandmother was going to have me committed to Blackwell's, so my cousin helped me get away and go join my brothers out West. They own a large ranch there. They are outside. Would you like to meet them?"

Tony and Maria were thrilled to have the chance to meet their beloved Megan's family. Megan called to them, and they filed into the store. Henri, Titus, Helena, and Carlton came in behind them.

"I am not sure my store has ever been this full. Like my heart. Next to Maria and Geno, Megan is close to my heart. She is a good, kind girl. We care for her. We like to thank you for taking such good care of my friend." Tony shook hands with each of the men and bowed to Helena.

Megan introduced her family to her friends, beaming. They could not stay too long; with the entire group in the store there was no room for customers.

Helena and Carlton extended an invitation to their wedding to the little family, and Tony accepted with pleasure.

Maria and Megan exchanged addresses so when Megan went home they could keep in touch. The Carters and St. Jameses soon took their leave with another round of hugs and handshakes, and then they were back in the carriages and on their way.

Chapter 21

Megan paused in front of the house she had lived in for years. She had rarely used the front entrance. She was shaking so hard her hat was trembling. How she wished Moriah was in the kitchen and she could sneak in the back way. With her brothers and Titus accompanying her, Adelaide could do her no harm, but the knowledge did not stop the fear rising in her throat.

"You ready?" Titus checked with Megan before knocking on the door. He didn't wait for an answer but swung it open and walked right in. Megan and her brothers followed.

Titus and Megan stopped inside the once-grand entranceway. Riley almost knocked his sister over, so surprised was he by their sudden halt. The large great room was empty. It had no rugs, no furniture, and not even the pictures were left on the walls. The enormous staircase was missing its oriental runner, leaving only dusty stairs and railings.

Megan was stunned. One look at her companions told her Titus was furious. Riley and the others were confused.

"Hello?" Titus called. "Grandmother?" His deep voice echoed through the empty hall.

"Excuse me, may I help you?" a tall, thin man asked. He eyed them up and down, his face a mask of disdain.

"Titus? Is that you?" a thin, reedy voice came from upstairs.

"Who are you?" the haughty man asked, standing between them and the stairs.

"We are Adelaide Carter's grandchildren. Who, may I ask, are you?"

The man's confrontational stance changed at Titus's announcement and he went pale.

"I beg your pardon, sir. I am Jeffries, the butler. Please wait a moment while I go check to see if madam wishes to see you." He scrambled toward the stairs, but Titus wasn't finished.

"Just a moment. What happened here? Where did the furniture go? Why is my grandfather's portrait missing, and the sideboard? What is wrong with Adelaide?" Titus had an iron grip on the butler's arm, and Megan's brothers flanked the two men.

"Speak, man." The steel in Titus's voice sent a chill down Megan's spine.

The butler's shoulders tightened, and his hands shook. His gaze flickered toward the kitchen as he clamped his lips tightly shut.

Megan glanced toward the kitchen to see someone dart back into the dark doorway.

"Sawyer." She called her brother's attention to the fleeing figure. Sawyer and Logan hurried into the kitchen with her. A heavy-set woman was trying to get out the back door.

"Stop," Megan commanded. The woman glanced over her shoulder but continued her escape. Sawyer and Logan would have pursued her, but Megan called them back.

"Let her go. The police will find her. Perhaps you should go find a policeman and bring him back here. The driver can help you. There are usually a few patrolling a few streets over," Megan said.

Sawyer and Logan stared at their sister for a moment. Without another word, they did as she bade.

Megan walked back into the entry hall. Titus was still trying to get answers from the butler, but the man was tight-lipped.

"Titus, we should check on Grandmother." Megan lifted her skirts and ascended the stairs.

"Grandmother?" Titus called as he followed.

"I am in my room." Adelaide's voice sounded weak.

Megan opened the door. "Hello, Grandmother." She worked to keep her features free of shock. The room was still as Megan remembered it, but Adelaide herself was much altered. Her normally perfectly coiffed hair hung loosely around her shoulders, and she was alarmingly pale. Never one to carry excess pounds, now the woman was skeletal.

Two pink spots appeared on Adelaide's cheeks, her nostrils flared, and her eye flashed with anger. "What are you doing here?" she seethed, then turned to Titus. "Did you bring her? If you have not come to apologize, I do not want to see either of you. Get out," Adelaide huffed, crossing her arms.

"Grandmother, what happened to you?" Megan was not deterred by the sick woman's anger.

"I broke my leg, chasing after Helena if you must know," Adelaide said. "I wrote her and asked her to come see me, but she never did. It is your fault." Her voice vacillated between petulant, sad, and hateful. "Who is lurking by the door? Has Helena come to see me?"

Caleb leaned forward. "No, ma'am. My name is Caleb. I'm your grandson. My brothers are here as well." He stepped back to allow them to come near the bed.

"Policemen are downstairs. They have Jeffries in custody," Morgan whispered to Megan.

"Jamison's boys?" Adelaide's face went pale as she took in each of the men.

"Grandmother, why is your furniture gone? And the portraits?" Titus asked.

"What are you talking about? It is all here. Do you not see it?" Adelaide's brow furrowed in confusion.

"Excuse me, ma'am. The boy is right. There is not a scrap of furniture downstairs. There is even more missing than when I was here last time." Officer Wainwright entered the room and introduced himself.

"What about my servants? Where is Jeffries?" Adelaide asked.

"Jeffries and his wife are being arrested. They confessed everything once they understood they had been found out. Sounds like your doctor was in on it as well," the officer explained.

"Well, who is going to take care of me? I can't get out of bed. I am still too weak." She lay back on the pillows, clearly using the opportunity to garner sympathy.

Megan didn't fall for it. The woman was sick, but not helpless. "It looks like right now you have two choices. I can stay and take care of you until you are back on your feet, or you can be placed into a convalescent home until you are able to take care of yourself."

"What about Helena? Couldn't she come and take care of me?" Adelaide wheedled.

"Helena is getting married in a few days. She will have a home of her own and wouldn't be able to care for you, Grandmother. Do you want her to give up her own life and happiness for you?" Megan attempted to appeal to Adelaide's love for Helena.

Officer Wainwright cleared his throat and motioned for everyone to join him downstairs for a moment.

"Would you like someone to stay with you?" Megan asked her grandmother.

"No, get out. I need time alone to think." Adelaide finished her statement on a kinder note.

"I am sorry things have turned out this way, Grandmother. I came to tell you I forgive you for what you did. The two men you sent to kidnap me succeeded, and they told us about your transactions with them. Despite those wrongs, I still love you. I have found a home in the West, but I am willing to stay here and help you if you need me to." Megan left the older woman with a sad smile.

Adelaide sat in her bed, seething. She could hear her blood pounding in her ears. Forgive *her*? After what that little wench had done, how dare she be so familiar as to say Adelaide needed forgiveness? She was disappointed in Titus, joining in and trying to make her believe her furniture was gone. Nonsense. The little imps were probably downstairs laughing about it right now. Well, she would show them. She would go downstairs and call their bluff.

She struggled to swing her legs over the edge of the bed. Pain shot up her leg when her feet touched the floor. Adelaide gripped the side of the bed until it subsided. She bit her lip to keep from crying out when she got to her feet for the first time in weeks.

Moving toward the door, she used the furniture to brace herself. Sweat was dripping down her back by the time she was halfway there. Her head swam as waves of nausea and dizziness crashed over her.

Time crawled as she lurched, stumbled, and inched forward until the door was within reach. One twist of the doorknob and she stumbled into the hall. She flung herself toward the balcony railing. Voices drifted from the hall below.

"We held the invitations and letters from you. Mrs. Carter never received them," Jeffries was saying.

"So she never knew about the wedding. That will make Helena feel better anyway, knowing Grandmother didn't ignore her." Guilt struck Adelaide's heart when she saw the relief on Titus' face.

"Did I do the right thing? Telling her either I would take care of her, or we would send her to a home?" Megan asked.

"I think so, miss. From what I hear, Mrs. Carter, while a victim of this man and his schemes, has a few things to answer for herself. She will be fortunate to not be put in the jail ward of the convalescent home, or Blackwell's," Officer Wainwright said.

"I would never send her to that horrible place."

A twinge of guilt struck Adelaide over Megan's words. No. She couldn't do it. She wouldn't be dependent on that girl to survive, and she wouldn't go to a home, either. She would not give anyone the chance to humiliate her ever again.

Her grandchildren had been right. Every stick of furniture was gone. All her beautiful things, gone. Her servants were gone. Helena, gone. She had nothing left. Not even her pride.

She staggered into her study and found the bottles of laudanum in her desk. She took two more from the bedside table. She poured four of them into a glass sitting next to the brandy decanter and topped it off with a generous amount of brandy.

Adelaide drank the entire glass as quickly as she could. She gagged on the bitterness of the medicine, but she finished every last drop. There. It was done.

∞ ∞ ∞

Megan waited at the bottom of the stairs listening to the men. Jeffries admitted he and Doctor Franks had kept Adelaide drugged with laudanum and had sold most of the furniture and jewelry, splitting the profits. He also alluded to a police officer as a partner but refused to say who it was. Megan knew very well he was talking about Officer Pietro but was afraid to say so. Titus had no such qualms and came right out and accused him. Officer Wainwright was not inclined to believe him, though.

Megan could hardly blame him. Even though she knew the truth, policemen tended to stick together. Accusing one of his fellow police officers could have serious consequences.

A crash from upstairs drew everyone's attention. Megan took the stairs two at a time and was the first into Adelaide's study.

Adelaide lay face down and unconscious on top of shards of broken glass. Riley and Titus carefully picked her up and shifted her to the bed. Several pieces of glass were embedded in her arm and face.

"The mirror must have been what we heard breaking." Titus's voice broke.

Officer Wainwright had assessed the situation immediately and had sent one of the other policemen for a doctor. A strange sound, similar to snoring came from Adelaide's throat, but her eyes were open.

Megan could see her pupils were small and not reacting to any light. A touch of her hand confirmed her grandmother's skin was ice-cold. Megan searched around and within seconds spotted the vials.

"Laudanum." Her quiet words silenced the room.

The policeman grasped Adelaide's wrist with one hand. He used his other hand to check his pocket watch. "Fast, but weak." He checked her pupils. "Contracted."

Megan found four empty laudanum bottles on the desk and handed them to the policeman.

"If she took all of that, even the doctor won't be able to help her. She is bleeding pretty badly from these cuts as well. I don't think there is anything we can do," Titus spoke from his place beside Adelaide's bed.

He and Sawyer were trying to stem the flow of blood from her arm. Adelaide took a deep shuddering breath, then all was still.

"Grandmother?" Titus shook Adelaide. Nothing.

Everyone moved aside as the doctor rushed into the room. He checked her pulse and her eyes. Resting his ear on her chest, he waited a moment. "She is gone," he confirmed.

"I am sorry. We will do everything we can to bring a satisfactory end to the case surrounding your grandmother's death. Please don't hesitate to contact us if there is anything else we can do." Officer Wainwright left.

Tremors hit Megan hard. Her grandmother was dead. She was finally free, but the cost for that freedom was terribly high. She covered her face with her hands and burst into tears. Titus was beside her in an instant, her brothers too. Everyone wrapped their arms around each other for a few moments.

"I didn't want her to die. I wanted her to know I forgave her, and I wanted her to love me," Megan cried. "How are we going to tell Helena? It will break her heart." The tears came faster and harder.

"I will tell my sister," Titus assured her. "Let's get away from here."

No one argued. Morgan and Riley took Megan's arms as they went downstairs. She was still crying, and was grateful for their support. More than once she would have tripped over her skirts if it weren't for their strong hold.

The police assured them they would take care of locking the house. Titus left his father's address with Officer Wainwright before he and the Carters headed home. Now, in addition to a wedding, they had a funeral to plan.

Chapter 22

The day of Adelaide's funeral was cold, rainy, and gray. Despite her former status in society, only her family attended the graveside service. Carlton was there to support Helena.

Moriah and Rollins had sent their condolences but were unable to come into the city. Their apples were ready for harvest. Helena's wedding was next week, and Megan consoled herself with the fact she would see them at the reception.

Helena leaned on Carlton, and Megan huddled into her black woolen coat against the biting wind. She longed for Andrew as she watched her cousin and her fiancé. She wished he was there, wrapping his strong arms around her in a hug. Instead, Megan leaned into Caleb. There was no shortage of loving arms to hold her, but it wasn't the same.

The funeral was short, and soon the family was back in the warmth of the St. James's parlor. Megan and Helena retired to their rooms, too tired to be much company.

Despite the funeral, wedding plans still moved on. Megan's dress fitting was the next day, and Helena and Carlton had a huge society reception to attend. Helena had invited Megan and her brothers, but the Carters had declined, deciding instead to accept an invitation to dine with Tony and Maria.

Megan had hardly closed her eyes when there was a light knock on her door.

"Come in," she called, sitting up and propping herself against her pillows.

The door opened and Helena poked her head around it. "Do you have a minute?" she asked tearfully.

"Of course, come in." Megan patted the side of the bed. Helena flopped down on top of the down coverlet. She kicked off her shoes and let her hair down, and Megan did the same, waiting for Helena to talk.

"I miss her," Helena said. Her eyes filled with tears. "I know at the end she was horrible, and mean, but I still miss her. She wasn't mean or horrible to me. I loved her deeply. She loved me. I don't regret the decision I made, but I am sorry I had to make it. Does that make any sense at all?"

"Of course you miss her. No one would expect otherwise." Megan hugged her.

"You don't hate me, do you? You should, you could, and I wouldn't blame you one bit. Please don't hate me for what I did. Or for loving Grandmother."

"Helena, I don't hate you. I couldn't hate you. I won't deny I was hurt by the things you said and did, but that is the past. We have both changed. We both loved Grandmother but in different ways. We had different relationships with her. She was my grandmother too, and I am sorry for the way she died. I am glad I have you, Titus, and Uncle Henri. I have found my brothers, and that wouldn't have happened without your help."

Megan sat back and considered her cousin's pale face and red-rimmed eyes. "We cannot change the past. We can only move forward. I forgave you a long time ago, Helena. I am happy we are friends again."

Helena and Megan cried together for a few minutes. Soon their tears became laughter as they reminisced about happier times in their childhood.

"Do you remember the time Uncle Henri took us to the farm? He had an experiment to do, and your mother thought it would be a good idea for us to see the farm."

"Yes." Helena dissolved into giggles.

"Titus and I were playing with the kittens near the house, and you screamed so loud I was sure the windows would break. We thought you were being killed." Megan was laughing now too.

"I didn't know Papa could run that fast, and I thought the poor farmer would have a heart attack."

"You were standing beside the fence, screaming and crying. The poor cow was as confused as we were." Megan laughed so hard, she slid off the bed and hit the floor with a thud. Helena lunged to catch her but instead ended up joining her in a heap on the rug.

The door to the bedroom burst open and Titus and Riley ran in. Henri and Logan came in right behind them. Seeing the concern swiftly turn to confusion on the men's faces, the girls laughed harder.

"Girls, what is going on?" Henri asked, leaning against the bedpost, amused.

"Helena got licked by a cow." Megan howled as Helena lay on the floor laughing.

"I remember that." Titus joined the laughter.

Megan's brothers were confused, so Henri explained, and soon everyone was laughing. Megan looked around at them. Family was a wonderful thing to have—complicated at times, but wonderful.

Chapter 23

Megan grinned at Helena in the mirror. The big day was finally here. Helena was getting married in a few minutes. Megan smoothed the bodice of her dress. The seamstress had done an amazing job. It fit her perfectly.

The seamed bodice skimmed her ribs, the eggplant taffeta was the ideal color for her, and the skirt was the right length. A lacy sash accented her waist and trailed down the skirt in a cascade of lace roses.

Helena's wedding dress had the same sash and roses but in white satin and lace.

Megan had turned to say something to Helena when the door opened. She closed her mouth with a snap as Officer Wainwright came into the room, his hat in his hands.

"I am sorry to interrupt your celebration, Miss St. James, Miss Carter." The officer's voice trembled, and he bit his lip.

"It is all right, officer. What can we do for you?" Helena smiled graciously

"I need to ask, do either of you recognize this?" The policeman held out a white-gloved hand. Sitting on his palm was a brooch. A bouquet of purple-jeweled flowers tied with a diamond ribbon.

"Yes, it was Adelaide's," Megan said.

"Yes, she was given it by my grandfather," Helena agreed.

"Yes, I recognized it as well. When I went to interview her, she was wearing it. She told me the story. Officer Pietro's wife was wearing it at the police ball two days ago. I saw it and reported it to my superior.

"Officer Pietro was confronted. He chose to run and was killed in the ensuing chase. Before he died, he admitted to a great many things, including holding you against your will and having you admitted to Blackwell's, Miss Carter." Officer Wainwright licked his lips nervously.

Megan sank onto the cedar chest with a sigh. Helena grasped her hands, sitting next to her.

"Are you all right?" the policeman asked them.

Megan nodded. "Please go on."

"You are both aware Adelaide Carter left her entire estate to Miss St. James. I came to return this to you." The police officer offered the brooch to Helena.

"Yes, you may be interested to know I have ordered the estate to be turned over to Miss Carter. She was the one who took care of Grandmother. The brooch belongs to her," Helena said.

Officer Wainwright held it out to Megan.

Megan shook her head. "Is it valuable?" she asked him.

"The jeweler appraised the piece at around ten thousand dollars."

"Do you want it, Helena? As a reminder of grandmother?" Megan asked.

"No, I have the things I want. Do you want it? It is pretty," Helena replied.

Megan's brow wrinkled in concentration. "You mentioned Officer Pietro's wife was wearing the brooch. Did they have children?"

"Four. Diana is six, Lucy is five, Henry is three, and Jack is only a few weeks old." Officer Wainwright's face twisted with sadness.

"Did his wife know what he was doing?" Helena asked.

"No, Olivia was completely ignorant of the matter, of that I am certain."

"Do they have any family?" Megan asked.

"Not around here. I believe Mrs. Pietro has family back in Virginia, but I am not sure."

"Sell the brooch. Give the money to Mrs. Pietro and her children," Megan said.

"Excuse me? What did you say?"

"You understood me correctly. Please sell the brooch and give the money to Mrs. Pietro and the children. What happened to them is not their fault, and it is difficult for a woman with no family and no fortune to make a living. They already lost their father; it would be a shame if they lost anything else. Perhaps the money will help."

"Miss, that is uncommon kind of you." The officer seemed to be at a loss for words. Tears filled his eyes, but he did his best to keep them from spilling over.

Megan smiled. A knock at the door signaled the women to make their way to the ceremony.

Officer Wainwright thanked them again and took his leave.

The doors opened, and Megan could see the auditorium was filled with well-dressed wedding guests, flowers, and flickering candles. The décor was beautiful, but it paled in comparison to the smile on her cousin's face.

Helena grasped her hand and squeezed it tightly. "Thank you, Megan."

"I love you, cousin." Megan smiled.

They walked serenely into the chapel, the events just moments before soon forgotten in the beauty of the ceremony joining Helena and Carlton as man and wife.

Chapter 24

Megan." A familiar voice attracted Megan's attention.

"Tillie," she cried, rushing forward to give her friend a hug. Tillie looked amazing, her cheeks rosy and full, and her eyes sparkling. A short, bespectacled man followed behind her holding a squirming toddler in his arms.

"Megan, I would like you to meet my wonderful husband, Stuart. And the rambunctious wiggle worm trying to escape from him is our son, Michael." Tillie was smiling from ear to ear.

"So nice to meet you." Megan nodded to Stuart.

He handed Michael to his wife and enfolded Megan in a heartfelt hug. "Thank you for what you did for Tillie. I will be forever in your debt for the kindnesses you showed her."

"She was helpful to me as well," Megan assured him. She was about to ask them how they liked the country when she found herself engulfed in another hug. This time she turned to see Moriah.

Megan returned the hug enthusiastically, reaching for Rollins as she held on to her dear friend. She introduced Tillie and her family to the older couple.

"Did you hear about Miss Nell?" Tillie asked.

"No, but here she comes now." Megan waved to the lady.

Another round of hugs and introductions interrupted the conversation as Titus and the Carter brothers joined them. A waiter brought by a tray of hot mulled cider for the guests to enjoy.

"What do I need to hear about you, Miss Nell?" Megan asked. "Besides how you got out of that horrible asylum," she added.

"It is all connected actually." Miss Nell smiled.

"Do tell," Megan implored.

"Well, to make a prolonged and gruesome story short, my husband refused to allow me to leave Blackwell's. Dr. Kent and Mr. St. James pleaded my case, but to no avail. A few weeks ago, my husband was killed in a hunting accident, and Dr. Kent and your cousin convinced the board to affect my release. Dr. Kent has been wonderful," Miss Nell said, her cheeks turning a pretty shade of pink.

"Tell her the rest," Tillie urged.

"Or I can tell her." Dr. Kent had come up behind Megan. "It is nice to see you. You are looking well, Miss Carter. I was sorry to hear about your grandmother." He put his arm around Miss Nell's waist. "And as for 'the rest' Tillie is eager for you to hear, Nell and I will be married in a few weeks." He grinned.

Megan's gaze flew to Miss Nell. She was holding out her hand, a huge diamond ring flashing on her finger. Megan squealed in delight and threw her arms around both the kind doctor and her friend.

After Megan had released him, Dr. Kent detailed the changes he and the committee were working toward at the hospital. Megan silently thanked God for all the wonderful things He had worked in her friends' lives.

∞ ∞ ∞

Megan squeezed Helena in a tight hug. She and Carlton were headed to Europe on their honeymoon. They were waiting to board the boat, saying their goodbyes to the Carters. Megan and her brothers were headed home the next day.

Carlton smiled at the women. "I am sorry, but we need to board." He enfolded Megan in a brotherly hug. "I am glad we were able to meet, Megan. Someday, I hope we can visit you out West as well." Carlton shook hands with the boys, and Henri, Titus, and Carlton's parents said their goodbyes as well.

Megan waved as the newlyweds walked up the gangplank. She was ready to go home. She missed Andrew so much that her chest hurt thinking about him. She crossed her arms.

"You feeling all right, sis?" Sawyer put his arm around her shoulders.

"I want to go home." She sighed.

"Any particular reason?" Sawyer winked at her.

"Many." Megan grinned at him. "There is one reason I think is particularly important, though."

"What might this reason be? Does it happen to be a certain man with a badge?" Morgan joined the conversation. "Or perhaps you miss Tiny? Or Mrs. Hernandez?" he teased.

"Yes, and the mountains, my bed, the piano—all of it. Mostly, though, I miss Andrew. I love him. I miss him. I never want to be parted from him for this long ever again." Megan sighed.

"Are you going to tell him?" Logan asked.

An idea formed in her mind. "Yes. As soon as the boat leaves, I need to go to the telegraph office, please." She grinned at her brothers.

"Megan, Mother Edwards, Father." Helena called. She and Carlton were standing at the side of the ship, waving down to them. The entourage waved back as the boat pulled away from the docks. The entire pier waved and cheered shouting bon voyage. The little group stayed until the boat was too far away to make out any faces.

"Megan needs to run by the telegraph office, but we will meet you back at the house for dinner," Riley informed the St. Jameses. The Carters piled into the carriage. It was crowded, but they fit.

Megan racked her brain, trying to think of what to say to Andrew. She needed him to know she was ready to marry him, but how could she tell him without broadcasting to the entire network of telegraph operators how she felt? She could fill volumes with how much she loved him, but she only had ten words. Ten.

The carriage stopped in front of the telegraph office, and Megan and Riley went inside. Megan carefully wrote her message on the telegraph blank and handed it to the operator. He counted the words.

"Cost for the telegram will be one dollar, miss," he said.

Riley handed him the money, and they were back outside in the waiting carriage in short order.

"What did you tell him?" Sawyer asked.

Megan beamed at him but wouldn't answer. No matter how much her brothers wheedled and cajoled, she wouldn't spill the beans.

∞ ∞ ∞

The trip home seemed to take forever for Megan. They were able to use the same train car, and the cooler temperatures made for a much more comfortable journey. This time she was prepared for the stage. Her clothes were more weather appropriate, and she had a new woolen coat that kept her toasty-warm.

It had been lovely to visit the city again, see the children and her friends, and visit with her uncle and cousins, but she was ready to be home. She missed everyone, though.

As the train slowed for the last time, pulling into Goodrich, she peered out the window. She had no reason to think he would meet them at the station, yet she hoped he would. Her heart felt like it would pound out of her chest.

A familiar silhouette stood on the platform. He was here. Megan jumped out of her seat and ran to the back of the car.

She wrenched the door open and launched herself into his waiting arms before the train came to a complete stop.

She didn't bother saying hello. Instead, she wrapped her arms around his neck and kissed him. He responded with enthusiasm, and it wasn't until one of her brothers cleared his throat that she realized the platform was filling with people.

All five of the Carter men feigned anger over the kiss, but Megan just grinned unrepentantly.

"Now will you tell us what that telegram said?" Sawyer's plaintive question made her laugh.

Andrew pulled the folded missive from his vest pocket and handed it over to her older brother as he leaned in to kiss her again. She didn't need to read it. She remembered exactly what it said.

COMING HOME STOP ORDER RED GINGHAM CURTAINS STOP LOVE MEGAN

THE END

Made in the USA
Columbia, SC
26 February 2021